ROMANTIC SUSPENSE

SPECIAL FORCES: THE SPY

Cindy Dees

NEW YORK TIMES BESTSELLING AUTHOR

HARLEQUIN®

ROMANTIC suspense

Heart-racing romance, breathless suspense

AVAILABLE THIS MONTH

ISBN-13: 978-1-335-66202-6

From passionate, suspenseful
and dramatic love stories to
inspirational or historical,
Harlequin offers different lines to
satisfy every romance reader.

New books available
every month.

HRSATMIFC0619

"Don't thank me. You should never have been here. Never gone through that."

Piper stared at him intently. Was he admitting that he'd purposely misidentified her? That it was his fault she was here?

"Why did you—" she started.

Zane cut her off, muttering quickly, "Not now. Not here, with them upstairs where they could hear something,"

"Who are you?"

"How's your jaw?" he countered quietly.

"Sore."

"Your side?"

"Same."

"Any serious injuries you're aware of?" he inquired.

"Why do you care?"

"Because I'm freaking trying to keep you alive and in one piece to the best of my ability," he snapped.

* * *

Mission Medusa: a fierce team of warriors who run into the danger zone...

* * *

Dear Reader,

Welcome to the next installment in the ongoing adventures of the Medusas. I hope you're having as much fun as I'm having with these stories of smart, sexy women warriors and the even hotter, sexier men they love.

This story grew out of a mental game of what-ifs that I played with myself very late one night when I couldn't get my brain to shut down and fall asleep. Two questions occurred to me, and it was out of those that this story was born. The first question was, what would happen if one of the Medusas was mistaken for a regular civilian woman who stumbled into an extraordinary situation?

The second question was, what would a no kidding, actual enemies-to-lovers story look like? I'm not talking about a hero and a heroine who bicker while making goo-goo eyes at each other before jumping into the sack and swearing their undying love. I'm talking about a man and a woman who are legitimately pitted against each other in some sort of life-and-death struggle. What would happen if *they* accidentally fell in love with each other?

And voilà! After one terrible night's sleep, several more weeks of working out the details of the story and several more months of writing it down, Piper and Zane's love story had taken shape.

So, make yourself comfortable, pour your favorite beverage and buckle up for one wild ride as Piper Ford and Zane Cosworth collide...and fall madly in love, of course...

Happy reading!

Cindy

SPECIAL FORCES: THE SPY

Cindy Dees

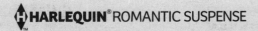

HARLEQUIN® ROMANTIC SUSPENSE

Recycling programs
for this product may
not exist in your area.

ISBN-13: 978-1-335-66202-6

Special Forces: The Spy

Printed in U.S.A.

New York Times and *USA TODAY* bestselling author **Cindy Dees** is the author of more than fifty novels. She draws upon her experience as a US Air Force pilot to write romantic suspense. She's a two-time winner of the prestigious RITA® Award for romance fiction, a two-time winner of the RT Reviewers' Choice Best Book Award for Romantic Suspense and an *RT Book Reviews* Career Achievement Best Author Award nominee. She loves to hear from readers at www.cindydees.com.

Books by Cindy Dees

Harlequin Romantic Suspense

Mission Medusa

Special Forces: The Recruit
Special Forces: The Spy

The Coltons of Roaring Springs

Colton Under Fire

Code: Warrior SEALs

Undercover with a SEAL
Her Secret Spy
Her Mission with a SEAL
Navy SEAL Cop

Soldier's Last Stand
The Spy's Secret Family
Captain's Call of Duty
Soldier's Rescue Mission
Her Hero After Dark
Breathless Encounter

Visit the Author Profile page at Harlequin.com for more titles.

Chapter 1

Relishing the morning sunshine pouring through her cozy bungalow's kitchen window, Piper Ford poured herself a cup of coffee and sat down at the table to catch up on current events. Of course, she didn't bother with newspapers. Instead, she browsed the classified briefing she and her teammates got each day covering every hot spot in the world.

It was one of the best perks of being a Medusa. She loved knowing the dirt that few besides her all-female Special Forces team had access to. But then, she always had been a poli-sci geek. Even at West Point, she'd reveled in getting into political debates with her classmates and instructors.

Her cell phone rang and she picked it up. Her next-door neighbor was calling. Susan and her six-year-old son, Jack, had welcomed her warmly to the neighborhood when she bought this place a few months back.

Piper had a particular fondness for the little boy, and he for her. Jack was a cool kid—funny, curious and smart as heck.

"Hi, Sus. What's up?"

"Hey, Piper. I'm stuck at the hospital. My day replacement called in sick at the last minute, and they can't find a nurse to sub in. I'm stuck in the ICU pulling a double shift. But my babysitter can't stay late this morning. Is there any chance you could run Jack over to his school on your way to work?"

"When does he need to be there?"

"Eight fifteen."

The Medusas had training at nine, but it was only about a twenty-minute drive from the town of Houma, Louisiana, to their classified facility, Training Site Vanessa, usually referred to as the TSV. It was tucked next to the Mandalay National Wildlife Refuge, deep in the bayous of southern Louisiana.

"Yeah, sure. I can drop him off on my way to work. Will he be ready to go around eight?"

"He should be. Rosie feeds him breakfast, gets him dressed and packs his lunch. I really am sorry about the last-minute notice. You're an angel. I owe you one."

Piper laughed, "I'm hardly an angel."

"Shrimp étouffée? My place, this weekend?" Susan offered.

"Deal. I'll bring the wine."

Piper dressed in jeans and a casual white oxford shirt, befitting her cover story of being a civilian historian researching pirate activity in this part of southern Louisiana.

She stuffed the daily intel brief into her backpack, along with her pistol, some basic survival gear she felt naked without and a uniform for running around in the woods with the Medusas. Vietnamese Special Forces instructors were in town this week teaching her and her teammates advanced jungle camouflage and ambush tactics—key skills for Special Forces operators like the Medusas.

Piper backed her little sports car out of the garage and pulled into the driveway next door. Susie's salmon pink front door opened and Jack darted out, all restless energy. Piper pushed the passenger door open for him and waved at Rosie, the babysitter, who followed him out the door at a more sedate pace, locking it behind her.

"Thanks for taking Jack to school!" Rosie called. "I have a doctor's appointment today in New Orleans, and I'm gonna be late as it is."

"No problem!" Piper called back. As Jack tumbled into the car beside her, she admonished, "Buckle your seat belt, squirt."

A bolt of envy for Susan and regret for opportunities lost shot through Piper's gut at the sight of Jack. Longing for a child tugged at her—longing for a family of her own. She'd have thought she would be over the sense of hollow emptiness for the children she would never have by now, given the career she'd picked. But it turned out biological clocks were powerful little bastards.

It had been a trade-off, and she'd made her choice. She had arguably one of the coolest jobs on the planet. But the sacrifice in return was no time for a private life.

In point of technical fact, she supposed a personal life was possible. But that would entail finding a man who didn't mind his partner being a lethally trained special operator, prone to running off at a moment's notice to who knew where to face who knew what danger.

The only man besides her boss who even knew the Medusas existed at this point was Captain Beau Lambert, the Medusas' operations officer. And her teammate, Tessa Wilkes, had that man locked down tight. The two of them were engaged and had set a wedding date next year. They made a great couple. Goo-goo eyes flew thick and fast whenever they were in the same room.

But that left her without any eligible prospects in the love department.

"I like riding in your car, Miss Piper."

"Why's that?"

"'Cuz your car doesn't have a back seat, and I get to sit in front."

"When you get bigger, your mom will let you sit in front with her."

"That's what she says. I'm eatin' as much as I can so I'll get big really fast."

"Patience, grasshopper. You'll be all grown-up before you know it. Enjoy being a kid while you can."

"Don't you like being a grown-up?"

"I do most of the time. But it's a lot easier being a kid. And more fun."

"My mama says you have a super boring job."

Piper mentally snorted. If Susan only knew the truth. The poor woman would run screaming from Piper. She smiled serenely. "I like my job."

"Lucky dog. I hate school. I suck at it."

"You do not. I happen to know you rock at all your subjects."

"School's boring."

"Maybe you're just too smart for the first grade."

"Mama says I'm smarter than my teacher."

Piper laughed, "I can believe it."

They pulled up in front of Southdown Elementary School, a dark redbrick building that Piper privately thought looked more like a prison than a school. As Jack jumped out, she called after him, "Have a good day. And behave yourself!"

He flashed her an impudent grin and dashed inside.

She made it nearly halfway to the TSV before she happened to glance down and spied a brown paper bag on the floor of the passenger side of the car.

Rats. Jack had forgotten his lunch.

If she hit the stoplights exactly right, she had just enough time to zip back to his school, run his lunch inside and make it to the training site on time. The Medusas' commanding officer, Major Gunnar Torsten, had no sense of humor whatsoever when it came to tardiness.

Classes had started by the time she got back to the elementary school, and the drop-off area was deserted. Parking quickly, she grabbed Jack's lunch and hurried inside. To the left of the front door was a large glassed-in office that looked like a reception area lined with institutional, Formica-topped desks. Several women sat at them. A little girl who looked about eight years old stood beside one, shifting her weight from one foot to the other.

Piper stepped inside. "Is this where I drop off a lunch a student has forgotten?"

"Yes, ma'am. Just a minute." The gray-haired woman who answered her went back to talking with the child. "Your mom says she'll be here in ten minutes with your inhaler—" The woman broke off, staring at something behind Piper.

A flurry of movement in the hallway outside caught Piper's attention out the corner of her eye. Something—someone—adult-sized had just run past.

Was there a problem?

As she turned to take a better look, a man dressed all in black with a black ski mask over his face burst into the office. Piper flipped into combat mode in a millisecond, her senses going on high alert and adrenaline rushing to all her muscles.

She noted several things at once. The weapon, held across the man's body, was an AK-47 with an extended mag, and he handled it like he was familiar with it. He was a shade over six feet tall. Athletic in build. Moved fast and silently, rolling from heel to toe with each step. *Like a Special Forces operator.*

"Everybody down!" he shouted.

The three women at their desks started to scream, and the little girl awaiting the inhaler froze, staring up at the man in openmouthed terror, like a rabbit in front of a wolf.

Stunned, Piper dropped to the floor with the other women. She was unarmed, alone and had no idea how many more men like this there were already inside the school. Terror and panic exploded in her gut in spite of all her Special Forces training.

God. Not a school shooting. A worst-case scenario on all counts. Nonexpendables everywhere—*children*—completely unequipped to defend themselves from harm. Targets handily clustered together in classrooms. Limited egress points. Even more limited sight lines. Chaos guaranteed.

Tragedy guaranteed.

By force of will and outstanding training, she pushed back all the paralyzing feelings and focused on acting.

Surreptitiously, she eased her cell phone out of her jeans pocket and dialed 9-1-1 by feel. She stuffed the phone under her hip lest the armed man brandishing the AK-47 hear the operator ask what the nature of her emergency was and kill her before she could answer.

She eased her hip off the phone and shouted, "What

do you want, barging into an elementary school with an automatic weapon like that?"

"Quiet, or I'll kill you!" the man shouted back. "Where's Mrs. Black?"

"She's out sick today," one of the other women quavered from the floor.

Piper eased back on top of the phone, praying the emergency operator had gotten the idea and called for the SWAT team. And the FBI and the National Guard and whoever else could be called.

Standoffs with kids caught in the middle were no picnic, but maybe when law enforcement got here, they could negotiate some sort of hostage release.

She calculated her options at the speed of light. She could probably take out the lone armed man—she did have all the necessary unarmed-combat training and the element of surprise on her side.

Question was, where were the other men she'd peripherally seen racing past, and how many of them were there? If she got the weapon away from this one, she could go hunting for the others...although hunting in a building full of children and teachers would be a dreadful environment for taking out bad guys. The odds of shooting an innocent bystander were far too high to risk.

As those thoughts darted through her mind, the armed man did an odd thing. He strode over to the little girl, grabbed her by her upper arm, glanced around, then led her over to a tall wooden coat cabinet against the wall.

He opened the door, pushed her inside and said low, "Stay in there until the police come for you and don't make a sound until then."

Piper stared, so confused she momentarily forgot her

terror. Did the intruder just save that little girl? Why on earth would an armed assailant do something like that?

He shut the closet door just before two more men raced into the office, dressed like him and similarly armed. Terrorist the First nodded tersely at his buddies.

What in the hell was this about? What did a bunch of men, attired and armed like bank robbers, want with a freaking elementary school?

"Where is she?" one of the newcomers demanded in Farsi. Piper's Farsi wasn't fluent, but that was definitely what she'd heard. These guys were Iranian? What on earth did they want *here*?

The terrorists commenced walking around the room, examining each of the women cowering on the floor. One screamed as an assailant grabbed her shoulder and lifted her up enough to see her face. These guys were looking for somebody? This was a hell of a violent and aggressive way of finding whoever they wanted.

The terrorists reached Piper, and she stared fixedly at their combat boots. Steel toes, nylon uppers, flexible rubber soles, quick-don zippers. Special operators' footwear.

Was this some sort of exercise aimed at her? The Medusas did some wild stuff in the name of training, but surely they wouldn't scare the hell out of a bunch of kids and teachers. Nah. This was the real deal.

A hand grabbed her shoulder roughly and threw her over onto her back. She rolled with the shove, not resisting. Unfortunately, the roll exposed her cell phone, and one of them kicked it away from her with his foot. Reflexively, her hand went out to retrieve it, but she froze as she made eye contact with the kicker.

Clear amber eyes stared down at her, the color of a

fine cognac. They were hard eyes, but they didn't contain the rage or fanaticism she'd expected.

He glanced at her outstretched hand splayed on the floor and did a double take. She swore mentally. Clearly visible on her fourth finger was her West Point class ring. In her guise as a civilian historian, she told people it had been her father's, but it was actually hers.

The man's eyes lit with recognition as he spied the chunky ring and its dark green central stone.

Dammit.

"Here she is!" he called out to the others in Farsi.

What? These men were here for *her*? How on earth did they know who she was? *Nobody* knew about the Medusa Project. It had been resurrected from ashes less than a year ago, for crying out loud.

Everyone had been led to believe the program was defunct and the military had abandoned the idea of training and equipping a team of female Special Forces operatives after the second Medusa team was wiped out in a mission gone terribly wrong.

The other two masked men grabbed her by her arms and hauled her upright. Adrenaline roared through her body, and it took all the discipline she had not to lash out and fight for her life against these men. She was hopelessly outgunned, and three on one was not the kind of odds she wanted to take into a fistfight.

She was a good hand-to-hand fighter, but she wasn't invincible. Martial artists won against three attackers only in the movies. Carefully choreographed and scripted movies. Not real life. Not in an elementary school full of children.

"You're sure this is her?" one of the other men asked the terrorist who'd hidden the little girl.

He stared at her indecisively. His gaze strayed to

a telephone sitting on the desk beside her, to the exit door and then back to her face. He exhaled hard. Regret glinted in his stare. "Yes. That's her." His voice was a rough baritone and sounded stressed.

Who in the *hell* did they think she was? Who *were* they?

Her only play was to delay these guys as long as she could. Give the police time to respond to her call.

"Who are you?" she demanded in English. No way was she giving away that she understood anything they were saying to one another. "What do you want with me?"

She didn't see the blow coming. A fist plowed into her jaw from the right side, snapping her head hard to the left and making her see stars. Dazed, she stared at the first man—the one with golden eyes—wincing silently in front of her.

Gingerly, she poked her right cheek with her tongue. No teeth felt loose, but the inside of her cheek was shredded. She opened her mouth, flexing her jaw experimentally. It didn't feel broken.

Well. That didn't go as planned. Dazed, she stared at her attackers. Real fear for her life flowed through her. She registered it, cataloged the emotion and forcibly pushed it down. She had no time for fear. Not if she wanted to live. And not if she wanted to protect the kids in this building.

She had to get these men outside, into the range of armed law enforcement officials, but slowly enough that said officials could get here before these guys fled.

"You're sure it's her?" the third man asked doubtfully in Farsi. "She doesn't look much like her picture."

"Yes, yes," Goldeneyes snapped back in Farsi. "Blonde. Tall. Thirty years old. And she does match the picture. These Western women wear a lot of makeup and it changes how they look. I'm used to that, and you're not. I'm telling you it's her."

With that declaration, Goldeneyes apparently sealed some sort of fate for her. The other two men nodded, accepting his word.

What picture? Part of becoming a Medusa was having her life scrubbed completely off the internet. *Completely* off. A team of cybersecurity experts did the initial wipe and then maintained continuous scans for any new images that might pop up. Even official public records were scrubbed. She did not exist in cyberspace.

So, how did these guys know her, let alone have a picture of her? She certainly had no idea who they were.

Belatedly, her mind working a couple steps slower than normal, she mentally corrected him. She was twenty-seven years old, not thirty, thank you very much.

In the distance, sirens became audible. God bless the 9-1-1 operator. She'd called in the cavalry, after all.

"Time's up. Let's go," Jaw Puncher bit out.

The men hustled her out into the hallway. She briefly considered making a stand right there in the entrance, but they had AK-47s, and one blow from the butt of one of those would knock her out cold. She would just as soon stay conscious if she could. Also, there were all those kids just down the hall. She had no way of knowing if there were any more armed men in the building, and she dared not provoke these guys to start shooting.

She did her best to slow the men down, though, shortening her steps and resisting moving forward between them in the guise of being too zoned out to do anything but shuffle along drunkenly.

Irritably, they overpowered her and shoved her outside into the parking lot. More sirens were audible now.

Lots of them. Unfortunately, they still sounded a half-dozen blocks away.

Goldeneyes stepped up close behind her and body-checked her hard but not painfully, shoving his hip into her lower back, helping the other two men throw her into a white step van. She tumbled to the floor, slamming hard into its metal ribs. Gasping for air, she noted a fourth man darting out of the building to join them. A fifth man drove, pulling away from the front door with a hard lurch of the van.

One of the men snapped at the driver not to leave tire tracks, and the vehicle lurched again as he slowed down abruptly.

Fear bubbled up again in her throat, momentarily choking her.

She did the four-step breathing technique she'd been taught. *In. Hold breath and count to four. Out. Count to four. In...*

It took several breaths, but calm prevailed once more over her panic.

Okay. She was being kidnapped. Major suckage.

But there had been multiple witnesses. Law enforcement would put out an APB for this van in a few minutes. Houma was a small town deep in the bayou country, which meant there were only so many roads these men could travel in between the copious waterways.

This would be okay. An hour. Maybe two. A standoff, perhaps. With her, a trained Special Forces operative, on the inside. She would be the police's secret weapon when it came time for a rescue. All she had to do was stay conscious and keep her wits about her. Trust her training.

The van pulled out of the parking lot and turned right. That would be south on Maple Street. They went straight for what she estimated to be five minutes, and then they turned left. A few minutes, another right turn and then they accelerated to highway speed. Maybe Bayou Black Drive heading west out of town?

Which would be ironic. That road would take them right past the unmarked turnoff to the Medusas' secret facility, where her teammates were gathering for today's training.

A sense of unreality washed over her. Surely, she was not being kidnapped by Iranian terrorists. This *had* to be a bad dream. It couldn't be happening to her. Was that shock lowering its protective fog over her brain? It felt just the way her instructors had described it. Everything was happening at a distance. Muted. Not really touching her.

One of the men admonished the driver in Farsi, but she didn't understand the command. In a second, she felt the vehicle slow down to a more sedate speed. Piper frowned. What on earth did Iranians want with her? She'd never had anything to do with that part of the world before—had never served or even traveled there and had no particular expertise on the region beyond reading her daily intelligence brief. What was going on here? She had to be missing something critical—

Something heavy smashed painfully into the back of her head, and she toppled forward as everything went dark.

Chapter 2

Zane Cosworth swore silently, wincing involuntarily as the terrorist calling himself Yousef clocked the woman prisoner on the back of the head with the butt of his AK-47. "Don't kill her," he snapped at the guy, the most volatile of the bunch.

"Shut up, Amir. I didn't like how she was looking at me," Yousef snarled back.

An urge to return the favor and clock the bastard upside the head made his hands twitch. Zane balled them into fists at his sides.

Amir was the name he'd used to infiltrate these SOBs' sleeper cell. Not that they were sleeping after this morning's little stunt.

They were a frustrating bunch, closemouthed and stingy with information for him, the new guy on the team. He was the only actual American among them, and he was convinced it was the sole reason he'd been brought on board. They called upon him to interact with other Americans and used him as their errand boy in any public situation where their accents might draw attention.

But that also meant he was completely expendable if he offended these guys or got in their way of whatever the hell their actual end goal was.

The team's leader, Mahmoud, was definitely taking instructions from someone who communicated via encrypted cell phone, or occasionally via a Dark Web site that was even more heavily encrypted.

Rolling his eyes at Yousef, Zane leaned over the woman, ostensibly to check her pulse. He grabbed her right wrist with his left hand while surreptitiously slipping the ring off her fourth finger with his other hand and palming the piece. No way in hell could he let his compatriots discover that this woman was a West Pointer. If he was gauging Mahmoud correctly, the guy would kill her instantly.

Mahmoud said practically nothing about his personal beliefs, but he made no secret of despising Americans, particularly military members.

Zane slipped the ring into his pocket. He was seriously grateful that chance had thrown a female soldier in his path this morning. What she was doing at some elementary school in a small town in southern Louisiana, nowhere near an active military base, he had no idea. Call it a small act of God that had gone his way.

Not that he was a whole lot happier about throwing a soldier to the lions than he would be about doing it to some random civilian woman.

But he'd been forced to make the best of an impossible situation.

Of the four women cowering on the floor in the school's front office, she'd looked to be by far the youngest and fittest of the bunch. Naming her as the target had been the least awful choice under the circumstances. Which wasn't saying much.

Honestly, he'd feared that if he told the others he didn't see their target in the office, where she normally worked as an assistant principal, they would start shooting kids to get the woman to reveal herself.

Mahmoud was a cagey bastard and had barely shared any information with any of his men about this fiasco. He'd briefed the cell members only about an anonymous woman they were supposed to find and kidnap.

Zane hadn't thought it was enough detail to pass on to his superiors. He'd assumed Mahmoud and his boys would spend days or weeks finding the target, doing surveillance on her, picking the perfect spot to abduct her and then launching an operation to kidnap the woman.

Zane *thought* he had plenty of time to find out who the woman was, slip away from the other men and send a message to his superiors about this little operation. It galled him to have been outmaneuvered by a freaking terrorist like this.

Mahmoud also hadn't given the team any indication whatsoever that today would be the actual snatch.

Zane had been nearly as shocked as the teachers and kids of Southdown Elementary School when they'd piled out of the van for real, armed with actual weapons and ammunition.

Mahmoud had passed around a picture and name of the target, Persephone Black—whoever the hell she was—in the van as they turned into the school parking lot. Zane hadn't even had time to send an emergency text to his handlers to let them know who the target was and that an attack was imminent before Mahmoud had ordered them out of the van and barged into a flipping elementary school, armed to kill.

The picture itself had been informative. It was fuzzy and taken from a distance. The woman had been with a man on a crowded street that looked like some place in Europe. She was looking over her shoulder at something, and the shot of her face had been snapped in that moment. For all the world, it looked like a surveillance photo taken by someone following the couple.

Did that mean Mahmoud and his men were in the US on behalf of some foreign government with an intelligence service of its own? Iran was the obvious candidate, given that they sounded like native Farsi speakers.

Regardless, they were some sort of black-ops team, and they'd proved this morning that they were not averse to using violence.

As soon as he'd heard that the real target was out sick, he'd known he had a big problem. Mahmoud and his boys wouldn't hesitate to shoot up a school full of little kids in retaliation for their victim being absent.

He felt really bad for this woman he'd inaccurately fingered as the target. He glanced down at her, crumpled on the floor of the van at his feet, and silently vowed to make it up to her somehow.

One thing Zane hated worse than just about anything else was being forced into a no-win choice. And God knew he'd faced one of those already today. He could either go along with assaulting a school, snatching a woman and scaring the hell out of a bunch of kids... or he could blow his cover, and throw away months' worth of work gaining Mahmoud's trust and worming his way inside what Zane's superiors believed to be a dangerous and violent sleeper cell.

He'd very nearly gone ahead and turned his weapon on his coconspirators to take them out this morning.

The one thing that had stopped him was being in an elementary school. The possibility of an innocent child being hit in the cross fire was the *only* reason any of these bastards were still alive.

If he just knew who they were, he would end this farce right now.

He did know one thing about them. They would *never* say anything under interrogation. They were all fanatic enough to die before giving up even their names.

He'd lived and worked with Mahmoud and his fellow psychopaths for months, and he *still* didn't have any idea who they worked for or what their ultimate goal was. That was how closemouthed these men were.

Normally, Zane would pull the plug on an undercover op like this immediately and get the civilian victim out. Hell, he was on the verge of doing that very thing right now.

The only thing stopping him was that ring in his pocket. If the kidnapped woman was a West Pointer, maybe he could let this thing play out just a bit more—a few minutes or a few hours—and get his answers before he called in the big guns to take these jerks down.

Thing was, if Mahmoud and company did work for Iran, they would only be replaced by another sleeper cell of trained killers when US authorities took these guys out.

Hence the urgent need to know who they worked for and what their end goal was. He didn't for a minute believe that kidnapping some woman from an elementary school was the primary reason this cell had infiltrated the United States.

They posed some much-greater national security threat. But *what*?

Nope, he'd had no choice today. He had to throw this

woman he'd never seen before under the bus and maintain his cover a little longer. He hated it, and he would do whatever he had to do to protect her.

Just a little while, he mentally promised her.

The unconscious woman beside him moved faintly and then subsided again. Yousef had hit her way too damned hard if she was still out cold. Zane knew from long experience in the field that if she was unconscious more than a few minutes, she would likely be out for the next couple hours.

Patience, Zane. Now was not the time to make his move to rescue her. He was probably her only chance of survival. But he would get one shot—and no more than one shot—at rescuing her. He had to wait until she was conscious, able to move fast and willing to cooperate with him.

He hoped to God she understood his choice and one day forgave him for it.

Did it make him a dreadful human being that he'd forced her into helping him figure out what these terrorists were up to? That he'd potentially sacrificed this woman's emotional well-being, and maybe her life, to save many more lives down the road?

Hell, he was already a dreadful human being. As an undercover agent, he deceived people and lied for a living. He'd even done criminal acts in the name of keeping his covers. He drew the line at hurting or killing innocent victims, although he was skirting dangerously close to that line today. Hell, sometimes he wondered if he was even one of the good guys anymore.

He owed this woman huge. When the time was right, he silently promised her he would find a way to save her from these men.

But how…and when…he had no idea.

Scowling, he leaned back beside her slumped body. He propped an elbow casually on his upraised knee. "Anyone following us?" he asked Bijan, the youngest of the crew, who crouched at the dirty rear window of the van.

"No. We're clear," the kid answered.

Zane had to give these guys credit. They'd run the grab-and-go to perfection, managing their time on scene to the second and getting away moments before the first police car arrived. His certainty that they were military trained—more specifically, Special Forces trained—intensified.

His concern for the woman intensified, as well. Men like this wouldn't hesitate to kill her if and when they figured out they had grabbed the wrong person.

He studied her face. She was pretty. Her hair was dark blond and her skin was smooth and slightly olive complexioned. The combination was unusual and striking. Her legs were lean in her blue jeans, and her shirt was currently twisted tight against some nice curves. Her fingers were long and slender with short, cracked fingernails.

Those fingernails surprised him. She looked put together enough to be the kind of woman to always have a perfect manicure. What did she do to beat up her hands like that?

"Pull over at the next gas station," Mahmoud, the team leader, ordered Hassan, the driver.

It took a few minutes, but Zane felt the van decelerate. They pulled around to the side of a tiny rural gas station advertising with a hand-painted sign that it also sold beer, fishing bait and, more alarmingly, gator bait.

After a quick check to verify that the gas station had

no surveillance cameras, Mahmoud and Yousef piled outside. Zane followed more slowly. The other men were already peeling off temporary decals on the side of the vehicle announcing it to be an air-conditioning service van. Meanwhile, Bijan used a screwdriver to change the rear license plate. *When had these guys set up this van as a slick getaway vehicle?*

Alarm slammed through him. Had they done it before he'd joined the team? *Or had they done it behind his back?*

Odds were they'd done it recently. Which was freaking scary. It meant they *still* didn't trust him.

Which also meant that not only was his life in mortal danger, but the woman's, as well.

The underlying tension that always hummed in his gut when he was undercover ratcheted up violently. He didn't like this. Not one bit. Was he a prisoner in this van, too? How fine a tightrope was he walking with Mahmoud and his men? He'd been useful to them as long as they were trying to keep a low profile and not be noticed by the locals. But if they'd completed their mission, these men would go to ground or flee the country and not need his services any longer.

His intuition screamed that he was blown. That it was time to bug out.

Normally, he never went against his gut feelings. Over and over through the years, his gut had proved to be right. And right now, it was telling him in no uncertain terms to abandon this operation *immediately*. The feds had plenty of ammunition to arrest these men and put them away for a very long time after this morning's stunt in the elementary school.

The authorities might never figure out what Mahmoud's

primary goal had been, but at least this particular terror cell would be off the street.

However, the woman changed everything. Zane couldn't possibly bail out now. Not as long as these men held an innocent woman captive. An innocent women *he* had put into these violent men's hands.

He mentally swore. He mustn't do *anything* to arouse these guys' suspicions. The danger of staying in this undercover assignment drove home hard, a punch in the gut that left him gasping.

Too tense to be still one more second, Zane walked around behind the van, pretending to stretch his legs. "Can I help with the signs?" he asked casually.

Mahmoud wadded up the last of the adhesive vinyl and tossed it in a trash can. He shoved a cigarette lighter down into the barrel, and a thin stream of smoke commenced rising from its contents. "No. We're finished. As soon as Osted gets out of the bathroom, we'll go."

Zane nodded slowly, trying to look impressed. "You guys are good. I'm grateful you let me learn from you, *almuelim alhakim*." He dropped in the Arabic phrase meaning "wise teacher" to gauge Mahmoud's reaction.

The guy nodded shortly and looked vaguely less irascible than usual, acknowledging the compliment.

Zane guessed they were assets of VAJA—the Iranian Ministry of Intelligence. But they never talked politics, not even in the most general of terms. They talked about European soccer and the weather for the most part. And such a degree of operational discipline scared the living hell out of him.

He strolled to the corner of the cinder-block building and, with a glance over his shoulder to make sure no one saw him, surreptitiously dropped the woman's class ring on the ground. There. One piece of evidence showing her to be a soldier erased. Now he just had to make sure she didn't have some other form of ID on her—dog tags, or maybe a wallet with a military ID in it.

For that matter, he needed to get rid of *any* identification she had on her. He had to keep up the ruse of her being Persephone Black for as long as he possibly could. Until both he and the woman could escape. Everything depended on it.

Including his life. And hers.

Tessa Wilkes eyed her boss cautiously. Major Gunnar Torsten was not a happy camper this morning. He barked, "Still no answer on Piper's phone?"

"No, sir," Rebel McQueen replied from her post at the ops center's communications panel. "I pinged her phone's locator function, and it puts her in Houma." Which was the nearest actual town to their secret training facility.

"Where in Houma?" Torsten demanded.

"Um, at an elementary school."

"What in the hell is she doing there?" he snapped.

Rebel didn't answer and instead threw Tessa a distressed look. She felt Rebel's pain. Torsten was usually a stern guy and all business, but this morning he really had a burr up his butt. Catching the silent plea for help, Tessa sighed and spoke up. "Do you want me to go fetch her, sir?"

"No! But I damned well want to know why one of my highly trained, supposedly responsible operatives has gone AWOL."

Rebel spoke from her console again, muttering, "That's odd."

Everyone looked at her. She glanced up and started.

"Oh. Um, I just pinged her backup locator. The one in her class ring from West Point. It's not in Houma."

"It had better be headed this way at a high rate of speed," Torsten ground out.

Man, the boss had seriously woken up on the wrong side of the bed today. Not that he was ever tolerant of screwups. He was fond of saying that seconds were the difference between life and death. He wasn't wrong, of course.

Rebel reported, "Her secondary locator is moving away from us on Bayou Black Road, heading northwest. It's about fifteen miles west of here."

Tessa, the first member of their new Medusa team and more at ease with Torsten than Rebel, leaned forward. "Something's wrong. Piper would have called one of us if she had a problem and couldn't get here on time. And she would *never* go AWOL."

Torsten huffed in irritation. "We can't wait any longer. Our Vietnamese instructors are only here for a few days, and I need you to learn as much as you can while you have access to them. Fall out, ladies."

Rebel and Tessa stood, trading worried glances with one another. It was supremely unlike Piper to blow off required training, and even more unlike her not to check in with someone. A note of worry started to vibrate low in Tessa's gut.

The major led the way to the reinforced steel door disguised to look like weathered wood siding, unsealing it and stepping out into the morning's steamy heat. Tessa fell into step beside Major Torsten.

She said soberly, "Sir, I'm worried something has happened to Piper. You taught us to listen to our intuitions, and mine says she's in some sort of trouble. I think one of us should go look for her."

He frowned, but at least he didn't rip her head off. "I'll take your intuition under advisement. If Piper doesn't show up in the next hour or so, I'll go looking for her myself."

Yikes. Piper was in a heap of trouble.

Chapter 3

Piper regained consciousness slowly. Her head throbbed painfully, and it didn't help matters that every time the van hit a bump in the road, the metal floor bounced underneath her temple, whacking her head again.

Her lips were dry, and her bladder was full, which meant she'd been out for a while. A couple hours, possibly. Dang it! They could've changed directions a dozen times without her knowing. She had no way of knowing where she was now!

A sense of disorientation swirled around her. As if she was completely disconnected from the real world. It was scary as hell, and she had to force herself to lie perfectly still until her breathing settled back down and the panic attack passed.

Questions peppered her mind almost too fast to catalog. Where was she? Who were these guys? What did they want with her? How much danger was she in? Where were they taking her? Would she have a shot at escaping them? Did they plan to kill her? Was this even real?

Cautiously, she cracked her eyes open and saw black pants and black combat boots. It hadn't been a terrible dream. She really had been kidnapped. The weight of panic landed on her chest again, and she struggled to control her breathing.

She could just lie here pretending to be unconscious... but just then the van hit a big bump and slammed her head hard into the floor.

Ow.

She probably had a concussion already from the blow that had knocked her out. No need to exacerbate the stupid thing. Piper pushed against the floor with both hands, sitting up groggily. At least none of the men stopped her from doing so.

The ski masks had come off, replaced by baseball caps pulled down low and dark sunglasses. Drat. She still wouldn't be able to identify her kidnappers in a lineup. She felt the weight of their stares upon her and did her best not to freak out and start screaming hysterically.

Whatever this was, whoever they were, she had to keep her wits about her, watch, wait and seize the opportunity to escape when it presented itself. And surely one would. She *had* to believe she would have a chance to get away, eventually.

Be calm. Breathe. Relax.

She did her level best to settle into the state of loose readiness that Major Torsten stressed over and over was absolutely necessary to peak performance.

At least they hadn't tied her up. It was a small victory, but she knew from her POW training that those were all a hostage could hope to achieve.

Choking fear bubbled up in her throat unbidden, and she stomped it down hard. She had no time for that.

This was a battle of wits and wills, and she needed all of hers. In the meantime, maybe she could figure out who these guys were, why they'd grabbed her and where they were going.

Pitching her voice to be polite and diffident, she asked, "Who are you?" A little rapport with her kidnappers could never hurt.

They stared back at her in stony silence. One of the men was seated beside her, between her and the driver. Which ruled out her making a dive for the steering wheel and maybe putting the van in a ditch.

"Why did you kidnap me?" she added.

Still nothing.

She debated starting up a one-sided conversation with these men to provoke them to talk, but ultimately decided she would be better served acting scared to death and letting them lead the conversation wherever they wanted to.

She craned her head to peer out the front window and saw a ribbon of interstate highway stretching away in front of the van. The sun seemed to be overhead, so she had no means of working out what direction they were going. But it confirmed she'd been unconscious for a while.

She realized her elbow was lightly rubbing the arm of one of the bad guys. Based on his build, she thought it might be Goldeneyes. Subtly, she shifted away from him. If she wasn't mistaken, she heard him exhale in irritation. What did he have to be irritated about? She wasn't his freaking girlfriend. And she wasn't about to cozy up to some homicidal terrorist.

Except, when they finally stopped at a rest area near a truck stop, that same homicidal terrorist was the one who helped her out of the van and steadied her elbow for a second while blood flow returned to her legs. Yup. Definitely Goldeneyes. He was the tallest and broadest of shoulder of the whole bunch.

He muttered in unaccented English, "Don't try anything, or my companions will shoot this place up and kill everyone here." Oddly enough, he sounded almost apologetic when he made his threat. What was the deal with this guy?

He also was the one who guided her over to the ladies' restroom, parked outside the door and said gruffly, "Two minutes, and then I'm coming in after you."

She went inside and checked quickly to see if there were any other women in there whom she could ask for help. The place was empty except for her. Damn.

But there was a window on the far end of the long bay of toilet stalls. She eyed it critically. It was small and high, but she might be able to squeeze through it. At least it was worth a try.

She climbed up on the nearest sink to the window and punched her fist through the screen covering it. The actual window was mounted on a hinge that swung out, and she forced it wide-open. It was awkward aiming her arms through the small opening while jumping up, but she managed to land her waist on the sill. Pushing against the outside wall with her hands and kicking her legs, she wriggled through.

She fell headfirst and caught herself with her arms, rolling into a somersault.

Yes. Free.

She jumped up and took off running as fast as she could. A large field of mowed grass separated her from the truck stop—and other people—perhaps a quarter mile away.

She sprinted for all she was worth. Her breath came

in huge gulps, and pounding blood roared in her ears. *Must. Get. Away.* Her thighs burned and her lungs screamed for air, but she pumped her arms hard and kept on going for all she was worth.

She was about halfway across the field when, without warning, something huge and heavy tackled her from behind, landing on top of her and knocking the breath out of her. She gasped frantically for air, but none came.

Dammit. She'd never even heard him coming.

A hard hand plastered over her mouth, which did nothing to help her regain her breath.

A male voice snarled low in her ear, "You and I are going to stand up. Then you're going to turn around and walk back to the van and climb in, all nice-like and co-operative." Hot breath wafted over her ear as her captor leaned close to add, "And if you don't, I'll knock you out and carry you back to the damned van."

A detached voice in a far corner of her mind registered that he hadn't threatened to kill her. But in the abrupt rush of adrenaline that accompanied the return of her ability to breathe, she ignored the voice and thrashed wildly beneath him.

She managed to get turned over on her back, but he was significantly bigger and stronger than she was, and apparently a trained wrestler. He flattened her with demoralizing ease. Their bodies pressed together in what would be a blatantly sexual fashion under any other circumstances.

As it was, she held herself rigid beneath him and did her best to ignore the way his thighs pressed against hers, the bulge of his crotch against the junction of her legs, the way his hard stomach pressed into hers and how her breasts smashed against his chest.

Goldeneyes, indeed.

She stared up at him in shock. Either his tackle or their struggle had knocked his baseball cap and sunglasses off, and she got her first good look at him.

If one human being could look any less like a violent criminal, this guy was it. His hair was a sun-tossed mix of brown and gold, nearly the same color as his eyes. His skin was tanned, his jaw chiseled, his features classy. All in all, he looked like he belonged on Martha's Vineyard, wearing chinos, a polo shirt and a white cricket sweater, sailing a boat on a crisp summer day.

Her brows twitched into a frown. She'd pegged all of these guys as Iranians from their use of Farsi. But this one didn't look even remotely Persian.

"Who are you?" she breathed.

"Get up." With a quick flex of powerful biceps, he popped to his feet. He had a crushing grip on her hand and gave a hard yank on it now, dragging her upright.

He frisked all her pockets and then did a weird thing. He checked her neck for jewelry. "What are you doing?" she demanded.

"Making sure you don't have a wallet with any identification in it or dog tags on you," he muttered.

Realization smacked into her, like a slap across the face. He didn't want any of the other terrorists to figure out her real name. If that was the case, then this wasn't about her being a Medusa at all. That was a relief, at least. Although it still left behind the glaring question of what in the world these guys wanted with some woman who worked with little kids.

With a quick jerk, he twisted her arm up and back behind her, shoving her along in front of him, back toward the rest stop building. The van was out of sight on the other side of the structure.

"What's your name?" she gasped.

"Amir."

"Baloney," she blurted. "That's not your name. You're named something preppy like Chad or Blaine."

He gave a warning tug on her twisted arm that was just shy of painful.

"You really should set me free," she tried. "I guarantee you don't want to face the criminal penalties when you guys get caught. *All* the law enforcement authorities will already be out looking for me. You'll never get away with this. If you let me go right now, by the time I can get over to the truck stop, call the police and wait for them to respond, you guys can be long gone. A clean getaway."

"The others will come out of the van any second to see what's taking so long. They have long-range rifles and know how to use them. You'd never make it across that field alive."

He almost sounded regretful about that. Weird.

"Be quiet," he bit out as they approached the building she'd broken out of.

He shocked her by walking her into the ladies' room and shoving her toward a toilet stall. He was still going to let her go to the bathroom? By rights, he should haul her back to the van, toss her in and let her suffer—or soil herself—after her attempted escape.

She used the facilities fast and was not surprised when she opened the stall door to see him looming just outside. He grabbed her elbow and steered her toward the van.

He growled low, "If my partners find out about your little stunt, they'll kill you—or worse. However, if you'll promise not to say anything about your failed escape attempt, I won't, either."

"Um, okay," she responded in confusion. Now, why

on earth did he make that offer? Surely it was only because he would get in trouble for her nearly getting away. Still. Something was off about this guy.

He hustled her back to the van and started to hoist her inside. "I've got this," she snapped, yanking her arm out of his grip. She got the distinct impression he chose to let go of her. His hand felt plenty strong enough to have resisted her tug.

"That took a long time," one of the other men complained in Farsi.

"Women," her strange captor responded, rolling his eyes.

The other man grunted in commiseration.

A frisson of satisfaction coursed through her. If they wanted to underestimate her because she was a woman, she was totally fine with that. Wait till they figured out she was a trained Special Forces operative. They weren't going to know what had hit them. Anticipation of the moment when she kicked butts and took names coursed through her.

Patience, Piper. Patience.

Not to worry. She would show them, all in due time.

She considered her captor's name. She supposed it was possible his name really was Amir, but it had rung false when he said it. He just didn't seem to own the name the way he would have if it had been his actual name. No, Goldeneyes fitted him better.

They drove for perhaps two more hours, taking back roads exclusively. The next time they stopped, she spied through the windows a tiny town boasting a single flashing red light, one gas station/convenience store/Laundromat and a Baptist church. Goldeneyes was the only man to exit the van. Which made sense if he was the only American in the bunch. He would draw a lot less attention than the others in this rural part of the country where few foreigners visited. He went outside to pump and pay for gas, and escorted her to the restroom again.

She didn't have a peanut-sized bladder, and in the absence of anything to drink didn't particularly have to use the restroom, but she still took the chance when offered. Who knew when they would stop again? And it felt good to get up and move around, get some circulation back in her legs. Wary of her captors killing the cashier, she didn't cause a fuss as Goldeneyes marched her inside.

She did, however, make a point of saying hello to the teen girl behind the counter and making direct eye contact with her. Maybe if this girl saw some sort of news story on a kidnapped woman, she would remember seeing Piper and call the authorities.

Goldeneyes had a painfully tight grip on her elbow as they walked past the store attendant, and Piper didn't test his unspoken warning to behave herself. There was no telling how far his goodwill would extend, and she'd pushed it pretty hard already.

He deposited her back in the van and went inside once more, returning after a few minutes carrying several grocery bags full of sandwiches and snacks.

Oh, no. That looked like road-trip food. Which meant they still had a ways to go before reaching their final destination.

"Where are we headed?" she tried.

Her captors just stared at her stonily.

The van pulled back out onto the road, and despair washed through her. The next time they stopped, she needed to let someone know she was in trouble and to call the police. But how? With Goldeneyes hovering over her every move and the threat that his teammates would kill innocent bystanders ringing in her ears, it wasn't like she had a lot of options.

He passed her a bottle of water. Silently, she took it and downed the whole thing. She had to give him credit; he was taking pretty decent care of her, all things considered. For the moment, at least, these men seemed interested in keeping her alive. Thank God.

At least she was able to tell by the setting sun that they were traveling more or less toward the north, and maybe slightly west. By now they had to have left Louisiana, which put them possibly in Arkansas.

They started to go up and down hills—which made sense if they were in the western portion of Arkansas, entering the Ozark Plateau. Which was both good and bad news. Good because it was lush country with plenty of food, water, shelter and cover for her eventual escape. The bad news was that it was isolated country with areas of very sparse population. She might have to evade her captors for days before she found help.

Why in the world had these men gone to all the trouble of kidnapping her just to haul her off on this extended road trip? Why not kill her in or near Houma? Did they plan to ransom her back to the Medusas? Surely they knew the US government adhered to a strict pay-no-ransom policy. And it wasn't like she had a rich family that would cough up money for her return. Her dad owned a small auto-repair shop and her mom was a preschool teacher.

Her captors took turns napping and driving into the evening, all except for Goldeneyes. He seemed to have appointed himself her personal guard, and the other men seemed to have silently agreed to let him assume all babysitting duties.

A small blessing for which she was grateful. He seemed generally concerned about her comfort and well-being, while the other men looked at her with open contempt as if she were of no more worth or interest than a bug crawling across the floor of the van. Their dismissive attitude would be their undoing if she had anything to say about it.

It had gotten dark outside when she noticed most of the men were dozing. Only the driver and Goldeneyes were awake. His disturbingly beautiful stare was locked on her like it had been for most of the past twelve hours.

"What's your real name?" she asked in a low voice.

"Amir."

"Fine. Be that way. I'll just stick to calling you Goldeneyes in my mind."

His right eyebrow lifted faintly, but he didn't show any other reaction.

"My name is Piper."

He replied firmly, "Your name is Persephone Black."

"I beg your pardon?" she blurted. He'd asked about a Mrs. Black when he'd first stormed into the school office. Was she a teacher? Why would these men kidnap an elementary school teacher?

"Your name. It's Persephone Black. You can pretend to be anyone you want. But we know who you really are."

What on God's green earth was he talking about? Had they kidnapped the wrong person?

"But...you looked right at me... You said you'd seen my picture...that you knew I was the right person—"

"Quiet," he bit out low, cutting her off.

She looked away from him and realized that the man who acted like the leader was awake, his eyes barely slitted open. How had "Amir" known the boss was awake? She hadn't gotten the slightest indication of it—not even a hint of intuition that she was being watched. Wow. Her powers of observation were messed up worse than she'd realized. And his—they were sharp and on point.

"May I please have some more water?" she asked meekly.

Goldeneyes passed her a bottle of water without comment.

She downed it and added the bottle to the pile of trash growing in the back of the van: food wrappers and soda cans. These men's discipline clearly did not extend to picking up after themselves. Either that or they planned to ditch the van at some point. Still. There would be fingerprints and DNA all over that trash.

With darkness, the team had taken off their sunglasses and hats, and she'd seen all their faces now. She'd watched them all evening, learning each man's features from many different angles. The bump on the bridge of a nose, the angle of a jaw, the shape and fullness of lips, even the timbre of their voices.

She was confident she could pick out any of these men from a lineup if it ever came to that. Now she just had to make sure she stayed alive and got away so it could.

All of them except Goldeneyes were black haired, dark eyed, and their skin was caramel toned, in keeping with a Middle Eastern heritage. Two of them looked quite young, in their early twenties.

The other three looked hard as nails and closer to their midthirties in age. The older men reminded her of Gunnar Torsten. They all had the same hardness and cool, lethal confidence as her boss. She made a mental note not to mess with any of the older men.

As for Goldeneyes, he was the odd man out. Besides his fair coloring, he looked about thirty years old, and he carried himself differently than the others. At least, he did now.

When he'd stormed into the school office, he'd exhibited all the deadly confidence of the older men. But now, he slouched in the back of the van, eyes down, shoulders hunched. As if he was trying to make himself invisible to the other men. Odd. He didn't strike her as the submissive-follower type. At all. But he was clearly acting like the low man in the pecking order.

The van slowed and turned off the winding two-lane road they'd been following up and down mountainsides for the past hour. It commenced bumping and banging over what was obviously some sort of bad dirt road.

They spent two or three more minutes getting tossed all over the back of the van, and then, just like that, the vehicle stopped. The driver turned off the ignition.

They'd arrived. Wherever that might be.

The silence and stillness were a shock to her system after spending the last twelve hours or so in the rumbling, vibrating van.

"Out," the one called Mahmoud ordered.

Bijan, one of the young ones, opened the double back doors, and Piper glimpsed the dark silhouette of a decent-sized log cabin with a long porch across its front. Trees—deciduous, she noted—crowded close, and there was no ambient light in the sky to indicate a city of any kind nearby. Yup. These guys had brought her out into the middle of nowhere to hold for whatever dastardly purpose they had in mind for her.

Goldeneyes hopped out of the van in front of her and turned around to help her out. She was tempted to shake off his hand, but her legs were numb, and as she stood on them, they tingled so badly she wasn't sure they would hold her full weight. She clung to his powerful forearm while circulation returned to her aching limbs. After a few seconds, she let go of his arm.

"Better?" he murmured under his breath.

"Uh-huh," she muttered back.

He stepped behind her, efficiently twisting her arm behind her, but putting no pressure on it that would be painful. His intention was clear: if she didn't fight him, he wouldn't hurt her.

For now, at least. As long as their silent truce held.

She didn't for a second believe these terrorists had brought her out here solely to enjoy the fresh air. They had some agenda up their sleeves. She just couldn't fathom what it was.

Which led her back to the same question that had been preoccupying her all day. Why her?

Chapter 4

It didn't take long after the report of armed men at Southdown Elementary School in Houma hit the news for the Medusas to put two and two together. They were taking a water break in the woods when Rebel, glancing at her cell phone, exclaimed.

Tessa piped up, asking, "Whatcha got, Reb?"

The communications specialist looked up from her phone grimly. "I just got a breaking-news alert. Armed men burst into Southdown Elementary School in Houma this morning and kidnapped an unnamed woman. She's described as tall, blonde and in her mid-to late twenties."

Tessa lurched upright from where she'd been lounging on a patch of moss. "That's got to be Piper!"

Major Torsten cut in. "Where are Captain Ford's cell phone and class ring locations now?"

Rebel answered, "I'd have to go back to the ops center to answer that, sir."

"What are you waiting for, then?" Torsten snapped.

Tessa got that he was worried about Piper. But he didn't have to bite their heads off!

Her train of thought derailed abruptly. Torsten was always tough, but he'd never been this snappish before. She traded worried looks with her fiancé, Beau, and his thoughts clearly mirrored hers. He was worried about the boss, too. Beau had worked for Gunnar Torsten for several years before being asked to help train the new Medusa team. If even Beau was worried about him, something was definitely wrong with Torsten.

When they hustled back to the vehicles to drive back to base, she made a point of climbing in the front passenger seat of the Hummer Torsten was driving.

"What's up, sir?"

He glanced over at her and bit out, "I've got a missing and possibly kidnapped team member."

"Besides that," she replied carefully.

"Isn't that enough?"

"You were way more tense than usual even before we thought anything was wrong with Piper…sir."

He exhaled hard and turned his eyes back to the road. "I got an intel report last night."

"And?"

"It indicates that Abu Haddad may not be dead."

"What?" she and Beau squawked simultaneously. The two of them had by a hair escaped dying in the explosion that had killed Haddad last year. The international, and very illegal, arms dealer, had to be dead! His entire yacht—and everyone on it—had been blown into bits not much larger than her finger. Beau had set the charges himself.

Torsten replied heavily, "We never did get a confirmation of death."

Beau leaned forward from the back seat and ground out, "That's because nothing but matchsticks and the occasional chunk of meat were left when I was done blowing up that bastard's yacht."

Tessa frowned at their boss. "Why does someone think Haddad may be alive?"

Torsten huffed, clearly as unhappy as she and Beau were. "A rumor has surfaced that the Haddad network may be doing some sort of big secret deal with a Middle Eastern nation. The source apparently has it on good authority that Haddad himself is expected to close the deal. It's possible that one of his flunkies has taken over the business. But there's also a very small chance that the bastard is back."

"What country is this deal with?" she asked.

"Rumor places the deal in Iran."

"For what kind of weapons?" Beau asked quickly.

Tessa wasn't sure that mattered. The Iranians were dangerous enough with the weaponry they already had. Although she supposed the last thing anyone needed was for that country's leaders to get their hands on something high-tech and truly deadly.

"No idea," Torsten replied.

"It's not like we have a ton of human information sources on the ground in Tehran," she commented. "If someone outside its borders could figure out who's making the sale and what the cargo is, we'd have a better chance of finding out what the Iranians are getting their hands on."

Appearing to give himself a mental shake, the major replied, "Not our problem, today. Right now, I need us to focus on finding Piper."

"Of course, sir." But curiosity about what a dead arms dealer was selling to a country like Iran continued to niggle at the back of Tessa's mind.

They parked in front of the one-story building that

was their communications facility and operational headquarters for Training Site Vanessa, named for Brigadier General Vanessa Blake, the founder of the Medusas over a decade ago.

Their headquarters squatted on stilts and looked like every other ramshackle fishing shack in this part of Terrebonne Parish. Notable only was the building's lack of windows, and the unusually bulky storage shed under the center of the building.

In reality, that shed disguised the elevator shaft down into the underground/underwater bunker that housed the heart of their ops center. The aboveground building mainly disguised antennae and receivers for the equipment below.

They piled into the elevator and stood in silence as it whooshed them down into the bunker. The door opened into the perpetual twilight of a room crammed with computers and monitors.

Rebel sat at her communication console and typed quickly. In just a few seconds, she reported without looking up from her screen, "Piper's phone is still at the elementary school where it was this morning."

"And her backup locator signal?" Torsten asked.

"It appears stationary about fifty miles west of here," she reported. "Reporters are saying a group of masked men were seen coming out of a white air-conditioning company van and heading into the elementary school. They left in the same vehicle. Presumably with Piper in tow."

Major Torsten left Rebel to man the ops center in case Piper called in, and loaded Tessa and Beau into his Hummer. They drove west, paralleling the murky waters of Bayou Black to the GPS coordinates Rebel had given them for Piper's backup locator signal. It turned out to be coming from a crappy little 1950s-era gas station in the middle of nowhere.

The gray-haired Cajun man inside the station swore he hadn't seen any woman fitting Piper's description all day. When Tessa showed him a picture of Piper on her cell phone, the attendant declared her hot, but again denied having seen her. Tessa was inclined to believe him.

Torsten called Rebel to confirm they were at the right place, and she was adamant that their position locators were literally on top of Piper's. And it was still pinging.

They fanned out to search the area, and after a minute or so, Tessa spotted a glint in the gravel at the corner of the building. She bent down and picked up Piper's West Point class ring. The one with the locator in it.

"I found her ring!" she called out.

"Don't move!" Torsten ordered immediately. He knelt down, examining the dirt between himself and Tessa. After a moment, he moved off to his right, toward the side of the building. Using his finger, he drew a rectangle on the ground. "Tire track. Recent," he commented, continuing to stare at the dusty clay.

Beau moved forward to join him in staring at the ground. He had a sniper's outstanding eyesight and was the best tracker of all of them.

"Looks like three men," he murmured. "They milled around beside the vehicle."

Torsten nodded. "And one walked over there to the corner of the building and back, close to where the ring was."

"Did he drop it, maybe?" Tessa asked.

Beau answered grimly, "I don't see any tracks small or narrow enough to be Piper's. These are all men in boots."

"Agreed," Torsten muttered. "I don't think she dropped it as a bread crumb for us."

"Either way," Tessa commented, "we know she was headed west a couple hours ago."

Beau crouched and studied the dirt a bit more, adding, "It looks like some of the tracks lead over to this burn barrel."

Tessa detoured around the footprints to stare into the rusty container at the pile of light gray ashes inside. It didn't look like it would hold any clues to Piper's whereabouts.

Torsten moved over beside her to gaze into the trash barrel, the contents of which were smoking lazily and stank of burnt plastic. He gingerly poked around in them.

"Do you see anything, sir?" she asked hopefully.

"Nope. Just ashes. If the guys in the van dropped anything in here, it's gone."

Damn.

Torsten moved away from her and pulled out his cell phone.

"Where's Piper now?" Tessa asked logically.

Beau looked up grimly from snapping pictures of the tracks. "I think it's safe to say she was kidnapped. Which leads to the even more salient question. Why her?"

They stared at one another grimly. Were the Medusas compromised?

How? Practically no one knew of their existence, let alone what their real mission was supposed to be. The only—deeply buried—paper trail that led to the team vaguely referred to it as an environmental research group.

"Back in the Hummer," Torsten ordered briskly. "We're going to New Orleans."

"What's in New Orleans?" Tessa ventured.

"An NCIS field office. It's time to bring in the big guns to track down Piper and figure out what in the hell is going on."

She wasn't about to voice the idea that, if Torsten had listened to her and Rebel earlier, Piper's kidnappers wouldn't have such a big head start on them. Torsten looked like he was probably having that thought all on his own, without her having to say it.

They climbed back into the Hummer in silence, and Torsten stomped on the accelerator, blatantly ignoring any notion of speed limits as they raced toward New Orleans at nearly a hundred miles per hour. No doubt about it, the boss was definitely more worried than he was expressing aloud.

They all were.

Zane goose-stepped the woman into the cabin as gently as he could. "Piper," she'd called herself. After a brief stop in the bathroom, he followed Mahmoud's order to take her downstairs into the basement and secure her.

The cellar was dirt walled and windowless, cool and dank smelling. He led her over to a four-inch steel pipe running vertically up one wall and pulled out the pair of handcuffs Mahmoud had handed him.

He looped them around the pole and then carefully snapped her wrists into the cuffs. He made sure they were tight enough that she couldn't slip out of them, but not so tight that they hurt her.

Zane brought over an armload of blankets and spread them out on the ground beside her. "It won't be the most comfortable place you've ever slept, but it's dry and you'll be warm enough."

"Why are you doing this for me?" she asked under her breath.

Why indeed? If he was one of the bad guys, he ought to be roughing her up, scaring the living daylights out of her and terrorizing her into unquestioning cooperation with him and the other men. But she was the innocent victim in this scenario, and he was the criminal who'd put her here.

He had already considered telling her who he was in hopes of gaining her trust and cooperation. But he'd reluctantly ruled out revealing his true identity to her.

If—when—Mahmoud and Yousef got around to torturing her, which Zane had no doubt both men were sadistic enough to enjoy doing, he really needed her not to blurt out that he was an undercover CIA agent. People in the midst of torture would say or do just about anything to make the pain stop. He dared not give her a grenade that she could lob to save herself.

As much as Zane would like to put her mind at ease and tell her he was one of the good guys, he couldn't. Not yet. Not until the two of them were out of here and clear of Mahmoud and company.

Her eyes were big and dark as she stared at him, revealing for a moment the fear that she was valiantly holding at bay. God, she was brave. Admiration for her coursed through him.

"Get some rest," he said gruffly.

Her brows furrowed in confusion.

"I'll take you upstairs to use the bathroom in the morning. If you have an emergency before then, let me know." He bent down and deposited a bottle of water and a protein bar on the floor next to the pole. "There's a drink and a snack right here, where you can reach them."

He headed toward the stairs and his hand lifted toward the light switch.

"Could you please leave the light on?" she asked.

"Of course." His hand fell to his side. He hated leaving her alone down here with her fear and uncertainty, but Mahmoud and the other men would be suspicious as hell if he hovered over her like a worried mother hen.

He hurried up the steps before he could lose his resolve.

"She tied up?" Hassan asked when he emerged into the kitchen.

"Yup. Not going anywhere."

Hassan nodded and set a TV dinner on the table for him. Turkey and gravy. Not his favorite, but he wasn't about to complain. Not with so much on the line.

Zane ate about half the bland meal before asking around a mouthful of pasty mashed potatoes, "What does Mahmoud want with the woman?"

Hassan shocked him by actually answering. Whether it was because the man already knew that Mahmoud planned to kill Zane, or because Zane had actually earned some trust today by participating in the kidnapping, he had no idea. "She's the wife of some guy that our employer needs to do something."

"So she's being held as leverage, then," Zane commented neutrally, leaping all over Hassan's rare chatty mood. "Got it. Keep her alive. Reasonably healthy. Just maintain control of her."

Hassan grunted in what Zane took as an affirmative.

"Do we know who her husband is?" Zane asked.

"Above my pay grade."

"And who exactly ordered the kidnapping?" Zane pressed.

"Above your pay grade."

He grinned and shrugged at Hassan. "Sorry. It's hard for me to keep operating in the dark all the time. At some point you guys are going to have to learn to trust me."

"I think you're okay. Don't take it personally. Mahmoud always plays everything close to his chest."

"Thanks, man." Zane got up and carried his empty dinner tray over to the trash can and tossed it in. "Tomorrow, you gotta let me go to a store and get us some real food if we're gonna be here awhile. That crap tasted like cardboard."

"No lie," Hassan laughed. "I'll ask Mahmoud in the morning."

"You want me to guard the prisoner overnight?" Zane offered.

"Don't you want to take shifts or something?" Hassan blurted.

"I don't mind doing it tonight. You drove most of the day and could use some rest. I can sleep at the foot of the stairs. It's not like she can get loose and go anywhere."

"You show admirable dedication to the work, my friend."

He shrugged and made eye contact with Hassan. "Just trying to prove myself to you guys. But you're tough nuts to crack."

Hassan grinned and merely dipped his chin at the compliment, reverting to his usual taciturn self.

By the time Zane went back down to the basement, the woman was curled up on her side next to the steel pole, nested in the blankets like a puppy. She was out cold. Exhausting day she'd had. He pulled one of the blankets over her gently.

Rough day for him, too. He unrolled the sleeping bag he'd carried down here and spread it at the bottom of the steps. His offer to stay with her was a two-edged sword, of course. Not only did it keep Piper from escaping, but it kept the other men from paying any extracurricular visits to her, as well.

Confident that she would be out cold for hours to come, he closed his eyes, knowing that sleep would claim him immediately. It was a combat trick he'd learned during his stint in the army, fresh out of college. When he'd never known when or where his next chance to sleep would come, he'd become expert at napping anywhere on a moment's notice.

A painful kick in his ribs woke Zane up sometime later. He tensed to do violence before he remembered where he was. He threw off the sleeping bag and rose, silent and fast, to his feet. Yousef was grinning at him and looking pleased with himself.

"Boss wants to see you," the man announced.

Zane suppressed an urge to bury his fist in the guy's face and merely gestured for Yousef to go first up the stairs. A quick glance at Piper confirmed that she was still dead to the world.

Yousef led him to the living room, where Mahmoud and Hassan already sat. These three were the senior members of this cell. The other two guys, Bijan and Osted, acted mostly as muscle.

Mahmoud held out a cell phone and a national newspaper to Zane, who stared at them suspiciously. After months without him having access to any kind of news or electronic communications, why in the world was the guy offering him both now?

"I need photographs of the woman," Mahmoud announced. "Clear ones where her face is easy to see. And she needs to be visibly tied up. We want her husband to understand in no uncertain terms that she is a captive."

"Of course," Zane responded. "Do you want them right now?"

"Yes."

"Back in five minutes."

Zane jogged down the basement stairs loudly, announcing his coming to the woman. Sure enough, when he looked across the space at her, she was awake and watching him.

In the middle of the cellar, he set down the wooden chair he'd carried from the kitchen, then moved over to her to unlock the handcuffs.

"What's happening?" she asked quickly.

"Picture time, Mrs. Black."

"You need proof of possession of me? To show whom?"

"Your husband, of course."

"Are you asking for a ransom? Blackmail? What's the play here?" she demanded.

An interesting, and decidedly military, turn of phrase. He responded, "The play is you're going to sit in that chair with your hands tied behind your back. You're going to look properly terrified, and I'm going to take a picture of you to send to him so he'll do what we want him to."

"Which is what?" she snapped.

God, he'd love to know that very thing. But he also wasn't about to admit to her that he didn't have the slightest idea what any of this was about. He propped the newspaper against her chest, being careful not to touch anything personal while he did so. When he was satisfied that the headline was prominently visible, he stepped back from her.

"Say *cheese*," he muttered as he pointed the camera at her.

"Are we doing just stills, or do I get a video, too?" she asked.

"So you can blink out an SOS or something clever like that?" he asked dryly. "Trust me. Your husband will know you're in trouble without you having to tell him."

"Jerk," she muttered.

"You have no idea," he muttered back.

"Do tell."

"Look scared, Persephone."

The end result was her scowling at the camera, looking more defiant than frightened. But her features were clear and readily recognizable.

Which was, of course, a gigantic problem for him. As soon as Mr. Black saw the photos and declared them not to be of his wife, and that information was relayed back to Mahmoud, this woman would be dead. How long did Zane have until all that happened? A day? Two, maybe?

Urgency to get this woman out of here and run far, far away from these bastards pounded through his gut. The only thing keeping him here with her was the fact that he still had no idea why she'd been kidnapped. That, and so far, the men upstairs had shown no inclination to harm her. If he kept his cool for just a bit longer, hopefully whatever Mahmoud had planned for this woman would be revealed.

He briskly led her back over to her pole and cuffed her to it once more. "Don't go anywhere," he said wryly.

"Are you kidding?" she retorted. "I love what you've

done with the place. Why would I leave this cozy little dungeon?"

One corner of his mouth turned up in sardonic humor. She was a sharp one, all right. "Don't try that sarcasm on any of the others. They'll kill you for showing them such disrespect."

"But not you?" she asked quietly.

"I'm the one with the sense of humor. Just don't push your luck."

She subsided, silenced by the admonition. Dammit. He much preferred her sassy and mouthing off to him over this silent, apprehensive version of her. If only he could tell her who he really was, what his mission was here.

"Look," he muttered under his breath, "I don't know what the boss has planned for you. I'm going to do my best to protect you from harm. But I need you to hang in there for a little while longer."

Her brow twitched into a perplexed frown. "Who *are* you?"

"I'm the guy giving you a wad of cotton balls. Keep them in your pocket for now, but if it looks like we're coming back down here en masse to rough you up, slip them in your mouth between your molars and cheeks. They'll protect the inside of your mouth, cushion any blows and help keep us from knocking any of your teeth out."

Her frown deepened sharply as he tucked several cotton balls into the front pocket of her jeans. The pocket was snug and warm against her body, and he jerked his fingers out quickly. Must not allow himself to feel anything for this woman. No attraction. No interest. No affection.

He scooped up the fluffiest of the blankets and breathed, "Lift your shirt."

"I beg your pardon?" she squawked.

"Keep your voice down," he admonished sharply. Using the knife out of his ankle sheath—a big fighting blade he kept razor sharp—he sliced the edge of the fleece and then tore off a strip of the soft, thick cloth as quietly as he could.

He reached for her, and she flinched away from him. He couldn't blame her for the reflex, but it cut at his soul and made his heart bleed a little. Reaching up under her shirt, he wrapped the length of fleece around her torso. His palms smoothed across her body, and it was slim and warm…and surprisingly muscular. This woman was in hella good shape. Thank God. She might just survive the worst of whatever Mahmoud and company threw at her.

He tucked the top edge of the blanket under the sides and back of her bra, then tugged the shirt down over the padding. He stepped back to examine his work.

"You can take another strip," he muttered half to himself. "You're leaner through the middle than I realized." He tore off another strip of the blanket and wrapped it over the first one.

"Sorry about this," he warned her, before tucking the second piece beneath the underwires of her bra. The backs of his knuckles momentarily rubbed against soft, resilient flesh, and his entire body tensed at the feminine feel of her.

Nope, nope, nope. Not going there.

Quickly, he tucked the blanket around the sides and back of her bra, too. "If Mahmoud gets any crazy ideas, that'll absorb the worst of the impact from his fists.

It'll still hurt like hell, mind you, but maybe you won't bruise so badly or break any ribs."

"Why are you doing this for me?" she mumbled as he tugged her shirt into place once more and stood back to observe his handiwork.

She looked a little thicker than before, but he didn't think the other men had been paying all that close attention to her, based on how they'd treated her so far. She'd been a target to them. An object to be seized and stolen. Not an actual human being.

"Do you by any chance know how to take a punch?" he asked in a low voice.

"As a matter of fact, I do."

This time it was his brow that twitched into a frown. How on earth did she know how to get punched? That wasn't the sort of thing many people had practical experience with. Not even graduates of West Point. He prayed she'd tried boxing at some point in her past, and not any less savory possible sources of the knowledge.

"Try not to dislodge that padding. I may not get a chance to fix it before you need it."

"Thanks," she mumbled. She looked up at him without warning, and their gazes locked. It was all right there in her eyes. Naked fear, confusion, questions.

She whispered, almost as if she wasn't even aware of saying the words aloud, "Am I going to die?"

"Not if I can help it," he answered, before he could stop to think about the words. An urge to wrap her in his arms, to surround her in safety and comfort, nearly overcame him. His arms even started to lift toward her.

No! He mustn't give himself away to her! Both their lives depended on him, and he had to keep his cover intact until they got out of here. He looked at her in silent apology, willing her to understand. To trust him a little bit longer.

She frowned faintly as if she sensed his unspoken message but was confused by it. "Why would you help me?" she whispered.

He stared at her, frustrated at his inability to answer her truthfully. God knew, she deserved a straight answer. "I can't tell you. But I promise you this—I will do everything in my power to get you out of this alive and unharmed."

She weighed his words, his sincerity—heck, him—for a long time. Then she nodded, apparently accepting him at his word. "Okay, then," she breathed. "Thanks again."

"No problem. I'm gonna be sleeping down here with you tonight. If you need anything, let me know. Quietly. Honestly, the quieter and less trouble you can be, the better."

"Don't draw attention to myself, in other words?" she asked.

"Exactly. I've learned that Out of Sight, Out of Mind is a good motto around these guys."

She stared hard at him, and mentally he cursed at himself for having been too revealing with that comment. He spun away from her and jogged upstairs to deliver the camera to Mahmoud.

Mission complete, he came back down and wrapped up in his bedroll at the foot of the stairs. He mustn't give away to her who he was. Not yet.

He tried to sleep, but it eluded him. Instead, he spent the time wondering who on earth she was. How did an army officer, obviously in fighting physical shape, end up in Houma, Louisiana? There wasn't an active military base anywhere near that town. Was she on leave, maybe? Visiting family in the area?

He could only be grateful for whatever twist of fate had thrown Piper in his path. She'd been braver and calmer than any woman should be about being kidnapped at gunpoint, thrown in a van and driven hundreds of miles into the wilderness. He just needed her to be brave for a little while longer. Just until Mahmoud revealed his orders, now that the sleeper cell had been activated.

Chapter 5

Piper was immeasurably grateful for the padding and cotton balls her friendly captor had given her, but she also was overwhelmed with dread at what it signified for her near future. As she lay in the quiet, dimly lit cellar, unable to sleep, she listened to the light, slow sound of Goldeneyes's breathing, and mentally braced herself for the torture to come.

In her POW training, the trainees had been slapped around some, and they'd all pretended it was an approximation of the pain they might experience as prisoners of war. But as she lay here now, she settled into the grim realization that nothing could prepare her for what was going to happen to her soon. She was going to suffer a real beating—or worse—at the hands of men who wouldn't hesitate to break her.

Her instructors had told the POW trainees that their endorphins would kick in and the pain would lessen. That women had an advantage over men because their bodies threw out more endorphins faster than men's, as a result of being biologically designed to withstand childbirth.

But she was still scared to death.

Goldeneyes had made it clear to her that the other men thought she was some woman called Persephone Black. Should she pretend to be that person, or was she better off denying being Mrs. Black? Would she piss off her kidnappers if she insisted she wasn't the woman they'd meant to kidnap?

But she had no idea who this other woman was. She couldn't correctly answer *any* questions about her. Her kidnappers would figure out soon enough that she couldn't possibly be the woman in question. Maybe she should just go ahead and stand by not being Persephone Black.

Of course, then her kidnappers would demand to know who she really was. And it wasn't like she was eager to spill her true identity or the fact that she was part of a highly classified Special Forces team.

The best bet was probably to go along with being Mrs. Black for now.

Working quickly, she built up a fake identity for herself. Originally from Minnesota, she decided to pretend she was from Wisconsin. Not that she expected any of the men except Goldeneyes would know a Midwestern accent when they heard one.

She would stick with the historian cover she already used in Houma: she was researching pirates in the early days of American history, particularly those who'd run through and hidden in the bayous of Louisiana.

She knew her captors thought she was thirty years old. How long had she been married? Three years seemed like a safe enough number. If only she knew what Mr. Black did. Since these people were obviously trying to coerce him into doing something, she probably had better avoid the topic of his work. If she was lucky, her captors already knew what work Mr. Black did and wouldn't bother to confirm it with her.

Since sleep was totally not happening in the face of impending pain, she opted to rest and meditate, practicing centering herself and separating her mind from her body. And she prayed for strength.

The long hours of the night passed, and eventually, she heard stirring overhead. Apprehension tightened across her skin, and she checked her padding awkwardly. Still in place, thank goodness.

She stood up and maneuvered the cotton balls into her palm just in case.

The door at the top of the stairs opened and daylight flooded downward. Goldeneyes stood quickly, just in time to meet three of her captors at the foot of the stairs. They held a quick, quiet conversation in Farsi, most of which she missed.

Goldeneyes threw her a single warning glance, touching his cheek briefly with his finger.

Damn. It was time for the cotton balls. Turning her back to the men, she quickly slipped them into her mouth and used her tongue to push them into place between her molars and cheeks.

"Bring her over to the chair," Mahmoud ordered.

Goldeneyes moved over to her and released one of her handcuffs. Using them like a leash, he dragged her toward the middle of the cellar. She resisted, unable to stop herself. She simply couldn't go meekly into whatever was coming.

She wouldn't say Goldeneyes was exactly gentle with her, but he wasn't rough as he forced her over to the chair and pushed her down onto it. Quickly, he threaded the handcuffs through the chair's back slats and pulled her free hand behind her back to recuff it.

Panic ripped through her and she looked up at him in anguish.

"Courage," he muttered without moving his lips.

Right. Courage. She was a Medusa and would acquit herself like one.

She hoped.

Mahmoud moved over to stand in front of her. He passed what looked like a video camera to Goldeneyes. "Film this."

Great. If this was going to be theater, then she could expect big dramatic punches. Blood. Pain. Lots of pain. She was all over giving these guys the best show she could. Maybe they would stop sooner if she did a lot of screaming and wailing.

Goldeneyes took the video camera, opened the foldout screen on its side and nodded. He didn't look up at her. Rather, he stared fixedly at the tiny monitor. Almost as if he couldn't bear to look directly at her.

The one called Yousef stepped up in front of her. He drew his arm across his body and backhanded her across the face. Hard. She let her head snap to the side with the slap, doing her best to move with the blow and minimize its impact.

But her entire right side of her face exploded with stinging fire. *Crap, that hurts.*

She glared at Mahmoud, standing behind and slightly to one side of Yousef. "Aren't you going to ask me any questions before you start slapping me around?"

The bastard's only response was, "Again."

Yousef struck from the opposite direction this time, smacking the other side of her face painfully. That was the same side that he'd punched yesterday at the school, and the inside of her mouth was already cut up. She was immensely grateful for the cotton ball to cushion the blow. Her eyes watered copiously, though.

She gritted her teeth, partially to keep the cotton balls hidden and partially because she was getting mad. Past her tight jaws, she ground out, "You guys are freaking cowards, hitting a woman who's tied up and can't defend herself. Does it make you feel like men? Because it makes you look like scared little boys."

Yousef punched her this time, burying his fist in her left side, at belly button height. She let her body pivot in the chair as the blow landed, tensing her abdominal muscles to protect her internal organs.

She yelled a curse as pain exploded in her gut, relieved not to have passed out from a drop in blood pressure from being hit in that location.

After that, she did her best to absorb each blow with a minimum of damage, but the toll started to add up. One of her eyes swelled nearly shut, and blood ran down her chin from her nose and mouth. Soon her entire body felt like hamburger, and the pain was so loud and steady now that more blows almost failed to register.

That must be the endorphins kicking in. Thank God.

Yet again, her attacker came back with a fist aimed at her face. She closed her jaw and kept her tongue well away from her teeth, prepared to let her head snap to the side, rolling with the punch.

"Stop!" Goldeneyes yelled.

Her eyes snapped open, and she stared at him, along with everyone else.

"What?" Mahmoud demanded.

"Unless our orders are to kill her right now," Goldeneyes ground out, "you need to stop making a punching bag out of her. As it is, you may have already seriously injured her. If she's got internal bleeding, hitting her again could kill her. What did your handlers tell you to do, Mahmoud? Are we here to kill her now or not?"

She looked at the leader of the cell. Fury was obvious in his eyes, but his jaw worked like he was struggling with some decision.

Goldeneyes added less belligerently, "She's plenty softened up. She'll answer your questions if you just give her a chance to." He threw her a significant look as if to say, *Answer his questions, for God's sake.*

Mahmoud turned to glare down at her. "What's your name?" he asked sharply.

She might need to help out her would-be rescuer and answer questions, but she didn't have to be nice about it. "You know my name," she snapped at Mahmoud.

"Say it for the camera."

She scowled at him, and only when Yousef drew back his fist, a glint of almost-sexual pleasure in his eyes, did she spit out, "My name is Persephone Black."

Goldeneyes's head snapped up from the video camera. She didn't spare him more than a glance because she had to keep her eyes on Yousef and prepare as best she could for a possible blow from him.

"Who's your husband?" Mahmoud demanded.

"Jack Black," she replied sarcastically.

Nobody said anything. They must not know the pop culture reference to the celebrity by that name. Goldeneyes looked up again, and after a glance at his cronies to make sure none of them were looking at him, shook his head slightly at her in warning.

Mahmoud demanded, "Where is your husband now?"

"I have no idea."

"What country is he in?"

What *country*? He wasn't in America? Huh. Who

was this guy, Mr. Black? Aloud, she responded, "I said I don't know where he is."

"What work does your husband do?"

She snorted. "Not enough, I can tell you that. I end up paying most of the bills, thank you very much. You'd think a man like him could bring home a decent living, but no. He sits around pretending to work when I'm slaving away like a dog—"

This time Yousef's fist caught her in the left eye. There was only so much she could do to protect herself from the blow and it snapped her head back hard.

She yelled a curse at the top of her lungs and took a certain small satisfaction from her loud outburst making the men jump.

"What do you want from me?" she shouted.

Goldeneyes jumped forward and grabbed Yousef by the shoulder. "You idiot. You're going to kill her, and then Mahmoud will be royally screwed. He'll be lucky if they only kill him. And it'll be all your fault."

Yousef's glare shifted to Mahmoud, who growled, "Stand down, brother."

This time, Mahmoud actually moved to stand between Yousef and her before asking, "Your husband is overseas right now, is he not?"

She blinked hard, her eyes watering like crazy as. blood from a cut over her brow dripped into them. She was going to get a hell of a shiner out of this.

"Well, um, yeah, he's overseas," she mumbled.

Mahmoud nodded in satisfaction. "And did he tell you where he was going this time?"

"He never tells me anything," she said bitterly. "I'm just the wife at home. I'm supposed to cook and clean and not ask any questions about his work."

Apparently, that was the right answer, for Mahmoud

nodded slightly as if that information jibed with what he already knew. He did surprise her by following up with, "What is your husband willing to do to keep you alive?"

So, this was a hostage situation, after all. She was supposed to be used as leverage against her "husband" to get him to do something. "What do you want him to do?" she asked.

"None of your business."

She looked back and forth between Mahmoud and the video camera. "Tell me what you want him to do, and I'll tell him to do it. You're filming me to show this video to him, aren't you? Let me help you convince him."

"Shut up," the man snapped, making a slashing gesture across his throat as a signal to Goldeneyes.

Mahmoud headed for the stairs, snatching the video camera out of Goldeneyes's hands as he passed. "We'll have to edit out that last part." He devolved into Farsi cursing. Something about women who couldn't keep their mouths shut. Maybe that they were a curse to men?

God, she hoped so. She would love to be a curse to him.

Yousef and the third guy, the one who'd driven the van most of yesterday, disappeared upstairs. Goldeneyes waited a minute, staring at the closed door at the top of the steps, before rushing over to her, swearing a blue storm under his breath.

"My God, I'm sorry," he muttered. "I had no idea they would go that far… My fault… Miscalculated terribly… You paid the price… Sorry, so damned sorry… Have to get you out of here…"

Her handcuffs popped free. Gently, he chafed her wrists, helping circulation return to her hands.

"That's it. I'm going up there right now and killing them all," he gritted out through clenched teeth.

Alarmed, she grabbed the front of his shirt to stop him from barging out of the basement then and there. She asked quickly, "Do you have a gun? An automatic weapon? You'll need it to put down four men before they can jump you and take you out. And that's assuming you're fast as hell and surprise them."

"No. But there are knives in the kitchen." He tugged at her grip on his shirt, but she tightened her hold frantically. She couldn't afford for her only protector to lose his cool and get himself killed.

"You won't win with a knife," she said urgently.

"But—"

She cut him off sharply. "You're no good to me dead. As furious as you are right now, I need you to calm down. Think. Keep your wits about you and be patient. It's the only way either one of us will make it out of this situation alive."

He stared at her in rage that very, very slowly faded to anguish. "But look what they've done to you."

"I'm alive. I was trained to survive stuff like that, and I did."

"You shouldn't have had to go through that—"

"Stop." He was starting to work himself up again, and she cut off that train of thought before it could leave the station.

He exhaled hard. Closed his eyes tightly. And when he opened them again, sanity had returned.

She let out the breath she'd been holding. Thank God. He'd come down off the precipice of breaking.

"How is it you're the one talking sense into me?" he muttered. "You're the one who should be hysterical."

"Oh, I am underneath. I just don't have time to let it

out right now. I have to think about staying alive first and foremost."

He pushed her tangled hair back from her face gently. "God, you're extraordinary."

Their gazes met for a moment of naked honesty. She let her fear show for a second, and he let his guilt show. Then, together, they forced down the emotions in an unspoken agreement that now was not the time for either feeling.

Eventually, when their stares had both hardened into determination, he nodded once at her. She nodded back.

From here on out, they were in this together.

"Are you okay?" he asked under his breath. "Can you breathe all right? Did that bastard crack any ribs?"

"No broken ribs."

"Teeth? Any loose? New cuts in your mouth?"

"Cotton balls worked," she sighed, suddenly feeling so exhausted she could barely focus. That was the adrenaline draining away after a near-death experience.

"What can I do for you? Name it. Anything. My God, I can't tell you how sorry I am you had to go through that. I had no idea Mahmoud would turn that sadistic bastard loose on you. I'm gonna kill them both one day soon—"

She cut him off gently. "I'll live. I could use some ice for my eye."

"I don't think there's any ice in the cabin." He wiped the blood off her face gently and then dabbed at her eye with the hem of his shirt.

Once the blood was cleared away, he examined the cut again. "Under normal circumstances, I'd tell you to get a few stitches in that. Or I'd sew it up myself. But I don't have any sutures. I think there's a butterfly bandage in the first-aid kit upstairs. I'll bring it down."

"And maybe a styptic stick to stop the bleeding?" she asked hopefully.

"Sorry. Don't have one."

He jogged upstairs and returned with a tube of antibiotic cream and the butterfly bandage. Very gently, he treated the cut and taped it together carefully.

"That's the best I can do. I wish it was more."

"Thanks."

"Don't thank me. You should never have been here. Never gone through that."

She stared at him intently. Was he admitting that he'd intentionally misidentified her? That it was his fault she was here?

"Why did you—" she started.

He cut her off, muttering quickly, "Not now. Not here with them upstairs where they could hear something,"

"Who are you?"

"How's your jaw?" he countered quietly.

"Sore."

"Your side?"

"Same."

"Any serious injuries you're aware of?" he inquired.

"Why do you care?"

"Because I'm freaking trying to keep you alive and in one piece to the best of my ability," he snapped.

"Why?" she demanded from between clenched teeth. She was really getting frustrated with not knowing what his deal was.

"I really wish I could tell you. Does it help to at least know that there *is* a reason?"

"How good a reason?" she retorted.

Without answering, he led her over to the steel post and latched her handcuffs around it once more. Once she was secured, he went back to applying pressure to her eyebrow.

"I thought it was a vitally important reason until I saw you getting beat up. Now, I don't give a crap for reasons. My only goal now is to get you out of here alive and safe."

What in the *hell* was he up to? She desperately wanted to trust him. But did she dare?

"Do you need to go to the bathroom?" he asked.

She glared at him. "Yes, but I'm damned well not walking upstairs into the midst of your friends so they can rough me up some more."

"Good point. I'll bring a bucket down to you."

"Oh, joy."

A faint smile bent his lips for a moment. "There's my brave and bold girl," he muttered as if to himself.

"I'm not your girl!"

He looked down at her bleakly. As he did so, his eyes gradually became harder and colder than she'd ever seen them before. His hand fell away from her eyebrow. "Right," he bit out. "I forgot. In your world, we're enemies."

Well, hell. She didn't mean to alienate the one person who was taking care of her and showing a modicum of kindness toward her. "I'm sorry," she sighed. "I'm not exactly at my best right now."

He stared at her a moment longer, and his expression softened. He fell to his knees in front of her, bringing their gazes to the same level. "I will never be able to make this up to you. I know that. I can only say I'm so damned sorry and that I'll do my level best to get you out of here unharmed. Well, not harmed any further. You're going to have to trust me. I don't deserve it, and you have no reason whatsoever to believe me. But I'm asking you to all the same."

He rose, turned and left the basement without saying another word.

How was she supposed to trust him when he wouldn't even tell her his name, let alone anything else about who he was, why he was here among these animals or why he'd dragged her into the middle of this? Whatever *this* was.

She sagged against her pole, hugging it forlornly, feeling utterly alone in a never-ending nightmare. This time the tears that slipped out of her eyes and down her cheeks weren't solely about pain.

Chapter 6

Tessa fretted while the NCIS agents in New Orleans were briefed on who Piper Ford really was and who the Medusas really were. Major Torsten also explained the importance of maintaining operational security around the Medusa Project and of getting Piper back as soon as possible before she was forced to reveal anything about the Medusas' training and capabilities.

When the agents made it clear they understood both the sensitivity and urgency of retrieving Piper, Torsten, Beau and Tessa climbed into a helicopter that would fly them to Barksdale Air Force Base near Shreveport, Louisiana, to await news. The FBI had received a tip from a convenience store clerk who she had seen a woman matching Piper's description with a man in that area.

As soon as they got to Barksdale, Torsten set up shop in the intelligence office there, and he put his team to work combing through intel reports from the past few weeks, in search of any clue to who might have snatched Piper.

"Keep an eye out for any references to Abu Haddad," he ordered them.

Beau and Tessa both scowled. Beau commented, "Hell, Gun. You saw the explosion. Do you think anyone made it out alive?"

Torsten shrugged. "You two did."

"Yeah, but we were on the deck and in the midst of jumping overboard when we blew the charges. The helicopter that was taking off went down, too. No way did Haddad get away."

Torsten replied grimly, "And yet I have a report that Haddad's organization is setting up some super secret deal with the Iranians and that Haddad himself is expected to close the deal."

"Does Piper's kidnapping have something to do with that?" Tessa asked. "Is there any way Haddad found out about us and spread word that the Medusas are back?"

The men looked at her grimly. Torsten eventually answered, "We can't take the possibility off the table. Back to work, people. The clock's ticking."

Zane dropped the grocery bags on the cabin's kitchen table in disgust. He'd hoped to go alone to get food and make a quick call to his superiors, asking for an extraction for himself and Piper, but Yousef had gone with him, and the bastard had kept an eagle eye on him. Which was a departure from the usual protocol. Mahmoud almost always used Zane as the lone white-bread American for any required public interactions by his team. The fact that Yousef had come along this time was alarming in the extreme.

It looked for all the world like Mahmoud didn't trust him, and had sent his number two man along to babysit. Which worried the hell out of Zane. He hadn't even had a moment to scribble out a fast note and pass it to the cashier at the grocery store.

Which meant he and Piper were still on their own in the middle of freaking nowhere. It had taken nearly an hour for Yousef to drive to the nearest grocery store, and that had been a tiny, run-down shop about a quarter of the size of a regular supermarket.

"Amir!" Mahmoud bellowed from the living room.

Bracing himself mentally and putting on his best subordinate face, Zane went as summoned. "We'll have decent food for supper tonight. I'm cooking," he announced.

"Praise Allah," Hassan commented.

Mahmoud announced, "I sent the pictures of the woman and the video you shot of her. They want more video."

It was on the tip of Zane's tongue to ask "They, who?" but he knew better. And given the apparent precariousness of his status, he dared not show undue curiosity. "What kind of video?" he inquired.

"We need to put her under more duress so they can raise the pressure on her husband, in case he doesn't give in immediately when we speak with him."

Thank God. The husband hadn't been approached yet. That meant he and Piper had at least another day or so to find a way out of here. "How much more duress?" Zane asked.

Yousef smiled aggressively from beside Zane. "It's not a sin to rape an infidel. They're not human, after all."

Zane's entire being froze. Rape? A little voice in the back of his head started screaming, *No, no, no, no, no!* No woman should endure that for any reason. Mentally swearing up a blue storm, he thought fast.

He said as casually as he could manage, "The problem with doing something like that is the forensic evidence it leaves behind. The FBI can lift DNA from a woman weeks after the fact—whether or not she's alive or dead. Right now, we're in the clear. No one can identify us. But after doing something that…" He trailed off and shrugged.

"You'll do it," Mahmoud declared. "And film it."

Abject relief pounded through him. No way was he assaulting Piper. But if this attack was up to him to perpetrate, maybe he could find a way to spare her.

But on the heels of that came indecision. Should he protest being chosen to do it? He probably should, given that he'd just declared it a bad idea. "Why me?" he whined.

Mahmoud snapped, "You weren't born Muslim. You've already lain with unclean females and are soiled in God's eyes."

Not to mention he would be the one to leave DNA evidence behind. Although there was no way he was actually going through with it. "Where's the damned camera?" he groused.

Hassan handed the video camera over.

"Make her scream," Yousef said, far too eagerly for Zane's taste.

"You wanna watch?" Zane snapped.

Yousef actually hesitated before declining.

Sick bastard.

"Do I get to watch some porn or something to get in the mood?" Zane asked hopefully.

Mahmoud snorted. "As if there would be Wi-Fi reception out here. Ha."

"Maybe on a cell phone?" he asked.

"We don't even have cell coverage in this godforsaken hole," Hassan muttered. "I had to use a satellite phone to send the images of the woman."

Well, hell. There went his plan to pilfer one of the senior men's cell phones and call for help.

"Fine," he huffed. Zane trudged out of the living room and through the kitchen. When he closed the basement door, he wedged a step stool across the door frame and under the latch. No way did he want any of the others to get a bright idea to watch, or heaven forbid, join in the "fun."

A faint smell of urine pervaded the basement now. Honestly, he hoped it would help keep the other men away.

Piper was awake and alert, sitting on the floor by her pole. "What now?" she asked quickly. She must've seen the grim expression on his face as he mounted the video camera on its tripod and pointed it at her nest of blankets.

She stood up as he approached her.

He leaned in close to her, putting his mouth near her ear. "We've got a problem," he said very low, vividly aware of the other men overhead.

"How bad?" she whispered.

"Bad. They want me to rape you and film it to co-erce your husband to cooperate."

Her eyes went wide with fear, but to her credit, her voice remained steady. "I expected something like this."

He breathed, "I have *no* intention of actually attacking you. Period. But we're going to have to put on a good show. Will you help me do that?"

"As opposed to the alternative? Hell, yes."

"Okay, then. I'll go turn on the camera. And I'm sorry in advance." He pushed away from the wall, hating this with every step he took toward the tripod.

He switched on the camera and turned toward her, his back to the lens. He gestured at his face, where he was miming fear, indicating that she should look afraid.

She cowered convincingly enough that a real spear of guilt stabbed his gut as he stalked toward her, considering how he was going to do this. He unlocked her right hand, but looped the handcuffs around the pipe, leaving her left hand chained to it.

"Take off your clothes," he ordered her loudly enough for the camera to pick up.

"No!"

Scowling, he grabbed the front of her shirt. He gave it a yank and buttons went flying. Piper's eyes widened in fear for real then. Her bra was a plain white cotton affair, but damned if it wasn't sexy as hell. Her chest wasn't huge but had lovely curves above the cups of her bra that begged a guy to cup them in his hands.

A guy whom she trusted and wanted to share her body with. Not him. Zane had no right to even think about touching her like that. God, he hated this.

"I'm sorry, I'm sorry, I'm sorry," he chanted over and over under his breath.

"Just get it over with," she muttered back from behind unmoving lips.

He reached for the zipper of her jeans, and she used her free hand to bat his hand away.

He wound up for a backhand slap, giving her plenty of time to see the blow coming. When she met his stare and nodded infinitesimally, he swept his arm dramatically across his body. He relaxed his hand as much as possible and mostly brushed it across her face. The slap still made a reasonably satisfying smacking sound, and Piper's head snapped to the side.

When she looked at him again, he slapped back the other way. "Whimper," he whispered.

She complied, and his skin literally crawled at the sound. Thank God his back was to the camera because no way could he keep the apology out of his eyes.

She made eye contact with him, and forgiveness shone in her gaze.

He was humbled by it. Nearly driven to his knees by it. Only the sure and certain knowledge that Yousef would happily rape her for real if he didn't go through with this pretend travesty kept him on his feet.

"God, I hate this," he muttered as he reached for her shoulders, shoving her up against the dirt wall, pinning her against it with his body. A host of sensations registered all at once. Her body was soft and warm through the cotton of his T-shirt, and it fitted against his just right.

He had no right to enjoy *anything* about this. His gut roiled with nausea at the mere idea of finding anything about this appealing.

"I'm so damned sorry," he murmured

"It's okay. I know you won't hurt me."

Her trust came within a hair of breaking him. He didn't deserve it. She didn't deserve any of this. It was his fault she was in this position at all. All. His. Fault.

Protectiveness surged through him as he covered her from the prying eye of the camera. "I won't let them hurt you again," he breathed. "I'll find a way to kill them all if I have to."

"Don't bother. Let's just get out of here."

"Working on it."

She stared up at him, and he stared down at her, silently begging her to see the truth in his words.

She nodded once. Slowly. And then she did the

damnedest thing. She relaxed against him, her body going sleek and soft and warm against him. She believed him. Thank God.

She burrowed closer against his chest as if relishing the human contact and safety that he represented. He lowered his mouth very slowly, slowly enough not to startle her in the least, to the junction of her neck and shoulder, relishing the silkiness of her skin against his lips. She tasted faintly of salt but was all woman.

"Fight me," he breathed against her neck.

"What?"

"The camera," he reminded her.

"Right."

She used her free hand to shove at his left shoulder, and he was shocked at how strong she was. She managed to push him back, throwing him off balance.

He stumbled back, wiped his hands across his mouth and snarled, "That's better. I like it when my whores fight."

Her gaze was momentarily stricken when she stared at him as if she'd forgotten for a second what they were supposed to be doing. This was acting. This was just acting.

Forgive me, he mouthed.

He stepped forward more aggressively, grabbing her by both shoulders and holding her against the wall as he kissed her too hard. Aww, hell. Her lips were as silky and soft as the rest of her. He ought to smash her lips against her teeth. *Bite her lip. Make her bleed.*

But damned if he didn't do the opposite, gentling the kiss, inviting her to open for him. He simply couldn't brutalize this woman, who'd already been so brave through so much.

Her mouth opened beneath his, and without thinking, he tilted his head to fit their mouths together better.

She kissed him back eagerly. Hungrily. Poor woman was so desperate for some safety, a pretense of normalcy, that she'd lost herself in this kiss. Not that he blamed her for a second. But when she found out who he really was, that he'd chosen to put her in this terrible situation, she was going to hate him forever. And for good reason.

Her hand, which had been shoving at his chest, fisted against his T-shirt, twisting the soft fabric in her fingers, tugging him closer. Thankfully, her hand was out of sight of the camera.

He moved his mouth across hers leisurely, enjoying the way she rose to meet him, lifting her mouth to his and kissing him back.

He shouldn't enjoy this. Shouldn't love the feel of her mouth against his, the scent of her feminine musk filling his nostrils, the resilient strength of her body sliding beneath his palms. Nope, he shouldn't love any of it.

And yet he did.

She was an amazing woman, and her mental fortitude astounded him.

As they continued to kiss, passion built between them, not a wild explosion all at once, but rather a gradual falling away of everything else that had led up to this moment. It left just the two of them kissing each other, sharing their stress and worry with each other, commiserating in their mutual danger and losing themselves in this new and unexpected attraction to each other.

Her free arm crept around his neck, her fingers twining in his hair, and abruptly, he remembered where they were and what they were supposed to be doing.

"Pull my hair," he muttered against her mouth.

She kissed him once more and then complied, giving a painful yank that made him yelp. He jumped back and made a fist, pretending to bury it in her solar plexus. She did a credible job of jumping up slightly and grunting hard as if he'd clobbered her for real.

He grabbed her jeans then and tore the button open. She thrashed from side to side, but he used his superior weight to force her back against the wall. It was surprising how much effort it took to keep her pinned against that wall. Reaching between their straining bodies, he managed to snag her jeans zipper and pull it down.

She let out a scream then, a primal sound of frustration. But hopefully Yousef would interpret it as something more akin to fear.

Zane shoved her jeans down around her knees and was privately relieved when the sturdy fabric tangled around her legs and slowed down her thrashing. He couldn't help but notice she wore bikini underwear—also white cotton, but with a sassy little pink bow and white lace panels on each side that took the panties from utilitarian to freaking sexy.

Piper's torso was golden and gorgeous. Her waist nipped in to a beautiful and feminine hourglass, and her stomach was flat and toned. Her thighs were muscular against his and as toned as the rest of her. He shoved his still-clothed thigh between hers and she froze reflexively, obviously galvanized by the sensation of sensually riding his thigh.

In *any* other circumstances, he would be so turned on he would hurt. But as it was, there wasn't the least thing sexy about forcing himself on any woman. And positively not this woman.

An urge to just get this over with washed over him.

He reached between their bodies and violently shoved her panties down her thighs. She jolted against him, letting out a gasp of shock and protest that sounded entirely real.

"It's almost over," he whispered in desperation. "I hate this as much as you. Just a little bit more to make it look real." He swore under his breath.

"Do what you have to," she was magnanimous enough to whisper back.

"I'm sorry. A thousand times sorry—"

"No more apologies. Just finish the damned video."

He reached for his own zipper and shoved his jeans down to the tops of his thighs. Silently, he prayed that his T-shirt was long enough to cover up most of his bare ass hanging out in the breeze for the camera.

Piper's eyes glazed over with real panic then. She fought like a wildcat, and he was sincerely grateful he'd kept one of her hands chained to that blasted pole. He'd met some strong, fast, fit women in his day, but Piper was in another class of athletes altogether.

Her fist caught him painfully on the side of his jaw, and he forcefully grabbed her wrist, yanking it up over her head. He had to use his height and strength to full effect to even stand a chance at subduing Piper. It took a couple hard-fought minutes, and he was breathing hard before she finally appeared to exhaust herself enough to stop flinging herself around wildly.

He noted a trickle of blood running down her hand-cuffed forearm. God, he hoped the camera caught that. Because no way was he doing anything else to harm her.

He shoved his crotch against her lower belly over and over, mimicking sex. His jaw clenched against a scream of fury at being forced into this travesty of what should be a beautiful, gentle and respectful sharing of souls.

He ground out, "Scream, Piper. Scream as loud as you can."

Man, she had a set of lungs on her. His ears rang from the piercing shriek she let out about four inches from his right ear. Grimly, he pumped his hips, bumping and grinding against her belly.

How long did he have to keep this up for it to look like a realistic rape, anyway? He had no idea.

The good news was that Piper dissolved into tears—real tears—just then. He felt physically ill for upsetting her that badly, but dammit, for her own safety it had to look believable. It wasn't like he had any choice about this, either. They were both victims this time.

He sped up his hip pumps and made grunting noises that disgusted him, hearing them coming from his own throat. He gave a shout and then collapsed against her.

He muttered against her sweaty neck, "May God forgive me. Not that I'll ever deserve it from Him or from you."

And then he stepped away from her. Keeping his back to the camera, he pulled up his pants and fastened them. Still blocking the camera, and without looking down at her unclothed body, he tugged up her underwear and jeans and pulled her shirt closed over her bra. The buttons were long gone, of course. But at least he could preserve a bit of her modesty for her.

Last, but not least, he reluctantly lifted his gaze to hers. Her good eye was huge and terrified, brimming with tears and accusation. The other eye was puffy and swollen from yesterday's video beating, but it still leaked a stream of tears that streaked her cheek.

Swearing at himself in a continuous mental stream of castigation, he stepped behind the camera and zoomed in on her face, catching all the betrayal and hurt in her expression in one last, intensely cinematic shot before he turned off the camera.

"Thanks for your help with that," he said quietly. "Can I get you anything?"

"Get out of here. I need to be alone. I don't want to look at you right now."

Yeah. He deserved that.

Feeling about as crummy as he'd ever felt in his life, he nodded miserably and unscrewed the video camera from the tripod. He turned to leave, then paused and turned back to her one last time.

"I am more sorry than words can convey. From the bottom of my heart. But I swear to you, there was no other way. It was them or me."

Chapter 7

In her rational mind, Piper knew she'd dodged a horrendous bullet. But in her emotional heart, feeling Goldeneyes's flaccid man parts thrusting against her belly over and over and over had been invasive, humiliating and degrading. It might not have been rape, but it certainly qualified as sexual assault.

She was intensely grateful to him for not actually raping her. But foremost in her mind, she was appalled that he'd been big enough and strong enough to overpower her like that. She'd deluded herself into believing that, with her specialized training, no man could do that to her ever. But he'd proved her wrong.

It wasn't his fault, of course, that he'd been picked to attack her. And it wasn't even particularly his fault that he was the man to puncture her false assumptions about her invincibility.

Granted, she'd been handcuffed to a pole, which gave him a distinct advantage. But still. She prided herself on being as strong as most men and better trained to fight. The fact that she was still that vulnerable to an assault was beyond appalling. It was terrifying.

What if next time one of the other men decided to have a go at her? What if it wasn't a simulated assault? Her mind shied away from even trying to imagine what that would be like. As it was, a protective fog of shock was lowering around her like a blanket.

She slid down the pole to huddle on the floor beside it. Using her as yet untethered right hand, she reached out and pulled one of the blankets around her shoulders. Then, hugging her legs, she dropped her forehead to her knees and sobbed out her fear and exhaustion.

A completely irrational sense of betrayal filled her that her one champion had put her through that. Rationally, she acknowledged that in some ways, he was also a victim in the scenario. He'd apologized profusely, over and over, clearly horrified by the whole situation, too.

He'd been as considerate as he could possibly be, given what they'd both been forced into pretending to do. But when he'd dropped his pants, all the reasonable explanations for being okay with any of it had fled her mind. It had become too real. Too personal.

She'd squeezed her eyes shut and refused to look at him. She couldn't bear to see him enjoy any part of what they'd done together.

As she forced herself to replay it in her head, something dawned on her. He hadn't been turned on by the encounter. At all.

His male parts had been completely unaroused against her belly as he'd shoved his pelvis at hers over and over. Thank God for that, at least.

Gradually, the initial shock of the simulated attack wore off, and she registered other small details that she'd failed to notice when the assault was happening. He'd never hurt her once, not the whole time she'd been fighting against him. And she'd landed a few pretty good punches on him.

He'd also carefully used his body to block her from the camera. The most anyone would ever see on that film was her face and maybe some of her legs.

She did note ruefully that he'd done a number on her shirt, though. It was ruined. Still, rather than give her captors the pleasure of taunting her with them, she collected the buttons she could reach off the floor and stuffed them in the back pocket of her jeans.

Her captors probably wouldn't cough up a needle and thread for her to sew the buttons back on. The garment had effectively become a jacket. Which meant she couldn't wear her blanket armor anymore, either. Not without a shirt to hide it.

She didn't relish parading around in her bra in front of these jerks, and she resorted to tying the tails of her shirt together to form a makeshift crop top. It exposed a strip of her stomach—which God knew would be plenty of temptation for a crew of terrorists. But her bra and most of her cleavage were safely covered up now.

Major Torsten would undoubtedly tell her in this situation to learn from it. To focus on taking care of herself and being ready to exploit any openings that came her way. Speaking of which, Goldeneyes had mentioned at the beginning of that awful encounter that he was working on an escape for both of them. Did she dare hope he was telling the truth?

If he indeed ran away with her, she would go with him initially, and then break away and strike out on her own. She didn't dare trust him, and honestly, her survival skills were probably vastly superior to his. He would be nothing but dead weight to her...

Okay. Fine. She was lying to herself. She mostly

didn't want to be alone with any man right now, especially not the man who'd just convincingly made a video of assaulting her.

Mentally exhausted and emotionally wiped out by the encounter, she rested her head against the pole, closed her eyes in genuine exhaustion and went to sleep.

Zane handed over the video camera without comment and made sure to give it directly to Mahmoud. It occurred to him yet again to wonder if, now that Mahmoud's superiors had this video, they might not need Piper alive any longer to act as leverage to force her supposed husband into action.

Ready or not, he was out of time to get her away from these men. The two of them had to disappear before this cell of violent thugs received orders to kill her and hide the body.

Mahmoud had the gall to ask, "Was she any good?"

Bastard. "Of course not," Zane replied scornfully. "She fought almost until the very end."

"Excellent," Mahmoud commented.

"Do you need anything else from me, or can I go cook us a decent supper now?"

"Go."

Zane mechanically went through the motions of making his grandmother's world-famous spaghetti sauce. Thankfully, he'd seen her make it a thousand times and he'd made it a hundred times himself because his mind was completely occupied with the woman downstairs.

He had to get her out of here sooner rather than later, identifying Mahmoud's real target be damned. Now that the taboo of raping the hostage had been broken, he didn't doubt that Yousef or one of the others would get the bright idea to have a go at Piper for themselves.

That, and he was certain that Mahmoud's superiors would give the green light to get rid of Piper any minute.

Man. If only he had some Rohypnol. He would totally roofie these bastards' food and knock them all out. He eyed the bottle of wine he'd bought to flavor the sauce with. Muslims technically weren't supposed to drink. But he'd found over the years that some of them would indulge from time to time. And this crew had not shown itself to be particularly religious.

Why would they be religious? After all, if they casually killed people without remorse, what was a glass of wine among friends? If nothing else, maybe a glass of wine would relax these guys and get them to sleep a little more deeply tonight.

He set the kitchen table for dinner and made a point of pouring glasses of wine at each place. He also made sure to give himself the smallest wineglass and to put only a splash of wine in it—just enough to make it look like he'd been drinking while he prepared the meal.

He piled big mounds of spaghetti on each plate and slathered them with sauce. What wine couldn't accomplish, maybe a carbohydrate coma could. He'd toasted a huge basketful of garlic bread as well, and put that in the middle of the table.

Then he called out, "Dinner's served."

The other men piled into the kitchen and dug into the meal with gusto. He made a point of refilling their plates over and over, stuffing them as much as he could.

Eventually, the men pushed back from the table, bellies overfull and their moods expansive. Zane got up and started carrying dishes over to the sink. "You guys go chill out and I'll clean up this mess," he said casually.

Bijan, the youngest of the bunch, commented, "Having you around is almost like being home with my mother."

He grinned at the kid. "I'm about to start yelling at you about it being past your bedtime, little boy."

The other men laughed and jumped in, ribbing Bijan about being a baby as they sauntered out of the kitchen in good humor. It was one of the few times he'd ever seen them let down their hair and relax. Maybe the wine was having the effect he'd hoped for.

He'd done all he could to ensure they crashed early and slept hard tonight. When the dishes were done, he carried a plate of spaghetti down to Piper. She was asleep, so he set it beside her quietly and retreated without waking her up. She'd earned some rest after her earlier trauma.

God willing, she would need to be rested before the night was out.

He joined the men upstairs and was delighted when Yousef produced the case of beer he'd added to the grocery cart earlier. They all lounged on the furniture and floor, drinking and watching an American preseason football game on the crappy box-style television hooked to an old-fashioned satellite dish.

Zane carried his beer with him when he went to the bathroom, and poured it into the toilet. He passed out fresh beers whenever someone emptied theirs, and just as important, he made sure everyone indulged about equally. He needed them *all* to pass out.

The game ended, and Mahmoud stood up, asking, "Who's taking first watch tonight?"

Nobody volunteered, and Zane sighed loudly, "Fine. I'll do it. Who's second?"

Mahmoud pointed at Osted, the quietest of the bunch.

Zane nodded at the young man. "I'll wake you up in, say, two hours?"

"Make it four," Mahmoud objected. "That way only two of us have to stand watch tonight."

Osted grinned and Zane flipped the kid off.

As the others headed for their beds, Zane stepped outside into the bracing chill of a mountain evening and took a lap around the cabin. Ideally, he would get the van keys and drive away from here with Piper. But Mahmoud kept the keys on his person at all times, and Zane wasn't interested in accidentally waking the guy up while trying to steal the stupid things.

He'd checked out the van yesterday, and it wasn't an ideal vehicle to hot-wire, either. Not to mention hot-wiring could get noisy as an engine tried and failed to ignite a few times before it caught and actually started. He couldn't afford to risk any sound waking up the other men.

Nope, the best bet was going to be for him and Piper to sneak away on foot. To disappear into the mountains. Thankfully, she was a soldier. Even though she was beaten up, she should be half-decent at hiking over rough terrain.

He made another circuit of the cabin, scouting for patches of loud leaves on the ground and noting logs and other obstacles to a silent departure. He also forayed out into the woods in several different directions, being sure to make obvious tracks each time. No sense making it easy for the bastards to track him and Piper.

Preparations complete, he went back inside the house to wait for the others to get fully to sleep. He noted that the kitchen door, which he used to enter, squeaked a bit.

While he waited, he quietly packed a rucksack with all the survival gear he'd secretly collected over the past few days in anticipation of bugging out with the hostage. He also dabbed a bit of olive oil on the door hinges to quiet them. There. Ready to go. Now he just had to let the others have plenty of time to fall into a deep slumber.

He timed it on his watch, waiting two full hours before he eased into the kitchen. And then he headed down into the basement.

Here went nothing.

Piper woke abruptly as a hand closed over her mouth. Her eyes flew open, and she stared up at Goldeneyes. Without uncovering her mouth, he leaned close to whisper in her ear, "You and I need to leave now. If you stay here any longer, they'll kill you. Or worse. Do you understand?"

Oh, she understood, all right. But did she dare trust him?

Frowning, she nodded up at him. If she could get him alone in the woods, away from here, she could at least sneak away or overpower him and make her own escape. But vivid in her mind was the memory of how easily he'd wrestled her into submission earlier.

He gripped her handcuffs to keep them from rattling against the steel pole, then unlatched them quietly, easing them off her wrists and tucking them in his back pocket.

She rubbed her left wrist gently, checking to see how bad the abrasions were from when she'd fought against the fake attack earlier. Two thin red rings of raw flesh encircled most of her wrist.

A hand appeared in front of her, palm up in offer, and she took it, letting Goldeneyes help her to her feet.

He held out a sweatshirt to her, and she glanced at him, making eye contact for the first time.

"Leave your shirt on and put this on top," he whispered. "It's cold outside."

She nodded and donned the sweatshirt. As it passed over her head, she recognized the scent. It was the smell of him. A little bit spicy, a little bit musky. All man. She'd gotten a good whiff of it when his body had been mashed against hers from neck to knee.

Residual panic flashed through her at the scent trigger.

Swearing silently, she tugged the soft fabric over her face and pulled it down her torso angrily. She was all right. She hadn't been raped for real. It had all been fake. She was lucky as hell that he'd been willing to merely simulate sexually assaulting her.

He grabbed the two thickest blankets and stuffed them into a rucksack. It wouldn't zip all the way up with the bulky blankets in it, but he slung it over his shoulder and gestured for her to follow him.

She trailed after him up the stairs, rolling from heel to toe with each step the way she'd been trained to move silently. He pointed at one of the stairs and then stepped over it, and she did the same. She'd already noted from his various trips up and down that it squeaked.

He held up a closed fist at the top, telling her to stop, and she did so. Huh. How did he know that she would know that hand signal? Oh. Right. He'd spotted her West Point class ring. He must presume—correctly—that she was a soldier.

He eased over to the back door and opened it gently.

Unbidden, a rush of adrenaline slammed through her. She was getting out of here. Away from her captors. The nightmare was over.

Well, not quite over. She and Goldeneyes still had to get away from here safely and get to help. But she was confident in her field training. Once they hit the woods, she would be in her native element. They would be fine.

She hoped.

Praying this escape was exactly what it looked like it was, she stepped outside and into the clean, cold, fresh night air.

Goldeneyes eased the door shut and then stepped around her, gesturing for her to follow him. She was impressed that he moved away from the porch at a snail's pace, placing each step with care not to disturb the leaves or make a footprint in any soft dirt. He, too, rolled from heel to toe with every step. Now, where had he learned that? Only Special Forces types routinely practiced walking like that.

She walked the same way, of course, additionally making sure to place her feet in the exact same spots he was stepping with his. No sense making it any easier to trail the two of them. Her footprints would be unique and noticeable to a decent tracker. Hence her disguising her steps within his.

They reached the shadow of a giant oak tree, and he signaled for her to stop. She did, and he squatted to examine their trail back to the cabin, checking to make sure they'd left no tracks. While his back was turned and his concentration elsewhere, she could totally take off into the woods and flee from him.

But she tamped down the urge. The thinking soldier's response to this situation was to play it out a little longer. Use him to get farther from the cabin. Far enough away that he couldn't easily rouse the others and put them all on the hunt for her.

He stood up, nodded the all clear and headed into

the woods. She had no idea what direction they were heading. Under the heavy canopy of trees, it was impossible to see any stars overhead and get her bearings. She would just have to trust him for now.

They moved with cautious stealth for ten minutes or so, gliding away from the cabin in complete silence disturbed only by the occasional swish of a leaf against their clothing. His silhouette was big and black in front of her, blending into the night as if he was a natural part of it. The guy totally had some sort of military training in his background to be moving so smoothly over the rough terrain.

Over the next half hour or so, her eyes fully adjusted to the darkness, and she began to pick out more features of the forest they passed through.

It was mostly big old oak trees. Which was good. The tannin from their roots had a tendency to retard the growth of brush under them, and the going was relatively easy. It wasn't exactly a stroll through a park, since dead branches and holes lurked under the carpet of leaves, invisible until stepped upon.

She estimated they'd been walking the better part of an hour when Goldeneyes finally stopped in the lee of a vertical outcropping of layered sandstone. He sat down on a boulder and eased the rucksack off his shoulders. He held out a plastic bottle of water to her, which she took and downed gratefully.

"Since we were never officially introduced… Hello, Piper. I'm an undercover operative for the CIA. And I'm truly, deeply sorry for everything that has happened to you."

Chapter 8

Zane held his breath. This was the moment of truth. Would she believe him—and trust him? Or would she continue to fight against him and make this a battle between them? Escaping and evading the men back at the cabin while fighting with her was going to be a bitch if she chose not to believe him.

He dared not tell her much about himself in case they didn't successfully get away from Mahmoud and gang. Although, if the two of them were caught, he suspected there would be only torture and pain before they were both killed. Mahmoud probably wouldn't bother to interrogate either one of them extensively. Still, Zane had to be cautious and keep his wits about him.

"Do you have some sort of government ID on you to prove who you are?" she challenged.

"Are you kidding?" he blurted. "Have you seen how dangerous those men are back at the cabin? No way would I carry something that damning on me. I only carry identification that goes along with my deep cover legend."

"What should I call you?" she asked dryly. Dryly

enough that she obviously realized any name he gave her would be an alias.

He shrugged. "I am conditioned to respond to Amir. Or your nickname for me—what was it? Goldeneyes?—will do for now."

"Why did you kidnap me in the first place? And why did you tell them I'm Persephone Black when you knew darned good and well that I'm not her?"

He sighed, "Like I said. I really am sorry about that. Mahmoud told us Mrs. Black was the assistant principal of that elementary school—and our target—about one hour before we barged through the front doors of the school, guns blazing. They weren't going to leave that place without Mrs. Black, and I was afraid that when they didn't find her, they'd shoot the place up. If you'll recall, one of the secretaries told me Mrs. Black was out sick that morning."

"So you told them I was her?"

"You seemed like the best substitute out of the available women in the front office. You were also the only person there who even remotely looked like the surveillance photo we were shown of the real Mrs. Black."

"Who is this Persephone Black woman?" Piper asked curiously. "Why would a bunch of terrorists be interested in the assistant principal of an elementary school in south Louisiana?"

He shrugged. "As far as I can tell, she's the wife of someone important. Her only value to Mahmoud's superiors appeared to be as leverage to get her husband to do something."

"What do you know about Mr. Black?" she pressed.

"Nothing. As soon as we get back to civilization, though, I'll damned well be looking into who he is and what's so special about him."

"You seriously don't have a cell phone to call for an extraction?"

He blinked. *Extraction* was a distinctly military term. That West Point ring had obviously been the real deal. "Mahmoud doesn't allow any electronics besides his, which are heavily encrypted. No phones, no tablets, no laptops. Nothing that can be tracked by the authorities."

She looked around at the trees. "How far are we from a phone or a human being with a phone? As soon as we reach one, I can call in considerable resources to come pull us out."

"So can I," he replied dryly. "Who are you, anyway?"

She frowned heavily enough that he was able to see the expression in the dim starlight filtering through the trees. She said cautiously, "As you saw from my college class ring, I went to West Point. I'm in the army."

"That reminds me," he said. "I've been dying to know how you ended up in Houma, Louisiana, in an elementary school."

"Bad luck, I guess."

Hmm. An evasive answer. He responded, "Well, it was great luck for me." Silence fell between them as they rested. He added, "How are your injuries? Do you need first aid? I have a small kit with antibiotic cream and some bandages. I can put a new butterfly on that cut over your eye—"

She cut him off. "I'm fine. Shouldn't we be moving on?"

"You're not too tired?" he asked.

She snorted. "I can hike all night, all day tomorrow and all of tomorrow night before I start feeling tired. Just get me away from those men and to the nearest phone as fast as you can."

"I'm actually not heading for the nearest town. That's where they'll expect us to go."

"Are we headed in the opposite direction?" she asked sharply.

"Actually, the nearest town is to the north. We're headed more or less east."

She subsided beside him, muttering only, "All right, then."

He would take that as approval for his choice of direction. He stood up, shouldering the pack once more. "If you get cold, let me know and you can wrap one of the blankets around you."

That garnered another snort out of her. "Once you pick up the pace to something decent, I'll be plenty warm."

"Would you like to lead the way and set the pace?"

He made the offer sarcastically, so was shocked when she nodded and said briskly, "Show me the last landmark you were headed toward, and I'll take point for a while. Let me know if I'm going too fast for you."

Her going too fast for him? Right.

Except when she did head out, she stunned him by setting a killer pace that had him huffing and puffing behind her to keep up. Cripes. He'd known she was in good shape, but he had no idea she was *this* fit. He would hate to see her pace when she wasn't bruised and battered.

She led the way toward a distant mountain peak for a solid hour before stopping again. She even had the gall to murmur, "Do you need a rest?"

"I'm fine, thanks," he replied. "Where did you get so buff? Do you run marathons for fun or something like that?"

"Something like that."

"Color me impressed," he commented.

"Do you want to take point for a while, or should I continue leading the way?" she asked matter-of-factly.

"I'll take over the lead." He knew it to be the more tiring role, and they would both have to pace themselves physically and mentally to make their escape.

"Who are those guys, anyway?" she asked as he passed her one of the last two bottles of water and downed the other himself.

"I'm not sure."

"But you lived and worked with them."

"They were incredibly closemouthed. The intel briefings that led me to infiltrate their group indicated they might be a terrorist cell. Whether they're state actors or freelancing, I couldn't tell you. I know they speak Farsi as their primary language, which pegs them as likely Iranian in origin."

"And?" she asked expectantly.

"And that's roughly all I know about them. Mahmoud, the leader, is taking orders from someone. He's the only one in the group who routinely uses a cell phone or the internet, and the encryption on both his cell phone and laptop is top-notch. Trust me. I've checked both."

"He and the two older guys—Yousef, and I never heard the other one's name—"

"Hassan."

"—and Hassan—struck me as military," she offered.

"Agreed. I actually think all of them have military training. Mahmoud, Yousef and Hassan also appear to have some sort of advanced training. Special Forces, maybe. And training in covert intelligence operations."

"Well, that's just special," she commented. "How much danger are we in of them finding us out here?

Do they have infrared or heat-seeking gear for tracking us?"

He considered her question. "I don't know. Mahmoud kept tight control of a couple large duffel bags full of gear. It's possible they have night-optical devices and other tracking paraphernalia."

"What I wouldn't give for a nice pair of NODs right now," Piper said wistfully.

NODs, huh? That was definitely military jargon for *night-optical devices*. Special Forces types, in particular, made frequent use of them. But it wasn't like he could up and ask her about where she'd learned the terminology. She was still refusing to tell him her full name, and he guessed he couldn't blame her. Not after all she'd been through.

And after all, he hadn't told her his name, either.

He had to assume that at least one of Mahmoud's guys was a skilled tracker and would be able to follow them. He didn't want to stress out Piper any more than necessary, but they really did need to keep moving. Quickly.

After the water break, he stood up and moved out, taking the lead and setting fully as fast a pace as she had. Thankfully, she kept up without complaint.

For now. At some point, fatigue would override her fear, and then he would have a hard decision to make. Did he push her to continue on, or let her rest and risk Mahmoud and company catching up with them?

He would cross that bridge later. In the meantime, he kept an eye on the ground in front of him and frequently scanned the forest behind them for signs that they were being followed—movement, sudden silence from the night creatures, anything to indicate that Mahmoud's men had found them.

He and Piper were dead if that happened. Between the two of them, they had his Ka-Bar knife strapped to his ankle and a pocketknife. Mahmoud's men had AK-47s. Their only hope was to outrun and evade the other men.

Around daybreak, it started to rain.

He'd managed to salvage a single large trash bag from the kitchen, and he slit its seams now to create a small makeshift tarp. They huddled together under it, doing their best to stay as dry as possible. But it was a losing battle.

They were both cold and wet, and he was tired, his eyes gritty.

Piper surprised him yet again by saying, "Take a fifteen-minute power nap. I'll keep a lookout while you rest."

It wasn't a bad idea. "Only if you'll do the same when I'm done," he replied.

"Deal."

He didn't exactly feel better after the catnap, but he knew intellectually that it had helped a little.

With daylight came ease of seeing their footing, and the rain made it silent going. But they also faced a whole new set of dangers. They had to be careful not to make themselves visible while topping ridges, and they were forced to stick to the heaviest tree cover they could find, which slowed them down somewhat. Not to mention it was nearly impossible not to leave muddy tracks. He could only pray the rain would erase the prints before Mahmoud's tracker found them.

Mahmoud and the others were surely awake by now and knew that he'd absconded with their hostage. He wasn't absolutely sure they would actually come after him and Piper. But if they did, it would be with the intent to kill both of them. Urgency to reach civilization and call for help ripped through him.

Cold and miserable, they pressed onward.

About midmorning, Piper asked, "Where are we with food and water?"

"I wasn't able to carry out much of either," he answered. "By my estimate, the nearest town in this direction is at least thirty miles from the cabin."

She responded, "In virgin forest, we can only expect to make, at most, something like five or six miles a day. So that means at least five days out here. Let's round that up to a solid week for caution's sake. I gather, then, that we'll have to forage for food and water while we hike."

"That's correct."

She nodded, seemingly not alarmed by that prospect.

He asked curiously, "Why isn't the idea of eating bugs and weeds freaking you out?"

"I've done a fair bit of wilderness camping," she replied evasively.

"How's that? Not many people can say that."

She glanced over her shoulder at him, her gaze giving away nothing. "I like the outdoors."

He frowned at her back. Man, she was being cagey with him. He got that he had no right to expect her trust after he'd put her in this situation to begin with. But it still stung. He'd blown a long-term operation for her, and he'd risked his own life to stick around to pull her out. But he wasn't in any position to explain that to her.

Hmm. Did she have secrets of her own that prevented her from being honest with him? If so, what could those be? He occupied himself for the next few hours turning over possibilities in his head. Was she AWOL from the military? Maybe she'd been discharged under less-than-honorable conditions.

The good news with the rain was that it created plentiful rivulets of runoff water. They found a good one running fast and clear, and he passed Piper a plastic bottle to fill while he filled one of his own.

He had managed to slip a bottle of water-purification tablets into his pocket in the grocery store yesterday without Yousef appearing to see him. He pulled that out now and passed it to Piper. As an experiment, he intentionally didn't say anything to her about how to use them.

She casually broke the wax seal, popped one tablet in the water and gave it a good shake. She stuck the bottle in the makeshift sling she'd made of one of the blankets across her body.

Huh. She definitely knew how to use the tablets. She knew to give them a little while to kill any bacteria in the water. He did the same, and they filled the two remaining water bottles and treated that water, as well. They commenced walking again.

They entered a valley with relatively heavy underbrush and pushed through it carefully, trying not to snag clothing or break branches in such a way as to leave a trail. It was slow going and hard work.

When he judged it to be midday—it was too cloudy to know for sure—he called a halt and offered Piper one of their precious protein bars.

"Are you going to have one, too?" she asked.

"I'll be okay for now. I had a big supper last night," he replied.

"Don't be a hero on me. You need to keep up your strength if you're not going to become a liability to me out here."

He managed not to stare, but just barely. *Him* a liability to *her*? Was that just her army training showing, or did she seriously see herself as more capable out here than him? Fascinating. Who in the hell *was* she?

The far side of the valley was very steep and rocky. It wasn't exactly a sheer cliff, but wasn't far from it.

"How are you at free-climbing rocks?" she asked him as they stared left and right at the long stone wall in either direction.

"I've done it before," he answered. "And it looks like a time-consuming detour to go around this."

"Up it is, then," she declared. "I'll go first. I've done a lot of rock climbing."

Of course she had.

She backed up and studied the face for several minutes, planning her route. Then she stepped up to the wall, reached for the first handholds and winced.

"What hurts?" he asked instantly.

"Ribs. Your buddy worked me over pretty good."

"He isn't my buddy. Yousef is a psychopath and a terrorist." He added, "If you've got broken ribs, we shouldn't try this climb."

"Your makeshift padding worked, as far as I can tell," she grunted as she hauled herself upward. "My ribs are just bruised."

"Still. If this climb is going to hurt too much, we can go around."

"Pain is weakness leaving the body," she commented absently as she eyed the next handholds above her.

He snorted. "The rest of that saying is, 'Unless you've served in the military. Then it's probably arthritis.'"

A burst of laughter escaped her. "Don't make me laugh. I'll lose focus and fall."

Grinning, he continued climbing behind her, privately enjoying the view of her tush and long, lean legs.

They were mostly silent during the climb, communicating only to warn each other of loose rocks, or to point out a possible change to their route up the wall. It took nearly a half hour to make the climb, and as they flopped on their bellies on the flat ground above, they were both breathing hard.

"Well. That should slow down Mahmoud and company a bit," he commented.

He climbed to his feet and helped Piper to hers. He noticed that she was moving distinctly more creakily than before. "Do you need to stop and rest for a while?" he asked quietly.

"No. Let's press on."

As impressed as he was by her fortitude in the face of pain and exhaustion, he said, "Look, we can't walk straight through for the next week. You're going to have to rest sometime."

"They're following us by now, right?"

"I expect so."

"Then now is the time to press on. Our tactical advantage will come from moving farther and faster than they can possibly expect us to. When they don't find us right away, they'll get frustrated. The rigors of tracking us will start to weigh on their minds, and we'll have won."

"Okay. Who are you?" he blurted. "That's seriously military-trained thinking."

"I told you. I'm in the army."

"Well, yeah. There's army and then there's *army*. Not that many women run around with field infantry units."

"There are plenty of women in the infantry, thank you very much. And we keep up with the boys just fine."

He threw up his hands. "I meant no offense. Suffice it to say I'm impressed by your training."

"I'll be sure to pass that on to my instructors."

He shook his head. "Fine. We'll press on a little while longer. But tonight, we stop, find or build a shelter, and get some proper rest."

"Fair enough."

She met his gaze, smiling a little as she did so. Hark. Was the ice queen's wall of suspicion actually beginning to thaw?

Chapter 9

Pain, exhaustion, relief and fear pulled at Piper in about equal amounts. The idea of building a nice fire, getting dry and warm, and curling up for a long nap sounded better than just about anything on earth. But she wasn't wrong. Now was the exact time to press on and push the hardest. When other people would stop and rest, this was the moment to put distance between herself and her captors.

The Medusas had a long history of capitalizing on their foes underestimating the capabilities of women, and this was definitely one of those times.

Thankfully, Goldeneyes was insanely fit himself and able to keep up with her as she pushed herself to her prodigious physical limits.

A CIA officer, huh? That certainly explained a lot. She was inclined to believe him. After all, he'd been unflaggingly protective of her from the very beginning, and he, too, had kept his cool in multiple high-stress situations.

It started to rain again as darkness fell. The rain became a downpour, and the temperature dropped precipitously.

She knew it didn't have to get colder than about sixty-five degrees for hypothermia to become a threat, and it was definitely colder than that now. Neither she nor her companion had proper clothing for cold, and their blankets were soaked, too.

Vaguely, it occurred to her that they should probably consider stopping and trying to find shelter. But where? She looked around and saw only trees and more trees. If they had a parachute they could build a great shelter. She couldn't remember what she was supposed to do if she didn't have one.

Alarm shot through her. Something was wrong with her.

She stumbled just then, and barely managed to right herself without face planting. Hmm. That was unlike her. She wasn't usually clumsy.

"Are you okay?" Goldeneyes asked from behind her.

"Uh, yeah. Fine."

"What's eight times nine?"

"What?" She turned around to peer at him in the thick darkness. The heavy cloud cover made it nearly impossible to see out here.

"What's eight times nine? Quick. Just tell me the answer."

"No fair. I suck at math."

"Answer me. Right now."

"Um…fifty-six—no. Seventy-two."

"Too slow. We're stopping," he announced.

"No! We have to keep going!"

"You're either exhausted or hypothermic or both. We're stopping. Now," he said firmly.

"Speak for yourself. I'm keeping going." She turned to face forward and disorientation swirled around her as she stared at the thick trees in every direction. Where was she supposed to go?

A hand closed on her upper arm. It was gentle but strong enough that she couldn't ignore it. "Listen to me, Piper. You need to take care of yourself now if you're going to be able to keep going tomorrow."

"But Mahmoud—"

"Mahmoud is no hero. He'll call it quits if the weather gets this nasty. He's just a guy doing a job. But his number one priority is saving his own hide and his own comfort and well-being. We've got some time to rest."

Should she believe him? As she considered that, it gradually dawned on her that her brain was fuzzier than it ought to be. A lot fuzzier. "I don't know…" she mumbled.

"There's a rock face about a hundred meters in front of us. Maybe we can find an overhang that's reasonably dry. Come on. Let's go have a look."

For lack of any better ideas, she fell in behind him. He followed the line of the cliff for a little while and stopped in front of a long, narrow ledge about waist high. It jutted out, forming a flat roof over an indentation caused by long-term erosion of the layers of sandstone below.

He announced, "It's not great, but this will have to do."

They crawled under the narrow overhang, which was only about eight feet deep. The good news was the dead leaves and debris collected at the back of the space were more or less dry. Which meant the ground beneath was dry.

He made her go in first, and then he stretched out

beside her with the garbage bag draped over his back to buffer the worst of the rain that blew in under the ledge.

As soon as they quit moving, the chill and the wet caught up with her, and she started to shiver. Over the next few minutes, the shivering worsened until her teeth chattered and her entire body shook violently.

Goldeneyes put his arms around her, but he didn't feel much warmer than her. After a couple minutes, he announced, "This isn't working. We're both getting more hypothermic. We'll be in serious trouble soon if we don't do something."

Hypothermia. That was bad. Deadly if not dealt with. She'd memorized something having to do with it somewhere before, a lifetime away from this moment.

She recited, "Dry clothing. Hot food and drink. Heat source. Share body heat."

"Did you get a merit badge in scouting for survival?" he asked humorously.

"Scouting? No. Medusas."

"Medusas? What?"

"Never mind," she mumbled.

He ticked off her list. "We have no dry clothing, and it'll take a fire to heat up drinks or food. For that matter, we could use a fire for the heat ourselves."

"Fire's a beacon," she mumbled.

"True. But we could die if we don't build one," he replied. "I don't think we have any choice."

"Shield it," she responded.

"Gotta build it first," he replied humorously. "And everything out here is wet."

"Not everything." She reached into her front jeans pocket and pulled out a handful of cattail fuzz.

He peered between their bodies for a moment, obviously working to figure out what she was holding in her fist. "Where did you get that?" he finally asked.

"Crossing one of the streams this morning. I grabbed some in case we needed a fire starter. My body heat dried it through the day."

He shocked her by dropping a fast, hard kiss on her mouth. "You are a goddess. You may have just saved us both."

She blinked, startled.

"Stay here while I go gather the driest wood I can find for a fire. I won't be long."

"Don't go far," she said quickly as fear of being alone out here roared through her. Weird. She didn't fear forests, and she certainly didn't fear being by herself.

"I won't."

And then he was gone. Only the sound of rain batting at leaves and water dripping nearby broke the heavy silence. She huddled inside the damp blanket, her fingers and toes numb with cold, and her brain at least as numb.

She had to move. Do something to increase her circulation. Otherwise, she was going to drift off to sleep and her core body temperature would drop even more. Gritting her teeth, she threw off the blanket and crawled out of what little warmth the thing had provided.

She cleared a wide space on the ground under one end of the overhang, collecting the relatively dry leaves and debris for starting their fire. In the center of the space, she used a stout stick and her hands to dig a hole. When it was knee-deep, she worked on widening it.

If they built the fire in the bottom of the hole, the worst of its light would be hidden from distant eyes.

To additionally protect the flame from being spotted, she draped one of the blankets over bushes just beyond the firepit. She left a small gap between the top of the blanket and the rock face so smoke and heat could escape without setting the blanket on fire.

Not only would it act as a light shield, but it would also protect the fire from wind and the worst of the rain. They'd sacrifice some warmth from the blanket for themselves, but the payback in heat from the fire should more than make up for the loss.

She was just finishing up when a shadow loomed suddenly, startling her badly. Goldeneyes. Wow, she was seriously off her game.

He dumped a big armload of wood on the ground and nodded in approval at her preparations.

"I've got one more thing to do before we hunker down and get warm," he murmured. He dug in his pack and came up with a plastic grocery bag.

"What's in that?" she asked curiously.

"Fishing line and mousetraps."

"You're going to trap the perimeter?" she blurted in surprise. "Do you need help?"

"Nah. You're too cold. Do you feel comfortable starting the fire by yourself?"

She threw him her best "are you kidding?" look and asked dryly, "Do you have some matches, or am I rubbing sticks together?"

He tossed her a cigarette lighter from his pack, which she snagged neatly in midair.

He grinned. "Good luck."

Smart-ass. She would show him.

She piled up her dry cattail fluff and a few of the dry leaves and small twigs to prepare a fire. Using her body as an additional shield against the wind and rain, she used the cigarette lighter to start it.

She bent close, blowing gently on her fledgling blaze and feeding in more leaves. It smoked heavily, but gradually, the twigs caught fire. She fed it more twigs, and then sticks the diameter of her fingers. It took perhaps ten minutes for the fire to really get established. But eventually, she laid down branches the diameter of her wrists and held out her hands to warm them over the growing flames.

Now and then a gust blew a sheet of rain under the overhang and the fire guttered. But it had established a bed of coals and, tucked down in the bottom of the hole she'd dug, was mostly protected. She broke all the branches she was strong enough to crack into smaller lengths, and ringed the firepit with the wet wood to dry out some before she had to stack it on the blaze.

Heat began to roll off the fire, but it wasn't enough to beat back the violent cold making her shiver uncontrollably.

Gradually, though, her hands dried, warmed and regained feeling. She stripped off her soaked tennis shoes and socks and draped them over logs near the fire. Her toes were white and wrinkled with wet and cold, and she held her feet close to the fire to dry and warm, as well. It hurt like crazy as circulation returned to them, but at least they were thawing and warming.

Goldeneyes was gone a solid half hour before he called out from the woods, "I'm coming in now." Which was kind of him. She would have hated to break his neck in reflexive reaction if he successfully sneaked up on her.

"Wires set?" she asked.

"Yes. The mousetraps won't be very loud, but they should silence all the critters around them. I set some about four hundred yards out and another group about two hundred yards out."

He was correct. Abrupt cessation of sound out here

would be as noticeable as a loud noise. Assuming the rain didn't drown out all sound. The good news: Mahmoud and his men had probably hunkered down in some sort of shelter to ride out this downpour.

"Give me your water bottles," Goldeneyes directed her. He set those beside the fire to warm up the water inside.

Good idea.

But then he stripped off his sweatshirt and T-shirt. His bare chest looked primal in the flickering firelight. He reached for the hem of her sweatshirt, as well.

"Whoa, whoa, whoa," she blurted.

"You said it yourself," he said. "We have to get dry. We need to dry out our clothes if we're going to have any chance of warming up."

She frowned at him, trying hard to come up with some reasonable argument to refute his logic.

Damn. She had nothing. She reached for her hem and winced as her ribs gave a mighty protest.

"Let me do that for you," he said quickly. Very gently, he slipped his hands under the wet cotton and pushed it up to her neck. He grabbed the cuffs and tugged while she pulled her arms free of the sleeves. A grunt of pain slipped out of her mouth.

"Easy," he murmured. He stretched the neck of the garment with his hands and lifted it very carefully over her battered face. The cold air hit her bare skin and she gasped.

He sucked in a hard breath as well, but it was probably the sight of the copious bruises across her torso that made him suck wind like that. She gathered the white cotton of her shirt across her middle, clutching it for a second in embarrassment before she steeled herself to shuck it off in turn. Still, after she took it off, she reflexively wadded it in her hands, clutched at her throat, clinging to its meager protection.

Carefully averting his eyes from her bruises and bra, he spread her sweatshirt out next to his on the far side of the fire, and then he held out his bare arm to her in invitation. He never once looked her way.

It was a small courtesy, but it meant a lot to her. She hadn't realized how embarrassed she would be by the evidence of her beating. Maybe it was a reflection of the helplessness she'd felt while she'd been tied to that chair taking punches.

Appreciation that he didn't force himself upon her in any way also registered. He waited patiently, his arm extended, not a muscle in his body moving. She stared at his chest for a long moment. It was muscular. Strong. It shouted of danger to her.

And yet she realized with a start that she trusted him. He had never hurt her before, and he wasn't about to start now. All at once, she shook out the torn cotton shirt and spread it on the ground. Then she scooted over close to him.

. He gasped involuntarily as she pressed her side against his. "You're an ice cube, Piper. Why didn't you tell me earlier that you were freezing?"

"W-was t-trying t-to ignore it."

"While I admire your efforts to be tough, we're in this together. Please tell me if you're cold or hungry or thirsty or tired, so I can take care of you."

"I'm all of th-the above," she admitted against his chest.

His arm tightened around her shoulders, protectively but not restrictively. An odd sense of comfort flowed over her, gradually sinking into her. Or maybe that was just his body heat.

"We probably need to take off our jeans, too," he sighed into her hair. "Mine are soaked, and I assume yours are, too. I didn't want to freak you out by suggesting all at once that we strip down."

She considered his words. What he said made sense. At least her mental functions seemed to be returning a little bit.

"You can take your jeans off and I'll leave mine on if you want," he offered.

"But that would mean you'd be sitting around in wet pants, not warming up," she objected.

"I put you through hell the past several days. It's the least I can do for you."

"We'll both take our pants off," she declared.

It was awkward working in the tight confines of the narrow space, and the wet denim clung to their legs stubbornly. They ended up having to take turns lying on their backs and holding their legs up while the other one peeled the jeans off.

Piper giggled as she yanked at his pants and accidentally got a fistful of his tighty-whities. He made a fast grab to preserve his modesty.

"It's not as if I haven't been exposed to all of your… equipment…already," she announced.

"I'm sorry about that."

"You can quit apologizing now. I got the message loud and clear that you deeply regret everything that has happened to me."

He shifted to lie on his side facing the fire, close to the back wall of their little shelter. She still sat upright, and he spooned lightly around her lower torso from behind.

"You'll be warmer if you lie down beside me," he

murmured. "Let me block the cold coming off the rocks at our backs from you while the fire warms your front."

"Won't you get colder?"

"Nah. I'm a furnace. Always have been. Once this fire gets a little bigger, you and I will both be toasty in no time."

She stretched out beside him, cuddling back against his body. He was fully as cold as she was. It was kind of him to lie about being all right. If nothing else, the fire could warm her, and her body heat would warm him up a little.

"As soon as the other blanket is dry, you should put it over you," she told him.

"By the time it's dry, most of our clothes should be dry, too."

"Not the jeans, though. Those will take a while," she replied.

Silence fell between them as they spooned next to the fire. She curled around the firepit, as close as she could get without being singed. With him pressed tightly against her back, she actually began to warm up and feel semihuman again.

"I'm doing better," she announced. "Do you want to switch places?"

"Nah. I'm good. You're warming me up."

With dryness and heat came awareness of the man pressed against her back from neck to ankles. His chest was muscular, his belly slabbed in muscle, as well. His legs were hairy, but the hair was soft against her skin. Whisker stubble on his face was rough against her shoulder. His knees tucked up under hers where they bent around the fire, and his arm was heavy across her middle.

She was surrounded by him. By his skin and muscle and sinew.

Not only did she feel almost warm, but she also felt almost safe. Finally.

She let out a big sigh, releasing the crushing fear and relentless stress of the past few days. Not surprisingly, a few tears escaped her eyes and ran sideways over her nose and dripped off her temple.

"Hey," he said in a low voice. "What's wrong?"

"Nothing. This is just relief."

"Ah." A pause. "That's good." Another longer pause. "Although I would be remiss if I didn't tell you we're not out of the woods yet. Literally or figuratively."

She smiled a little. "I hear you. But being chased by bad guys and evading them in the woods is more in my regular wheelhouse. I'm trained to deal with doing that, and it doesn't freak me out."

"Ri-i-ight."

Damn. She'd given away too much again. This guy lulled her into a sense of safety and relaxation where she spoke without thinking and kept tossing him hints about who she really was. She had to stop that!

"For the record," she said reflectively, "I really appreciate everything you did to take care of me and protect me. Everything except that tackle in the field when I tried to escape. That hurt."

He chuckled into her ear. "I would have let you go except one of the guys would have stepped out of the van to look for us any second. I was afraid we would get mowed down by an AK-47 before we got to the truck stop."

"Speak for yourself. I'm pretty fast."

"I know that now," he replied. "But I didn't then."

"Are you really in the CIA?" she asked.

"I really am. And that's classified, by the way. When we get back to the real world, I'll need you not to tell anyone about it."

"Or what? You'll have to shoot me?" she quipped.

"I could never shoot you. I—" He broke off.

"You what?"

"I care too much about you."

She froze in his arms, and he went just as still.

At long last, she mumbled, "You don't know anything about me."

"I know you're braver than just about any woman I've ever met, and you have a great sense of humor, even in the face of terrible, terrible events. You're unbelievably calm in a crisis, and you keep your wits about you under pressure. You tried to protect me by telling Mahmoud you were Persephone Black, and you sure as hell didn't owe me a damned thing in that scenario. Which tells me you have a noble and self-sacrificing streak a mile wide. And, of course, you're freaking beautiful. But that goes without saying."

She didn't know what to say. Eventually, she mumbled, "You still don't know most of the important stuff about me."

"Okay, tell me something important about you," he murmured.

"You first."

He sighed, "When are you going to learn to trust me? I mean, I get why you're cautious, but I promise, we're on the same side."

That might be true, but her secrets weren't the kind she could share with anyone. Her life, and those of her teammates, depended on total secrecy around the Medusa Project.

He surprised her by continuing. "Fine. Something

important about me. Let's see. I'm from New Hampshire originally. I was amused when you said my name should be Chad or Blaine. And yes, I have actually been sailing off Martha's Vineyard. I grew up being the preppy you accused me of being."

"Ha. Nailed it."

His arms tightened a bit around her. "Remind me to add being perceptive to your list of virtues."

"Trust me. I have plenty of vices," she retorted.

"Name one."

"I love junk food. If I could get away with it, I would live on pizza, chips and soda. Oh, and ice cream. Lots of ice cream."

"What do you do to stay so fit, then?"

"I do my job. I run around in the woods, do calisthenics and swim and run basically all day long every day."

"What's your job?" he asked, sounding surprised.

She paused. "Here's the thing. My job is classified."

"So I gather. You know what NODs are. You walk and talk like a warrior. Your survival skills are outstanding. Are you an infantry officer?"

"I was one."

He went still, obviously thinking hard.

Dammit, she'd done it again. She'd gone and revealed way too much about herself to him. She didn't need him making the next leap of logic that she'd moved beyond plain-Jane infantry to the Special Forces.

She half turned in his arms so she could look up at him. He stared down at her intently, obviously weighing everything he knew of her and drawing his own conclusions.

"Can you do me a favor?" she murmured up at him.

The thoughtful look in his eyes was abruptly replaced by sharp alertness as he stared back at her. "What's that?"

"Would you kiss me, please?"

Caution leaped into his eyes. "Why do you ask for that? I would have thought that after I, um, attacked you, you would want nothing to do with me."

"In the first place, you didn't attack me. You simulated attacking me, and you were as much of a gentleman as it's possible to be in a situation like that. In the second place, I would like to replace the bad memory of that event with a good one."

"You're sure?" he asked soberly.

"Positive."

His chin dipped, his mouth moving toward hers slowly. Carefully. Like he expected her to change her mind—or maybe attack him. When their lips were no more than a few inches apart, his upper torso pressing her opposite shoulder down into the ground, he murmured, "Are you okay?"

Hell, no. She wasn't okay. The fake attack had been traumatic no matter how nice he'd been about it. It had been a chilling demonstration in what it felt like to be helpless and at the mercy of another human being. What if he hadn't been such a decent guy? What if he hadn't taken care of her and only simulated the attack?

She mumbled aloud, "Yes, I'm okay. And thank you for practicing good consent behavior. But could you kiss me already? The suspense is making me nervous."

Which was to say, she was terrified her courage would desert her and that she would back out of her request. Worse, if she didn't get back in this saddle right now, with this man, she had a sinking suspicion it would be a very long time before she trusted any other man to kiss her.

"It's only the suspense making you nervous?" He almost sounded disappointed that it wasn't him doing so. News flash: *he* was making her nervous. More than she wanted to acknowledge, in fact. She'd just spent the past half hour more naked than not, pressed against him skin to skin, vividly aware of his body against hers.

Her heart raced and her breath hitched as he closed the final gap.

His lips brushed across hers lightly, a bare caress, so feathery she might not have felt it if she hadn't been looking straight at him.

She froze, and he stopped, apparently waiting for her to gauge her reaction to the bare touch of their mouths.

She lifted her chin to kiss him this time, a little more firmly. A little more actual mouth-on-mouth contact.

It was his turn to freeze. Had her hand not been resting on his chest directly over his heart, she would've missed the abrupt acceleration of his heartbeat, pounding hard against her palm. Well, then.

What *was* she going to do with this man? She certainly knew what she would like to do with him. Did she dare?

If the past few days had taught her nothing else, it was that life was too short to let chances like this pass her by.

She kissed him again, more passionately this time. Was he aware that his hips were rocking a little against hers? Oh, yes. She wanted him, too.

"You okay?" he breathed.

"Getting there…"

Chapter 10

Getting there, indeed. Zane was way ahead of her, racing toward desires that were surely far, far beyond what she had in mind. He'd spent most of the past few days watching this woman, practically around the clock. He knew every curve of her face, had memorized every angle and curve of her body, the expressions that flashed across her mobile face—

Get a grip, man. This was the woman he'd kidnapped, for crying out loud. Guilt roared through him that he'd put this wonderful, warm, generous woman through hell. The last thing he wanted to do was take advantage of her vulnerable, emotional state. Hell, for all he knew, she was suffering a case of Stockholm syndrome, where the prisoner began to empathize too much with his or her kidnapper in a psychological-defense reaction to extreme duress.

She captured his mouth with her soft, sweet lips. She felt like an angel and tasted like heaven—

His brain reengaged sharply. He had no business kissing her. Yes, he got that she wanted to reassure herself that she was not traumatized. He was willing, happy even, to help her with that.

But no more than that. He owed her complete self-restraint on his part. If he cared about her at all, he would leave her the hell alone.

He went perfectly still, letting her call the shots. But damned if she didn't continue letting her warm, re-silient lips linger against his. Her mouth was fully as warm and pliable as it looked and he loved how her lips molded to his.

She deepened the kiss just a tiny bit.

Mistake, mistake, mistake!

She shifted beside him, rolling more fully onto her back and twining her arms lightly around his neck to take him with her. He propped his left elbow between her and the edge of the firepit. He partially covered her body with his but was careful not to let much of his weight come to rest upon her. No need to scare her when she was just starting to relax.

What are you doing, you idiot?

He answered himself that he was helping her move past the trauma of her near rape. That he was letting her use his body to heal herself.

Liar. You totally want this woman.

The fire was hot on his forearm, but it didn't hold a candle to the heat suddenly pouring off the women beneath him. Her fingers slipped into his hair and tugged his head down to hers once more, pulling him more urgently into their kiss now.

Ignoring the warnings of logic and his better im-pulses, he obliged her and kissed her even more deeply, opening his mouth a little in invitation, but letting her set the overall pace. Her tongue traced the outline of his lips and then the sharp edges of his teeth. He held himself stock-still, not moving a muscle throughout her explorations.

She tilted her head to one side, fitting their mouths more tightly together, giving herself even deeper access to his mouth. Her chest lifted off the ground slightly, arching up toward his body. Her cotton-covered breasts rubbed lightly against his chest, and his breath hitched. Hard.

Man, that felt good. He silently wished for her to do it again. But no way would he ask such a thing of her. This was her show. She called the shots tonight. Whatever she wanted, he would give her. No less, and no more.

Their tongues swirled together, mimicking the sex act in a carnal dance that made him wild with desire.

He reined in his urges ruthlessly, refusing to give in to his baser impulses.

Her right hand slid across his shoulder, over the bulge of his biceps, and trailed down his arm. Then her fingers lifted away from him momentarily. Mentally, he howled a protest. But then her hand touched his waist, tracing a path of destruction across his ribs, following their length around the front of his torso toward his sternum.

Her hand dipped lower, her palm coming to rest upon his belly where the muscles were contracted so hard already that they were painful. He wasn't trying to show off—her touch just did that to him. It made him tight and hard all over, in fact. Schooling himself fiercely to be still and let her set the pace of their embrace, he actually shook from the effort of holding himself perfectly still.

At least he wasn't cold anymore. Far from it. Suddenly, he felt as if he was burning up. With need. And lust. For her. So much for hypothermia. One kiss from this woman and he was in danger of going up in flames.

What he really wanted to do was surge up over her, rid them both of their underwear, position himself between her legs and pump mindlessly into her body until the universe went supernova around them.

Instead, he gritted his teeth and suffered in silence, loving and hating the slowness of her explorations as her hand wandered at a snail's pace across his bare skin.

It was torture.

He owed her this.

In a way, it was fair payback for the torture he'd put her through.

But he was getting the better end of that deal by a lot.

His breath caught and then stopped altogether as she slide her hand down his stomach, lower and lower yet. Her fingers slipped inside the waistband of his underwear. They tangled briefly in his pubic hair, and then her hand encircled his engorged erection.

"Oh, thank goodness," she sighed.

"I beg your pardon?" he blurted out.

"I was worried when you didn't get at all aroused during our fake attack that you didn't find me attractive."

He snorted. "I don't find the idea of forcing myself on any woman the least bit attractive. In fact, I can't think of a bigger turnoff than that."

Her fingers gripped his erection firmly, sliding up and down the shaft experimentally. His hips lurched and he inhaled hard.

"I can't tell you how relieved I am to learn that a) you don't relish assaulting women, and b) that you do relish me at least a little."

He buried his face in her hair and mumbled, "This is not me being turned on a little. This is me being turned on like crazy."

"Hmm. What are we going to do about that?" she teased.

"We're doing nothing at all about it. You may do whatever you like to me and with me, Piper. But I refuse to lift a hand to you in any way, lest you feel the least bit threatened." To that end, he rolled onto his back beside her.

She raised up on an elbow to stare down at him. In the firelight, she looked like some primal goddess bathed in warm light, her hair glinting like spun filaments of gold, her eyes darker than the night around them.

"Are you serious?" she breathed. "I can do whatever I want to you?"

Whatever encompassed a very broad range of possibilities. But he owed her more than he could possibly begin to repay. This was the least he could do. He nodded firmly. "Whatever you want. My body is yours."

She rose on her knees beside him. Dry leaves crunched under the blanket he lay on, and the ground was hard and unyielding beneath him. Piper reached for his underwear, and he lifted his hips, helping her strip them off him. His erection jutted up, as hard and hot as newly forged steel. No help for it. And she seemed to want to look at all of him. So be it.

She ran her palms lightly over his torso, and he jumped occasionally as she found ticklish spots. Then she shocked him by stripping off her panties quickly and throwing a leg over his hips to straddle him.

"You'll get cold," he protested.

"The rocks overhead have warmed up and are radiating heat down on me," she countered.

"I don't have any condoms," he ground out from between his clenched teeth. The control it took to stay still beneath her as her lady parts rubbed up and down his shaft was almost more than he could muster.

She murmured, "I have a long-term birth control pellet in my arm. As long as you know you don't have any sexually transmitted diseases and haven't had sex with anyone else in a while, we're good."

"God, I love how prepared you are for every contingency," he muttered.

She laughed a little and then her moist, hot opening was poised at the tip of his penis. He reached up to grab her hips. To stop her.

Lord, man. Have you lost your mind?

Shut up, horny me. I'm trying to do the right thing here.

Aloud, he bit out, "Are you sure about this?"

She reached for his hands and drew them away from her hips. Slowly, she drew his hands up over his head and pressed them to the ground. Her breasts were right there, only inches from his mouth. He would love to suck and lick at them, to make her scream with pleasure—

But this was her night.

"Don't move," she murmured.

Such sweet torture. "I won't move," he ground out.

She sat back up and reached between their bodies. Her fist gripped him strongly and he couldn't stop the groan of pleasure that escaped his throat.

And then she was sliding down onto him, impaling herself by slow degrees. The heat and tightness of her body nearly made his eyes roll back in his head with pleasure.

His hands jerked reflexively, started to reach for her. "Keep your hands over your head, please," she whispered.

He slammed them back down to the ground as she

started to move on him, easing herself up and down his erection. Gliding in and out of her tight sheath was almost more than he could stand. A need to explode into her rolled through him, and he clenched his teeth against it.

Long and slow and easy, she rode him. Gradually, her eyes glazed over with pleasure as she angled herself just right for maximum sensation. Her body undulated in the firelight, and was without question the sexiest thing he'd ever seen. Stretched out on a rack of pleasure beneath her, he lost himself in the blissful agony of letting her use his body however she wanted to.

And use it she did. She rode him faster, harder, until he was groaning aloud with the struggle not to come inside her then and there. She took pity on him and slowed her pace, letting him almost, but not quite, recover his composure before she rode him hard again.

Over and over she took him right to the brink of losing it and then backed off. Thankfully, she seemed wired for pleasure and achieved orgasms quickly, shuddering hard around him once. Twice. Three times.

Finally, when her body glistened with perspiration and his literally shook from the effort of holding back his own orgasm, she took pity on him.

Placing her hand in the middle of his chest, she leaned forward a little and rode him like a wild creature, a fey being of the night who'd come to him to take him on a fantasy adventure into a realm beyond humans.

"You can move a little if you want," she panted.

His hips bucked beneath hers as he surged up into her over and over, completely lost in the pleasure she'd created between them.

"Now!" she cried. "Let go now!"

He surged up into her with abandon, and she

slammed down onto him, their bodies raging together toward release. His entire body arched up off the ground and she slapped her hand over his mouth hard as he coiled, clenched, and then his entire being exploded up into her. Up into the night. Up, up into the magic spell she'd woven around them both.

The power of it tore away everything, leaving him raw and exposed, his soul bared before her. He fell back upon the blanket and stared up at her as she panted above him. Her muscular legs were relaxed now around his hips.

Both her hands were planted on his chest now as she leaned on him, catching her breath. He knew the feeling. Running a marathon didn't even wipe him out like this.

She stared down at him in what he hoped was a modicum of satisfaction. Maybe even a bit of wonder shone in her clear, serene gaze.

"Warm enough?" he finally managed to gather his scattered thoughts enough to mumble.

She smiled knowingly. "I'm going to have to cool off and let the sweat dry before I dress again."

"That's a better problem to have than freezing half to death."

"I'll take this any day over being cold," she murmured.

He reached up to wrap his arms against her, and she came down to him willingly, sprawling across him bonelessly.

"Am I crushing you?" she murmured.

"Little thing like you? Nah."

"I'm not that little. I'm almost five foot nine. And I'm solid muscle."

"I'm six foot two, which makes you a shrimp in my

world. And you may be muscular, but you're still lean. And may I say, beautifully proportioned."

"Thanks."

"Thank you," he replied fervently.

"I'm pretty sure I'm the one who should be thanking you for that," she retorted, pushing up on his chest to stare down at him.

Her hair fell in a curtain around them and he pushed it back and tucked it behind her ears. "Tell you what. I'll stop apologizing for getting you kidnapped and everything that followed if you'll stop thanking me for what we just shared. I assure you, I got at least as much pleasure from it as you did."

"Fair enough. But it was very nice of you to let me do whatever I wanted like that."

He laughed up at her, "I'm definitely adding that to my regular rotation of things to do in bed with beautiful, sexy women."

"Oh, and you have a lot of women in your bed? Your last name isn't Bond, is it?"

"No. My name is Zane." He added reluctantly, "Zane Cosworth."

Very, *very* few people outside of his immediate family knew his name. For him, it was the ultimate signal of trust he could give to anyone.

She stared down at him, looking deep into his eyes. At least she seemed to understand the significance of him giving her his real name.

"Nice to meet you, Zane Cosworth. My name is Piper Ford. Captain, United States Army."

"Nice to meet you, too, Captain Ford." And then he added, "Who are the Medusas?"

Chapter 11

She rolled off him and sat up, hugging her knees and staring into the fire. "How high is your security clearance?" she finally asked him.

"High enough that the name of it is classified," he answered quietly, sitting up beside her.

They really did need to get dry again before they thought about getting dressed. Ah, but what a way to get damp. He checked their clothes and turned over the sweatshirts and jeans to let their other sides dry.

Piper surprised him by saying, "The existence of the Medusas is a well-kept secret and needs to stay that way. I actually will have to kill you if you blab about it to anybody."

"You don't have to tell me about it if you don't want to," he responded seriously.

"No. I want to. You shared with me who you are, and if I don't miss my guess, risked your life to do that. I owe you no less."

He shrugged. "You're not wrong that knowing my name gives you a lot of power over me." He threw a couple logs on the fire and then settled beside her again.

"This isn't a tit-for-tat relationship, Piper. I don't think in terms of you owing me anything. If you'd like to tell me about it, I would love to hear more about how you acquired your...atypical...skill set."

"The Medusas are a joint military task force, manned—or womanned, as the case may be—by women from all the branches of the military. We're a small all-purpose, all-female Special Forces team."

"All female?" he exclaimed under his breath.

"Correct."

"Well, that certainly explains a lot about you." He fell silently, obviously thinking back to everything he'd observed her do over the past several days. At length, he asked, "What were you doing at an elementary school in Houma, Louisiana?"

She laughed ruefully, "Dropping off my neighbor kid's lunch that he forgot in my car. I gave him a ride to school that day."

"What a stroke of luck that was. I couldn't have asked for a better hostage."

"Thanks, I think?" she replied wryly.

"You know what I mean. If Mahmoud and his guys were going to snatch anyone, you were the best possible person to end up being their prisoner. Have you had enhanced prisoner-of-war training?"

"Oh, yeah. We've had all the training."

"I thought so. When you knew how to take a punch, and you knew just how long to hold out under interrogation, and just how much information to eke out to your interrogator, I wondered where you'd learned that."

"I didn't tell Mahmoud much. I just parroted back stuff you'd already told me and then followed Mahmoud's lead from his questions."

"Like I said. You were the perfect hostage."

She poked at the fire with a stick, and the flames flared. This fire was life to them out here. It was recovery from hypothermia, dry clothing and hot water to drink and bring up their core temperatures.

"What kind of missions do these Medusas of yours run?"

"The previous Medusa teams did all sorts of missions. They guarded high-value female targets, went undercover on rescue missions, even freed a hijacked cruise ship. We mostly go into nations where women are ignored and marginalized, or where we can work under the radar because the locals aren't looking for women operators."

He nodded thoughtfully. "I can think of some situations where you ladies would be handy assets."

"Next time you need a woman, give us a call."

He laughed a little. "Next time I need a woman, I'll give *you* a call."

A blush made her cheeks feel even hotter than the fire did. "You know what I meant. Next time you need a female operations team, call the Medusas."

He grinned at her, and she ducked her head, embarrassed at her slip of the tongue and secretly a little delighted that he would consider calling her again. Most of the men she met were intimidated by her confidence, intelligence and self-possession. That, and her utter failure to be impressed by their macho posturing and mansplaining.

To his vast credit, Zane hadn't done any posturing or talking down to her ever. He had always treated her with complete respect. Even when he was pretending to rape her, for crying out loud.

"We need to get some sleep now that we're out of

danger from hypothermia," he said, jerking her thoughts back to the situation at hand.

"We'll need to take turns sleeping and tending the fire," she responded.

"Are you tired now?"

She shook her head. "If you can sleep now, I'll take the first shift on fire-guard duty."

He pulled on his underwear and now-dry T-shirt, then stretched out along the back wall of the crevice on his side, facing her and the fire.

"Here." He held out his Ka-Bar knife to her, hilt first. She took it easily, hefting it in her hand, getting the feel for its balance.

He murmured, "Wake me up if there's any trouble at all."

"I will." She added, "But I can generally take care of myself, and I don't get afraid of the dark. It's my preferred work environment."

One corner of his mouth curved up as he planted his head on his bent elbow for a pillow. "Duly noted."

She added wood to the fire as the night grew colder around them. The rain came and went, sometimes nearly stopping, sometimes coming down hard.

During a lull, she pulled on her sweatshirt, which was mostly dry, and her jeans, which were damp but not sodden, and went out to gather more wood. She dug under the leaves for branches that were less soaked than the stuff lying above the deadfall, and hauled it back to their little camp.

On the way back, she noted with worry that the glow of the fire was still somewhat visible through the blanket they'd hung to screen it. Hopefully, this awful weather would drive Mahmoud and his men back to their cabin.

If they knew what was good for them, Mahmoud and his guys would leave the United States altogether. They had no way of knowing how soon they would be reported to the authorities and when a massive manhunt for them would be launched.

But one thing she'd learned in her Medusa training: there was no accounting for the logic of terrorists. If they were zealots, they might get it in their heads that she and Zane needed killing at all costs.

She spread out the wood to dry around the fire and stripped off her clothes to let them dry again. She passed the time alternating between watching Zane sleep and gazing out over the valley below for any sign of pursuit. Of course, the night was pitch-black with the total cloud cover, and she wasn't likely to see anything out there, let alone a team of stealthy bad guys. But it didn't keep her from staring apprehensively out into the darkness.

When she'd judged that several hours had passed, she reached out to touch Zane's foot. She was glad to feel that it was warm and dry. His eyes opened, and she reveled in their beautiful golden color. She'd nicknamed him well indeed.

"Hey, beautiful," he murmured in a sleep-roughened voice that made her toes curl in delight.

He sat up, stretching lazily and throwing off the blanket he'd been wrapped in. "Feels like it has gotten colder."

"It has. Rain's letting up, though."

"Okay. To sleep with you, Piper. I've got the watch and the fire."

They traded places, with her tucking back under the ledge on the bed of dried leaves, while he took her place huddling by the fire. The ground still held a little of his body heat, and the heat of the fire had collected under the overhang and warmed the rocks. They radiated that heat back gently now. It wasn't exactly a spa hotel room, but on a wet, freezing night, it wasn't half-bad.

And the blanket smelled like Zane with a hint of his male musk. She went to sleep with a smile on her lips.

Zane replenished the fire and settled down beside it, his feet stretched out beside the pit. He leaned back against a big rock, and alternated staring out into the darkness and glancing over at Piper. Her face was relaxed in sleep, and she was beautiful with the firelight glinting off her satin skin.

He couldn't get enough of looking at her. Which was a first for him. He wasn't the type to sit around gazing at any woman. He was all about the job. Always the job. In his line of work, anything less than total concentration spelled a mistake, and a mistake spelled death.

But then Piper had become the job.

The rain trailed off and finally stopped about an hour before dawn, according to his watch. He was glad for the earlier nap, but his eyes were gritty again, and his eyelids heavy. This was the worst time of day to stay awake. His biorhythms were declaring in no uncertain terms that this was sleep time.

He got up to gather more wood and check his trip wires. Moving around would help him stay awake.

He was on his way back to camp, just inside the inner ring of trip wires, when he heard a sharp snap behind him.

He froze. That was one of the outer mousetraps. He had set the wires thigh high specifically so that small and even medium-sized animals wouldn't set them off. It would take a bear—or a man…to hit the fishing line stretched between trees.

Gliding back toward camp on silent feet, he moved swiftly nonetheless. He had the advantage of having walked around out here a fair bit last night, and he knew his way back to Piper well.

He barged into the camp and dropped to his knees beside her, pressing his hand urgently over her mouth. She woke instantly, her eyes alert. He signaled fast, holding up three fingers and pointing in the direction of the tripped mousetrap. She nodded and yanked on her jeans and shoes at lightning speed while he pushed the pile of dirt near the firepit back into the hole, dousing the flames. He packed the water bottles, wadded up the blankets and shoved them in his rucksack, and helped Piper scatter leaves all over their little site.

They had no more time to cover their tracks, for another, closer snap sounded in the woods. Whoever was moving around out there was headed this way. And was now two hundred yards away.

He hand signaled for Piper to take the lead. She took off, heading out of their little camp away from the sound. She moved so fast through the trees that he seriously struggled to keep up with her.

Damn, she was good.

Which might just save their lives out here. He would never in a million years have guessed that a woman could run that silently, that quickly and sure-footedly through terrain like this.

After about fifteen minutes, he was breathing hard. After a half hour at the killer pace, he was sucking wind.

Thankfully, Piper stopped without warning, ducking under the spreading branches of a pine tree and melting into the deep shadows there. The sky was just starting to turn gray in the east.

You okay? she mouthed.

He nodded, concentrating on breathing deeply and exhaling fully. He had to get as much oxygen to his screaming muscles as possible.

In exactly one minute, she breathed, "Ready to go?"

He nodded resolutely. At least when she took off like a bat out of hell this time, he was expecting it. There was no way Mahmoud and his guys could move this fast. Not if they were having to track his and Piper's movements. And to her credit, she was following anything but a straight line out here. At varying intervals, she made direction changes of at least thirty degrees or more. Assuming they were even making a trail that could be followed, she was giving Mahmoud's tracker hell.

They settled into one pattern, though. Every ten minutes, she stopped for about a minute to let both of them catch their breath. They didn't speak. They just breathed deeply and then took off again.

Dawn came and went, and early morning came and went. And still they ran. She slowed the pace a little, to a ground-eating run that allowed them to pass quietly through the forest but put a ton of distance behind them. Hopefully, they were putting a ton of distance between themselves and whoever was behind them, too.

In a perfect world, that had been a bear.

But in a worst-case world, they had to assume Mahmoud and his men were hot on their trail.

On and on they ran, until Zane was so exhausted he could barely see straight. How Piper was continuing to hold this pace, he had no idea. Maybe she was superhuman. They had to have covered four or five miles before she finally stopped again, just shy of a wooded ridgeline.

"I'll top the ridge first and have a look on the other side," she whispered in his ear. "Wait here."

He nodded and turned automatically to keep a lookout behind them, searching for any sign of pursuit or movement back there.

Piper was gone maybe sixty seconds before she came back grinning ear to ear. "C'mon," she murmured.

He followed her across the ridge and stared into the valley. Cleared pastures stretched below, and two long, narrow barns made of galvanized aluminum pointed toward a small house at the far end of the valley.

"Praise the Lord and pass the potatoes," he muttered.

Piper took off down the hillside, fully as fast as she'd run from the campsite initially. He felt it, too. The burst of adrenaline at the idea of this nightmare being over was huge. He rode the wave of renewed energy to fly down the hill beside her. They hit the edge of the pasture and she veered into the trees beside it.

They would have gone faster in the cut grass beyond the barbed wire fencing but would've been out in the open. He had to give Piper credit for proper caution.

It took them almost ten minutes to run the length of the big pasture, parallel the barns and then swerve toward the house. A rusty pickup truck was parked beside it. Please God, let someone be home.

They raced across the front yard and up onto the covered front porch. Piper knocked on the door. The next few seconds were perhaps the longest in Zane's life as he prayed for someone to be in. For there to be a working phone. For him and Piper to be safe.

The front door opened, and a man of about fifty years stood there. "Little early to be out selling stuff, isn't it?" he growled.

"Please forgive us for bothering you," Piper said

politely. "My friend and I have been out hiking and got lost. We desperately need to use a telephone and call for help."

The farmer looked her up and down and then did the same to Zane. For his part, Zane smiled and did his best to look nonthreatening. But the truth was, he and Piper probably looked like ax murderers. He had several days' growth of beard going, and both of them were covered in mud and debris from their wild run through the woods.

"You look like you got lost in the woods," the farmer grunted. "Come on in. Phone's in the kitchen."

Piper stopped by the phone and looked at him questioningly. "Who can get here faster—your people or mine?"

"Mine," he answered without hesitation.

She gestured at the old princess-style phone hanging on the wall, and he picked up the receiver and dialed. He chose the emergency number he'd memorized before this mission. It went straight to a CIA crisis-response desk.

He rattled off his identification credentials and waited impatiently while they were verified.

A female voice said, "You are authenticated. Go ahead."

"I'm blown on an undercover assignment and need immediate emergency extraction. Armed hostiles are in close pursuit of me." He looked at the farmer, whose mouth hung open. "What's the street address here?"

The farmer shook himself and answered. Zane relayed the address and then said, "We need a police helicopter here ASAP, along with armed law enforcement response."

"We?" the woman at the other end of the phone asked briskly. "How many people need extraction?"

"I have a civilian female with me. I brought her with me from the undercover operation, and she will also need transport. She's a material witness in the investigation."

"Understood. Is this a good call-back number?"

"Yes."

"Shelter in place. We'll have people out to you as quickly as possible. I show you being in a fairly remote area. Police response may take up to an hour."

"Tell them to hurry," he bit out.

"Will do." .

Zane disconnected the call and passed the receiver to Piper. She dialed quickly, and her call was answered immediately, too.

"Hey, Rebel, it's Piper."

Zane heard the exclamation from the other end of the line. But Piper cut off whatever the other woman was saying. "Look, Rebel. We're in trouble. I've got a team of foreign terrorists on my tail. Same guys who kidnapped me. Police response has been called in to this location, but if you could have Major T call in any military assets that are close by, that would be helpful. If he can get a National Guard helicopter scrambled to this location, and maybe a gunship, that would be good."

Zane listened as she relayed the farm's address. There was a pause, and then the person at the other end of the line spoke for several seconds.

Piper's expression went grim as she listened. "Understood. Thanks."

She hung up and surprised Zane by turning to the farmer. "Is there anyone else here besides you, sir?"

"Nope. Wife already left for work."

"Do you happen to have any guns and ammunition here?"

The farmer frowned. "Why do you ask?"

"A satellite looking down at this position reports a team of five humans moving in this direction. They're about a half mile from the ridge at the back end of your pastures. We've got about fifteen minutes until they get here. And my source said they looked armed."

Zane winced. Mahmoud and his guys would come in hot with AK-47s blazing, and possibly more weaponry than that.

The farmer appeared hesitant.

Zane said quietly, "Look. I know you have no reason to trust us. But I'm a federal agent, and she's a military officer. We're running from some very, very bad men. We all need to get in your truck and drive away from here as fast as possible."

"Truck's broken down."

"Can we get it running in fifteen minutes?" Zane asked urgently. "The government will buy you a new truck—hell, I'll buy you a new truck—if we can at least get it moving and get a few miles away from here."

"Naw, man. It's dead. Won't even turn over, let alone start."

"Tractor?" Piper bit out.

"It's parked behind the chicken sheds—"

"Too far for us to reach before Mahmoud's guys would be within shooting range," Zane responded.

Piper nodded in agreement. "Sir, we need you to bring us any firearms you have in the house. What's your name? Mine's Piper, and this is Zane."

"Irv Smith."

"Nice to meet you, Irv. I'm so sorry we've brought this trouble to your door. My partner is right. The government will compensate you fully for any damage to your property today."

Zane was impressed with the calm, confident, soothing tone of voice Piper used on the man. It had the desired effect, too. The farmer smiled a little and nodded at her.

"Guns?" Zane prompted gently.

The farmer headed for a spare bedroom, and Zane followed close on the guy's heels with Piper close on his. They had to step around and over an elaborate model train set that took up most of the floor.

Irv opened a closet and pulled out a .22 shotgun and a larger Remington rifle. He rummaged on the upper shelf and emerged with four boxes of ammo, two for each weapon.

Zane looked at Piper. "You wanna shoot long range or short?"

"Long. I've had a fair bit of sniper training." She picked up the Remington, and he picked up the .22.

She looked over at the flabbergasted farmer. "How true do these fire?"

"I been huntin' with 'em for nigh on twenty years. Don't miss much."

Piper nodded. "Do you have any more weapons in the house?"

"My wife's got a little peashooter she carries in her purse from time to time. She don't usually carry when she goes to work. Lemme see if it's around."

Zane gave the .22 a quick once-over, checking for rust, familiarizing himself with the trigger action and practicing loading it. Piper did the same with the Remington, handling it with smooth ease.

"Aha!" the farmer exclaimed. From a drawer that

looked to be full of ladies' lingerie, he extracted a dinky little handgun.

Zane said, "You keep that. Use it to protect yourself if it comes to that."

"What's in the barns?" Piper asked. "Chickens?"

"Yup. Nearly a thousand laying hens. Raise 'em free-range, I do."

Zane said quickly, "The barns are made of aluminum siding. No protection from gunfire. Might as well be inside a tin can."

Piper nodded tersely. "This house will offer the best cover, then. If you head down to the barns, Irv, you can hide there. We'll draw the gunfire up this way and you'll be safe. The bad guys want us, not you."

"You sure? I'd be a third gun."

Zane smiled warmly and patted the older man's shoulder. "We appreciate the offer, but that little pop gun isn't going to do much good against the firepower these bastards are going to bring to bear on us. Piper's right. You need to head on down to the barns and stay out of this. We don't want you to get hurt. And Uncle Sam will build you a new house and renovate the whole farm after this. So don't panic if you hear stuff getting shot up."

Piper added, "Go look after your hens. We'll take care of the bad guys."

"All right, then." Looking worried, Irv headed out the back door and hurried toward the barns, pistol in hand.

"ETA?" Zane asked Piper as they moved furniture out of the way of windows and created clear pathways from one window to the next.

She looked at the clock on the kitchen stove. "Ten minutes."

He commented, "If they try to search the barns, we'll shoot at them and draw them up here, yes?"

"Yes." She asked, "Will they try to surround us or will they take up protected firing positions and pepper us for a while?"

"Mahmoud will want to kill us both. But he's got several young guys on his team. My guess is they won't be experts at field-of-fire control. I don't see him fully surrounding the house because he won't trust the youngsters not to shoot him or his more experienced guys. I could see him trying to burn us out."

She nodded. "Then we shoot just enough to draw them up here to us and then lie low until they try to close in on the house."

"Fair enough. And then we'll improvise when the plan goes to hell," he added dryly.

She smiled at him. "Exactly."

Her grin was almost wolfish. "Are you enjoying this?" he asked incredulously.

She shrugged. "I want to protect that farmer, and I have to admit I'd like to drop a few of these bastards. Particularly that Yousef guy who took so much pleasure in beating me up. I'm not afraid, if that's what you're asking me. I'm trained for this stuff."

"Thank God," he replied fervently.

She disappeared into the kitchen and emerged with two big, sharp butcher knives. She passed him one, presenting him with the handle. "Mahmoud won't expect me to know what to do in a firefight. He still thinks I'm the assistant principal of an elementary school."

Zane grinned. "He's in for a hell of shock when he sees what you can do." If this came down to hand-to-hand combat, his money was on Piper. He tucked the knife in the back of his belt, checked the load on his weapon one more time and settled down to wait with the extra ammo on the floor beside him.

Piper went into the kitchen and made another phone call. Zane listened as she said quietly, "ETA on our hostiles?"

There was a pause, no doubt for the satellite technician to get a fix on their position and look for warm bodies. Piper listened for a minute and then stayed on the line.

She called to him in the living room, "ETA three to four minutes. They're about halfway down the side of the pasture. Five incoming."

They had tipped the refrigerator over on its side across the back door, and they'd pulled a bulky wood stereo console across the front door to barricade it. Piper knelt behind the refrigerator now, watching the approach to the house from that direction.

She called, "My eyes in the sky say they appear to be circling wide of the barns to approach the house from the west side."

That would put Mahmoud and company facing the living room's side wall. "Will you have a shot at them from the kitchen?" he called back.

"Yes. I can shoot out the window over the sink."

They had already opened every window in the house a few inches so they could put the barrels of their weapons on the sills to steady them. He moved to the living room window on the west wall of the house and scanned the tree line a little over a hundred yards away.

From that distance, the AK-47s should shred the house's siding and quickly start putting rounds into the living room. Zane glanced about and spied a hefty coffee table in front of the television. He jumped up, grabbed it and dumped it on its side in front of the window for extra protection. It was made of oak planks a good two inches thick. That sucker would stop bullets for a good long time.

"Have you got decent cover in there?" he called.

"The kitchen sink is enameled cast iron. I've got my shooting nest all set up. You?"

"My nest is built. I've got a two-inch thick oak table in front of me," he replied.

"Check. I'll let you know when they emerge from the trees. If they head for the barns, I'll call the shots."

God, it was nice working with a highly trained Special Forces operative. He couldn't think of anyone he would rather have beside him in a gunfight.

There was one last thing he needed to do before this show went down. He propped his rifle at the ready and went into the kitchen, where Piper was looking out the back door.

"Eyes in the sky have us covered," he murmured. "They'll see our hostiles well before you will."

"I know," she sighed. "Looking for them just gives me something to do." She turned away from the door to gaze at him questioningly. "Are you really as calm as you look, Zane?"

He stepped forward and drew her into his arms. "I am. I've done everything in my life that I ever wanted to, and I found you. My life is complete. If today's my day to die, I'm at peace with that."

He dipped his chin and kissed her reverently, doing his best to convey just how genuinely extraordinary she was to him. Her arms went around his neck and he swept her body up against his, holding her tight as she kissed him back desperately.

Her intensity sucked him in, wrapping him in the scent and feel of her, drawing him into that special magic the two of them created between them. It was a place of trust and safety, where nothing could touch either one of them.

As their mouths joined, so did their bodies, pressed together from chest to knee. Even though they were fully clothed, he felt every contour of her, remembered the feel of her skin against his, her heat embracing his, her arms and legs wrapped around him in the throes of passion. It was all right there again. Everything they'd shared between them last night.

It hadn't been a dream. It was real, and it was here, right now.

"I won't let anything hurt you," he murmured against her sweet lips.

"Same," she breathed into his mouth. "I've got your back."

He plunged his hand into her thick, soft hair, washed clean by the rain. "Don't be a hero on me. I need you to come out of this alive. Promise me, Piper."

"I will if you will."

"I promise. No heroics," he said as sincerely as he could. It was a total lie. He would do whatever it took to get her out of this day safely. Including sacrificing himself.

The phone rang, jarring both of them out of the moment.

She grabbed for the phone and he spun away, moving quickly back to his shooting nest and settling in for whatever happened next. *C'mon, Mahmoud. Show your face. Give me a clean shot so I can blow your head off.*

He had never been more eager to end a mission with a kill than this one.

The house went silent as he and Piper waited, mentally preparing themselves for the chaos to come. He focused on draining all emotion from his mind and becoming cold and calm. A killing machine. He had no doubt whatsoever she was doing the same.

"One minute out," she announced.

Thank God. Her voice was calm, cool as a cucumber. She was mentally ready to rock and roll.

So was he...almost. Only one emotion refused to go away. Fear. Specifically, fear for Piper's safety. Dammit.

He concentrated fiercely on transforming it into utter determination to do what was necessary to keep her safe. When it had become a hard kernel in the middle of his chest, he took one last deep breath. He was ready, come what might. Even if that included sacrificing himself for her.

Piper spoke quietly from the kitchen, her voice pure ice. "Here they come."

Chapter 12

Piper saw the men emerge from the woods at almost the exact same moment that Beau Lambert murmured through the telephone receiver, "Hostiles moving into the open. Inbound to your position. Contact imminent."

"Roger, I have visual contact. How's that gunship coming?" she muttered into the receiver.

"Airborne. ETA your position, eighteen minutes."

"Tell them to firewall it."

Beau murmured, "You should've heard Torsten bully them into launching. They know to get to you ASAP."

"I'll keep the line open, but I'm gonna have to put down the phone now and get ready to fire," she reported to her operations officer.

"I'll shout if I need to relay information. Good shooting, Piper."

"Will do."

She laid the phone receiver in the kitchen sink and took up a firing position, kneeling on a chair in front of it. Mahmoud's men were moving cautiously, fanning out as they approached the farm. Dammit. Two of the men peeled off to head toward the barns.

The whole game now was to engage in a delaying action until reinforcements could arrive. To that end, she watched and waited as Mahmoud, Hassan and Yousef went out of sight behind a shed.

"Have you got eyes on Mahmoud plus two?" she called quietly.

"Affirmative," Zane replied.

"I'm watching the young guys. When they've almost reached the barns, I'll fire and draw them back here. If your three move before then, you fire first."

"Ammo's very thin," he warned. "Only take kill shots if able."

She smiled against the stock of her rifle. She was fully versed in ammo management. He was worried about her. "Roger. Will do," she replied quietly.

She settled back into emotionless concentration on the scenario unfolding in front of her. She picked the spot where, when the young guys reached it, she would fire at them. She probably wouldn't hit them at this distance, but she hoped to use the shot to check the accuracy of the weapon's sights.

All those endless hours on the firing range rolled through her, with neural pathways and habit patterns built over hundreds of shooting sessions and thousands of rounds fired clicking into place. *Relax completely. Breathe long and slow. Exhale and hold.* One last gun sight correction; her finger touched the trigger…

The pair reached the spot, and she squeezed smoothly through the trigger. The sound of her rifle firing was deafening, shattering the morning's silence shockingly.

The young men reacted violently, flinching and ducking and then racing back toward Mahmoud's position behind the shed. She took note of the hole that appeared in the side of the barn. Slightly high and right of where she'd aimed. Duly noted. She would adjust her aim a tiny bit low and left.

She swung her rifle toward the shed, following the zigzagging path of the two terrorists until they disappeared from sight. She would love to be a fly on the wall to hear the discussion happening behind that shed right now. The terrorists had lost the element of surprise, and now they knew their prey was not entirely without teeth. That had to be a nasty shock to poor Mahmoud.

She waited with detached interest to see what he did next. She and Zane were badly outgunned, but they had excellent cover inside this house, and Mahmoud and his guys would have to come out in the open to use their assault weapons.

He and his guys would also be running around with only the ammunition they could carry. And ammo was heavy, which meant they had a finite supply of it and would have to be careful with their firing habits, too.

A drawback of a weapon like an AK-47 was that it could chow through a whole lot of rounds very fast. If Mahmoud's guys didn't control their fire tightly, they would spray a few impressive fusillades against the side of the house and then be clicking on empty.

From her and Zane's end, this was purely a delaying action, buying time for that gunship to get here. Which gave them the tactical advantage.

If any of Mahmoud's guys weren't particularly experienced with combat, they were very likely to be excitable and fire off all their ammunition too quickly. She figured Mahmoud, Yousef and Hassan probably would keep their cool. But the younger two…they might be convinced to behave stupidly and unload their weapons all at once.

In Mahmoud's position, she might order the worst

shot of the young guys to go ahead and empty his AK-47 magazines against the side of the house just to gauge what kind of reaction she and Zane had to offer.

Sure enough, one of the young guys jumped out from behind the shed with his weapon held at waist height, one hand on top of the barrel to hold it down as it tried to climb.

"Incoming," Zane bit out. "Take cover."

She crouched on her chair behind the sink, making as small a ball as possible. The weapon cut loose, roaring like a dragon as the side of the house was peppered with dozens of rounds. Some of them penetrated the wood siding and missed wall studs, zinging past her to bury themselves in the far wall.

"They're rushing from behind the shed to your left!" a voice shouted over the phone.

"Incoming!" she called out to Zane. "Left side of the shed!"

Two more men rushed around the corner just as the first round of fire ceased. Piper took quick aim, fully exhaled and pulled off a single shot.

Hassan, the driver, spun back behind the shed. The other guy, one of the young ones, lurched, obviously hit. He spun for cover more slowly than Hassan. But she knew as well as anyone that a single gunshot wound rarely took a combatant completely out of a fight. The other men would be tying a strip of cloth over the wound and telling him to get back in the fight right about now. Shock and adrenaline would mask any pain the kid felt.

"Hostiles on the move again," Beau reported over the phone. "Looks like they're spreading out."

"I've got no visual," she called back, loudly enough for Beau to hear. More quietly, to Zane, she asked, "Any visual?"

"Negative."

They must be crawling around in some sort of swale that provided them with cover from the house.

"Position report?" Zane asked quietly from the living room.

"Where are they, Lambo?" she called.

"Straight line. About ten yards apart. Thirty yards from your position. They look to be taking up prone firing positions," Beau replied.

She relayed the information to Zane, relieved that he was as disciplined as he was and prepared to wait out the bad guys with her. Amateurs would be firing away like crazy by now, panicked and burning through their ammo.

All at once, Mahmoud and his men started firing at them. They were, indeed, conserving ammunition, firing single shots and taking turns, keeping up a fairly steady barrage, one shot every fifteen seconds or so. Still, they were going to burn through their ammo quickly that way.

"ETA on that chopper?" she asked Beau.

"Thirteen minutes."

"Still too long," she replied tersely.

Beau announced, "Hostiles are advancing, but appear to be prone. Do you have visual to fire?"

"Negative," she bit out. "Once they hit the front yard, though, the only cover they'll have is the pickup truck."

Another voice came on the line. Major Torsten's. "That truck is only about twenty feet from the house. When they charge you from behind the truck, you'll only have a few seconds to neutralize all of them, or your position will be overrun. Do you have an egress route?"

"Not really."

"Can you create one in the next minute or two?" he asked. "Look for chemicals. Can you blow a hole in the back wall of the house?"

"I'm no MacGyver, but I'll try."

A quick inventory of the cupboards in the kitchen yielded enough chemicals to create a low-order explosion, but nothing that would punch through a wall.

"Wait a minute," she exclaimed under her breath. "The guy who owns this house has a model train set. Don't they use something fairly nasty as fuel?"

Rebel interjected, "Some model trains use nitromethane."

"Now we're talking," Torsten said sharply. "Can you disengage to go look?"

"Zane. I'm leaving my position for a minute. Call if you see movement."

"Roger. What's up?" he asked without looking away from the window as she raced through the living room.

"Boss thinks we need an emergency exit. I'm gonna set up an explosion to create an impromptu door on the other side of the house."

"Um, okay."

She smiled a little at his apparent confusion. *Welcome to working with the Medusas.* They were trained to think and operate outside the box. And he—along with the jerks outside—was about to get a taste of what that really meant.

She ducked into the spare bedroom and found a gallon jug of model-engine fuel. Sure enough, it was volatile nitromethane. She carried it and the chemicals she'd brought from the kitchen into the bathroom. Working fast, she unscrewed the toilet tank from the seat and lifted it quickly. Water cascaded all over her feet and the floor as the tank emptied.

Working quickly, she plugged the bottom drain hole with duct tape she'd found in the kitchen, then ran a rag through the taped plug to act as a fuse. She tucked the other end of the rag in a bottle of flammable cleaning solvent and set the other containers of chemicals beside it inside the ceramic vessel. She pointed the open tank top directly at the wall. It was a crude-shaped charge at best and might not even work, but it was worth a try.

Worst case, she and Zane could jump out the bedroom windows. But that was a harder maneuver than it looked when armed, trying not to get hurt and needing to land, fall, roll and come up running. Particularly when one or more of Mahmoud's guys were likely to be waiting for them to come out the windows.

"They're closing in!" Zane called from the living room.

She raced back to the kitchen and resumed her position in the window. And just in time, too. The long grass on the far side of the yard was moving; five trails of moving grass were headed straight at the house.

"ETA?" she bit out into the phone.

"Hostiles? Twenty seconds. Gunship? Eight minutes."

"We don't have eight minutes. We've got maybe three," she snapped.

"Roger. You know what to do. Just relax and let your training take over," Torsten said calmly. All the faith in the world was packed into his voice, and it steadied her. Focused her on the job at hand.

She called to Zane, "You good?"

"I'm good."

"Ops thinks they'll cluster behind the truck and rush us from there. We'll have a few seconds to take out whoever we can, then we need to retreat to the bathroom, blow the wall and run like hell for the trees. We'll need to evade until the gunship arrives. Rendezvous when able even with the chicken barns, a hundred yards into the trees."

"Got it," he muttered absently. "I've got the right-hand field of fire. You've got the left."

"Roger, I'm left," she replied, making the reflexively ingrained response. She would shoot at whoever came around the left end of the truck. And if all the bad guys came from the same side of the vehicle, she would take the left-hand targets in the cluster.

She watched in total concentration as the trails of swaying grass converged and disappeared behind the truck. The show was about to get real.

Any second now.

She was glad she was in this with Zane. He'd been her rock through everything, and even now he made her feel safe. Protected. The bubble of caring and concern he'd surrounded her with in that kiss a few minutes ago still cocooned her. She still felt his arms around her, the bulwark of his big body shielding her from harm.

She trusted him. With her life.

And then she emptied her mind of even that thought. It was go time.

"They're gathering themselves to charge," Beau announced.

"Get ready," she relayed to Zane.

Without warning, all hell broke loose. Two men rushed from behind the truck and two rushed around the front. Showing as little of herself as humanly possible, she fired at will at the rushing men. She knew without a shadow of doubt that she hit with multiple shots on multiple targets. But the bastards kept on coming.

When they'd almost reached the house and she and

Zane were losing any sort of decent angle to fire without showing too much of themselves, he yelled, "Go now!"

She ran for the bathroom and used the cigarette lighter she'd found in a kitchen drawer to light the fuse. She spun into the hall, estimating that she had ten seconds—

It was more like three seconds. A tremendous explosion deafened her, slamming into her body like a physical blow. The whole house rocked violently, and she peeked around the corner. Debris was everywhere, and there was a ragged man-sized hole in the wall.

"Come to me!" she shouted.

Zane spun away from the living room window and sprinted toward her, waving her through the hole ahead of him.

"I've got the left," she called as she jumped outside. Her sweatshirt caught on something and tore, but she yanked violently and pulled free, spinning left to clear that corner of the house.

She felt Zane land beside her and spin right.

They took off running at top speed, crossing the fifty feet or so of lawn in a few seconds and diving into the trees.

They separated to make harder targets of themselves and divide the force brought to bear against them. She dodged and zigzagged, using as many trees for cover as she could. She worked her way up the hill and then cut right, toward the prearranged rendezvous point.

A shot rang out on her right, but she thought it wasn't aimed at her. She pressed on grimly, not bothering to look over her shoulder. Doing so would only slow her down, and seeing who was behind her wouldn't make him go away or change where she was headed.

As she neared the rendezvous point, she slowed and

veered left, higher up the slope into some heavy brush. The going was very slow through brambles and bushes, but the cover was excellent. Confident she wouldn't be seen by her pursuers, she eased forward to approach the spot from above.

Peering out from the bushes, she scanned the forest around her both for Zane and for hostiles. Knowing he was out there, she would refrain from shooting at any movement she saw until she had a positive ID on the person.

She hunkered down to wait for Zane to show up, scanning all the while. Her brain raced, replaying the events of the past few minutes quickly, seeking information or mistakes by Mahmoud.

Why had only four men rushed around the truck to attack them? It wasn't like Mahmoud had come around behind the house to lie in wait for them as they'd blasted their way out. Where had he gone? Had he headed for the barns...and Irv?

Crap. If Zane didn't show up soon, she would have to head down to the barns to make sure Irv was all right. How much longer should she give Zane before she had to assume he was hurt or pinned down? Did she need to go rescue him?

Who to rescue first? The innocent civilian, or the man who'd saved her life and, not to mention, was her lover?

Her duty was to Irv. But her heart belonged with Zane. And Zane could help her rescue Irv. They would be more than twice as effective working as a team than her alone.

Dammit, she was trying to rationalize going after Zane first.

She wrestled with the decision a few more seconds,

praying that he would show up and erase the dilemma, and then spotted movement below her. A man, creeping forward stealthily. Wearing a dark sweatshirt with the hood up—no help. She couldn't see hair color.

Crouching, she eased around the bushes, heading off to her left. She'd moved maybe twenty feet when she spotted another man. This one stood still in the lee of a large oak tree.

And his hair was light brown touched with gold. Zane.

As she looked on from her perch above, the second man—the first one she'd seen—crept toward Zane.

She lay prone on the ground, propped her rifle on a downed log in front of her and took careful aim. The target, the height and build of Hassan, would pass in front of her about fifty feet away. His profile didn't make for the world's biggest target, but she was going for a head shot, anyway. A body shot wouldn't stop a man like him. It would have to be an outright kill.

She tracked him until he was directly in front of her and paused for a moment, appearing to listen for movement around him. She pulled the trigger.

The shot rang out, and Hassan dropped. She couldn't see if she'd hit him or not, for Zane took off running to her left, abandoning the rendezvous point. He had no way of knowing it was her who'd fired, of course. She leaped to her feet and paralleled his position, doing her damnedest to keep sight of him as he raced through the trees.

Whenever she could, she angled to her right, down the hill, closer to his path. If someone besides Hassan had been on Zane's tail, it brought her into danger, too, making a single target of both her and Zane. But she dared not lose him out here. She might never find him again.

She put on a burst of speed as she crossed a tiny clearing, jumping for the brush on the other side, the back of her neck twitching at being exposed like this.

She dived into the thicket and jolted as an arm snagged her waist, yanking her down violently. She reached for the knife in the back of her jeans, and her hand had just closed on the hilt when Zane's face appeared in front of hers.

Oh, thank God. Relief that he wasn't one of Mahmoud's men made her knees weak for a moment. But in the next breath, her tension ratcheted back up. They were still being hunted out here.

And frankly, she'd had just about enough of that. She didn't like being the rabbit. She much preferred being the tiger. And given how shot up Mahmoud's men had to be, she figured this had to be close to an even fight by now.

Zane hand signaled that he'd heard one hostile behind them, farther down the hill.

She leaned forward, putting her mouth directly on his ear. "Time for us to go hunting."

He nodded, and they moved out together.

Chapter 13

Zane liked the way Piper was thinking. He was pretty much over skulking around in the woods getting shot at.

Moving slowly, they circled back toward the barns and whoever might be behind them. Stealth was on their side now. Piper did something odd in front of him. She moved up the hillside purposefully, gazing from side to side as if she was looking for something.

After about three minutes, she tensed, then stalked forward slowly, her cheek pressed to the Remington rifle in a ready position. He did the same.

She stopped and he spared a glance down at the ground in front of her. Hassan's sightless eyes stared up at the sky. A large kidney-red hole in the side of his head announced that he was very, very dead.

One down. Four to go. Although Mahmoud and his guys couldn't possibly be at full strength. As they'd closed in on the house, the men he'd seen had all been bloody and injured.

Piper leaned close to whisper to him, "Is this who you heard behind you, or is there another one tracking you?"

"I don't know."

"Did they use earpieces?" she asked.

He glanced down quickly and realized that in what remained of Hassan's ear there was no earbud. Piper used the tip of the rifle to turn his head. There was no listening device in the other ear, either.

"They trained with earpieces and mikes," he replied under his breath.

She nodded. "One of the others may have already found Hassan and taken his earpiece so we can't eavesdrop on them. He would have headed back toward the others rather than be out here alone with both of us."

"Barn?" Zane asked tersely. Poor Irv must be losing his mind hiding out with his chickens and hearing all the gunfire.

"Roger that," she breathed.

Piper took off ahead of Zane. He probably ought to offer to take point, but she was the Special Forces soldier who trained in armed combat every day. As an undercover operative, he had the training, but he didn't use it often. He ran around in the woods like this at his recurrent field ops training only every other year. He wasn't ashamed to let the better soldier lead the way.

They met no opposition at all as they headed for the barns. They'd almost reached them when Piper froze in front of him. The two of them were right at the edge of the woods, where it came within about a hundred feet of the nearest long barn. Close enough to smell the odor of a thousand chickens.

Three armed men came around the far side of the barn. Zane recognized Yousef, Bijan and Osted. All three looked bloody and battered. Twigs and leaves stuck to their clothes, and Bijan was limping badly.

Yousef was holding his weapon weirdly, like he had an injured arm or hand.

Yousef raised his AK-47 and fired a short burst through the end of the barn, peppering the big metal sliding door with bullet holes.

Piper eased down to a crouch, rifle ready, and Zane mimicked her. When Yousef loosed another burst, Piper fired her weapon at him, and Zane did the same an instant later.

All three men pivoted and shot wildly at the woods. Spooked, were they?

Behind them, the big sliding door opened without warning, squeaking violently. The men started to turn toward it, then pivoted back as Zane and Piper fired again at them.

And then a cloud of frantic chickens swarmed out of the barn, some running, most flapping and flying, all of them panicked.

Osted screamed and took off running back around the barn, and Yousef wasn't far behind. Bijan followed more slowly because of his limp, but appeared no less freaked out by the attack of the flying chickens.

In the distance, Zane heard the thwacking of a helicopter. It got louder rapidly as he and Piper advanced toward the now open barn door.

"It's me, Irv!" Piper called before approaching any more closely. "Are you okay in there?"

"Bastards shot at my chickens!" Irv bellowed.

It sounded as if he was headed toward the other end of the barn, and Zane risked peering around the door. Sure enough, the farmer was charging down a long concrete aisle, brandishing the teeny handgun threateningly in front of him.

Zane sprinted after the farmer and Piper spun into

the barn behind him, pausing only long enough to shove the big door shut again.

Zane caught up with Irv a dozen feet from the front door and grabbed the farmer in a horse-collar tackle, throwing his arm around the big man's neck to stop him. Urgently, he whispered in Irv's ear, "Don't go out there! That's an army gunship and it'll kill anyone who moves outside with a weapon in hand."

Piper caught up with them, panting hard. "Have you got a cell phone on you, Irv?"

"Yeah, but coverage is spotty out here. Middle of the barn's your best bet."

She grabbed the phone he held out and took off running. When she reached the middle of the barn, she placed a quick call and talked into the device urgently for a few seconds. She ran back to them.

"Gunship's been told we're in here. They passed a message to come out with our hands over our heads. They've killed two targets on the ground and the third one has fled into the woods on the other side of the road. They were instructed not to pursue him, but rather to stay here and provide support to us."

"Thank God," Zane said fervently.

He laid down the shotgun and made sure Irv did the same with the pistol. Piper put the Remington beside the other two weapons, and then all three of them stepped outside. They were met with violent downwash from the chopper that all but knocked them off their feet. Irv's baseball cap flew off his head. The farmer started to grab for it, but Zane barked, "Let it go."

"Oh. Right," Irv grumbled.

The chopper hovered over them for perhaps two minutes before moving off to hover over the woods across the road from Irv's destroyed house. A second helicopter, this one a Huey with a police paint job on it, landed between the house and the barns.

A man in full body armor raced out of it and over to the three of them. "Your names?" he demanded, weapon trained on them.

"Piper Ford, Zane Cosworth and Irv Smith," she shouted over the noise of the choppers.

"I wasn't told about Irv Smith!" the cop yelled back.

The farmer bellowed, "I own this place! Or what's left of it!"

"He's with us!" Zane shouted.

The cop waved all three of them over to the helicopter and loaded them aboard. Three other fully armored and armed police were inside, and it was a tight squeeze. Piper ended up sitting on Zane's lap, and Irv sat on the floor. The aircraft lifted off the ground and swooped away from the house quickly.

They landed at a state police barracks about fifty miles away, and Zane grinned as Irv declared, "Well, hell's bells, that was a fun ride! Can I get a ride home that way?"

The police led the farmer off to take his statement, and tried to separate Zane and Piper to get statements from them, too.

But Zane objected. "Sorry, gentlemen. This mess is above your pay grades. I'll be happy to give you my supervisor's phone number in Washington to confirm that, of course."

"Same with me," Piper said regretfully. "Although I'll have to give you a different phone number."

The police still insisted on putting Zane in an interrogation room and Piper in another until their identities were confirmed, which actually pissed Zane off to no end. He hadn't been apart from Piper for days now, and he hated not being with her.

What was up with that? He never got attached to people. Never mind that they'd made love last night and he felt closer to her than he had to anyone in years.

Cripes. When had he fallen for his hostage?

While he sat there staring at himself in the two-way glass, he had plenty of time to wonder about it. That, and what in the hell he was going to do, now that he had fallen for Piper.

His grim reflection gave him only one entirely unhelpful answer. He was screwed.

Piper hated being away from Zane. He'd been her only source of support and safety for days, and she felt naked and vulnerable with him gone to who knew where. He was probably sitting in another interrogation room like this one, thanking his lucky stars this mission was over and he could get back to his regular life.

Now that they were both safe, where did that leave them? Did they still have a relationship? Or was everything that had happened between them purely a reaction to the crisis they'd been caught in? Had any of it been real?

Doubt speared through her.

Major Torsten had been blunt in their classroom instruction for advanced prisoner-of-war training; weird things happened to people under that extreme amount of pressure. The brain did all sorts of bizarre things to protect itself from the unimaginable, including normalizing crap that was no way normal.

Was that what she and Zane had done? Had they been attracted to each other and formed a relationship rather than face the horror of what they were both experiencing?

For she had no doubt that being undercover with violent terrorists had been fully as stressful as being their prisoner had been. Except he'd lived in that environment for months. She'd been under that kind of pressure only for a few days, and it had pushed her to the breaking point and beyond. What would it have been like not to have been rescued for *months*?

Her mind shied away from even thinking about it.

So where did that leave her and Zane?

Had they shared a one-night stand of pure relief? Had their connection been based only on fear and mutual survival?

A police officer poked his head in the door, interrupting her mental spiral. "You're still refusing to write up a report for us?"

"I'm sorry, but I can't. The information in it would be classified if I wrote it down. I'm sure the military will give you a redacted version of my formal report if you ask for it. Can I go now? Or can I at least make a phone call?"

"Some dude's here to pick you up, anyway. Wearing a military uniform and scaring the hell out of the rookie cops. C'mon."

She leaped to her feet and followed the cop eagerly down the hall. "Big blond guy? Eyes like ice?"

"That's the one."

"That's Major Torsten. And he doesn't scare *you*?"

The cop grinned at her. "Semper fi, ma'am. Once a marine, always a marine. Guys like him and me get along just fine."

They rounded the corner into the squad room and Rebel and Tessa raced over to hug her tightly. She might or might not have shed a few tears of relief in the midst of the hugs at seeing her teammates again.

Major Torsten came over at a more measured pace. "Welcome back, Captain Ford. I hear you acquitted yourself well."

She shrugged modestly and started to speak, but then caught sight of Zane coming around the corner. His gaze riveted on her immediately, and she nodded slightly at him. A smile lit his eyes but didn't escape to the rest of his face.

Thank God. He cared about her at least a little. Or at least he was prepared to be civil to her. That was better than nothing. Right?

God. If only she knew him better. Then maybe she could guess where his head was at.

She made the introductions quickly, using no last names, given that a bunch of police without security clearances surrounded them.

Torsten said to Zane, "Can I give you a lift to the nearest secure telephone?"

Zane nodded. "That would be helpful."

Piper piled outside with the others and jumped in a big Hummer Torsten had obviously commandeered from someone local. Zane ended up in the front passenger seat, and she ended up stuffed in the back of the vehicle as far from him as it was possible to get. Had Zane engineered that? Or maybe Tessa and Rebel had tacitly arranged it.

Either way, it felt strange to be this close to him and yet feel so far away.

"Any chance we could get something to eat?" Piper asked. "We ran out of food a while ago."

Without comment, Torsten drove them to a diner and loaded them both up with tall stacks of pancakes, and then they headed to a regional airport and boarded a small business jet.

"Where to, sir?" the pilot asked Torsten as they approached the plane.

Major Torsten turned to look at Zane. "If you don't mind, I'll get my debrief from you two first, and then you can give your full debrief to your people, Zane. I expect yours will take some time, since you were embedded with those men for the long term."

Piper interjected. "We have a more pressing problem than debriefs."

Everyone turned to stare at her.

"The real Persephone Black is still out there, somewhere. And by now, it's entirely possible that Mahmoud and his boys have been informed that the woman they kidnapped was not her. Forgive me for feeling a special connection to her after experiencing what was meant for her, but I think we need to go find her with all due haste and secure her safety."

Torsten nodded tersely. "What about you, Zane? Do you want to come with us, or do you need to get back to your people?"

Piper's gaze shot to Zane's face. She saw it. The moment of hesitation.

Her heart fell, thudding to the ground somewhere in the vicinity of her feet.

He said emotionlessly, "I'd better come with you. I'll feel responsible for Mrs. Black if something bad happens to her."

Right. Responsibility. That was all he'd felt toward Piper, after all. He was a naturally protective guy. Which made him a decent human being but also meant what they'd shared had been nothing more than general compassion. Nothing personal. He'd just been comforting the exhausted, cold female and making up for any trauma he'd caused her.

The knife twisting in her gut served one purpose, at least. It told her she'd actually had some real feelings for him that extended beyond mutual survival or clinging to safety in the midst of terror. Not that those feelings meant a damned thing now that the two of them were back in the real world.

Well, hell.

An urge to cry made her eyes burn and the back of her throat tight.

She was not going to break down!

She fought back the urge. *I'm just overwrought— whatever that actually means.*

"Captain Ford makes a good point," Torsten declared. "Zane, where did your group's surveillance of Mrs. Black indicate that she can usually be found?"

"We did no surveillance at all on her. We just barged into that elementary school to snatch her."

"Then that's where we'll start." To the pilot, he said, "We need to land as close to Houma, Louisiana, as you can take us."

The pilot nodded. "It'll take us a few minutes to write up and file a flight plan, and then we'll be out of here."

It was a cool morning, and they all lounged in the back of the airplane with the door open while they waited to take off.

Piper asked no one in particular, "Where do you suppose Mahmoud and Yousef took off to after they fled the firefight?"

Torsten responded tersely, "They had better be on their way out of the country. The manhunt that's about to go after them will be the end of them if they don't get the hell out of Dodge."

Piper looked over at Zane sharply. "Did you give their identities to the police?"

"Yes. Along with surveillance pictures of them that I uploaded to the cloud before they took my cell phone away. The authorities have the photographs and a list of every fake ID I saw any of them use."

She nodded in satisfaction. "I hope they die horribly."

One corner of Zane's mouth turned up sardonically. "I hope so, too, personally. But professionally, I'd love to get my hands on one of them and force him to tell me exactly what they were in this country to do."

"Kidnapping Piper wasn't their main objective?" Torsten bit out.

Both Piper and Zane shook their heads. Zane added, "She was definitely a side job. They were collecting resources slowly and methodically while training together as a team to hone their skills."

"What sort of training?"

"They ran all kinds of armed-assault scenarios. Along the lines of a hijacking or taking over some space filled with civilians to use as hostages."

That sounded scary.

Piper spent part of the hour-long flight trying to imagine what target she would go after if she were part of an Iranian sleeper cell specializing in taking hostages. The problem was not coming up with targets. The problem was narrowing down the possible list.

Chapter 14

It was early afternoon when they landed at Houma-Terrebonne Airport with a bump onto the runway that woke Piper from a deep, disorienting sleep. Fortunately, her Medusa training had prepared her to go long periods of time with little or no sleep and to wake instantly on full alert even when exhausted. Which she was.

They deplaned and climbed into the Hummer Beau Lambert had driven over to the airport to meet them. He sat in the driver's seat and Tessa and Rebel sat in the back. Obviously, Torsten had spoken with him from the plane, for as soon as they were in the vehicle, Beau took off toward Southdown Elementary School without having to be told where to go.

They arrived at the school and pulled up in front of it. As they approached the front door, the police officer lounging in a chair beside it went tense. His hand drifted toward the revolver at his hip.

But thankfully, when Torsten pulled out his military ID and asked the cop to escort them to the office of the assistant principal, Mrs. Black, the guy relaxed.

A wave of déjà vu rolled over Piper as she turned

left into the glass-walled front office. Had it been only a week ago that she'd walked in here with Jack's lunch? It felt like a lifetime.

She didn't look over at Zane. What must this feel like to him? Last time he was here, he'd been brandishing an AK-47 and terrifying women and children.

Torsten told the receptionist, "We're here to see Mrs. Black. It's urgent."

"Um, I'll let her know you're here," the woman said nervously.

A tall, pretty blonde who actually did look a bit like Piper stepped out into the large room. "Who are you?" she asked a tad sharply.

"Major Gunnar Torsten, US Army. We're here in connection with last week's school invasion. Can we speak in private?"

"All of you?"

Torsten shrugged. "If you'd be more comfortable, I can pare it down to, say, three of us."

"Please do."

Torsten nodded at Piper and Zane, who followed him into Persephone Black's office, while the others stayed outside in the main area. Zane closed the door behind them.

Piper sympathized when the woman went around behind her desk and sat down, clearly using it as protection from these threatening strangers. Reading the stress in the woman's eyes, she dived in to speak before the men could.

"Mrs. Black, we know why those men barged into your school last week, and it has to do with you. That's why we're here today. To explain to you what happened, who those men were and what it means for you."

"Really? The police have nothing. No motive and

no identities." Then she blurted, "I'd love to hear your theory."

Piper nodded in Zane's direction. "This gentleman here is a federal agent. He has spent some months… observing…a group of men he believes to be Iranian operatives. The same group that invaded your school."

"Iranian? Does this have to do with Mark?"

"Who's Mark?" Piper asked quickly.

"My husband. He's working in Iran right now."

"You are correct," Piper replied gently. "Those men came here to kidnap you."

"One of the secretaries said they were asking about me. But I couldn't believe I was that important to anyone. I mean, I'm an assistant principal at an elementary school in a small town no one's ever heard of."

"The secretary was also correct. Those men planned to kidnap you, take pictures and video of you, and send the images back to Iran, where somebody planned to coerce your husband into doing something. Do you have any idea what they might have wanted from him?"

"Well, yes. He's a nuclear facility inspector on an international team. I imagine the Iranians would want him to falsify a report or maybe pretend to have inspected a facility he hasn't seen."

Piper stared at the woman in shock. Ho. Ly. Cow. She glanced over at Gunnar Torsten, who also stared grimly at the woman. Looking sidelong at Zane, Piper muttered to him, "Does that jibe with what you know of Mahmoud and company?"

"Yes. Perfectly."

"Then maybe she was their main mission, after all."

Zane shook his head. "I don't think so. I still think she was a side gig. If they're hostage-taking specialists, they would be the logical choice to be activated and sent in to kidnap a civilian."

"What are you two talking about?" Persephone interrupted. "How do you know what these men wanted? If they actually wanted to kidnap me, why didn't they come to my home when I wasn't here at school and grab me there?"

Piper answered, "Because they thought they had you. One of the men identified me as being you."

Persephone stared at her. "I don't understand."

"I was here that day. Delivering my neighbor kid's lunch that he forgot in my car. When they barged into the office and saw me, they mistakenly identified me as you and kidnapped me instead."

"Oh, my God!" Persephone exclaimed. "But you're okay? They didn't hurt you?"

Although the worst of the swelling in Piper's black eye had gone down, she still had a cut over her left eyebrow and her eye was turning a rainbow of various colors. It was patently obvious she hadn't gotten out of the experience unscathed. She answered honestly, "They did hurt me, in fact. And they would have done the same to you."

"Oh, my God!" This time when the woman exclaimed, she actually rose out of her chair. "This can't be true! I don't believe it."

Zane leaned forward and spoke grimly. "Believe it, ma'am. I'm one of the men who attacked the school, and I'm the one who identified her as you."

"You're one of the assailants?" Persephone gasped. She reached quickly for the phone on her desk. It was obvious she intended to call the police.

Major Torsten leaned forward and pressed his hand down on top of Persephone's, stopping her from lifting the receiver. "We told you. He's a federal agent. He was undercover, infiltrating the team. He was instrumental in getting those men out of your school without anyone being harmed."

"How can you say that?" Persephone's voice rose toward a screech. "The children are traumatized! My teachers are terrified—"

Torsten cut across her unfolding tirade. "They're alive. The attack on this school could have gone immeasurably worse. That team was trained killers with no capacity for remorse. They wouldn't have hesitated to mow down everyone in this building if they hadn't found you—or a woman they believed to be you—right away."

Persephone looked unconvinced, and Torsten continued tersely, "My operative, Captain Ford here, was beaten and brutalized on your behalf. Ask her how capable of violence those men were if you don't believe me."

Persephone looked at Piper in horror and woman whispered, "Is that true?"

Piper leaned forward and looked her squarely in the eye. "Yes. It is. Had I not had the highly specialized training that I do, and had I not had the surreptitious help of this agent, I would have suffered even more serious attacks than I did and very likely would have died. *That* was what those men had in store for you."

Clearly appalled, Persephone pressed a hand over her mouth and stared at Piper, her eyes full of silent questions over just how bad it had been.

Piper stared back at her implacably, doing her best to convey that it had been every bit as dreadful as the woman was capable of imagining.

Torsten's voice cut through their silent communication, woman-to-woman. "Where exactly is your husband now, ma'am?"

"Last I heard, he's in Tehran."

"Do you have a direct phone number for him?" the major pressed. "We need to warn him. Tell him to head for the American embassy immediately for his own safety."

"Um, yes. Of course." She pulled her purse out of a drawer, set it on her desk and fumbled inside it. She emerged with a cell phone. Unlocking it, she pushed a few buttons and then listened intently.

She murmured in alarm, "He's not answering."

"It's late evening over there," Torsten replied. "He's probably asleep."

"Yes, but he always picks up my calls."

"Can you leave a message?" Torsten responded.

She nodded and said into the phone, "Mark, it's me. Please call me the second you get this."

Torsten leaned forward. "Tell him to go to the embassy first."

Persephone continued, "Umm, you need to go to the American embassy right now. You're in danger and need protection. I'll explain it when you call. Just get to the embassy and then call me. I love you. Be careful, and be safe."

She laid the phone down, her expression troubled. "Something's wrong. Even if he were asleep, he would wake up and answer a call from me."

Torsten swore under his breath, and Piper silently echoed the sentiment. Her antennae were wiggling wildly. Mark Black was in serious trouble.

Then Torsten said, "Would you consent to entering into protective custody, Mrs. Black? I'll have some of my people stay with you and guard you until FBI agents can come from New Orleans and pick you up."

"My job—"

"It will wait." Torsten cut her off. "Your life is in danger, ma'am. Two of the terrorists got away this morning, and it's possible they're headed here to kidnap you for real."

"What about Mark?" she demanded, sounding near panic.

"We'll locate him and put him under guard, as well. But I can't in good conscience leave you without protection. The sooner you agree to let me take care of you, the sooner I can get on with finding and protecting your husband."

Piper was impressed. It was a low blow by Torsten to use the woman's husband to manipulate her into agreeing to protective custody, but Piper got why he'd done it. Right now, time was the enemy. The major was only doing what was necessary to move the mission along.

It had been one of the more difficult transitions to special operations thinking for her. Lies and subterfuge were standard tools of the trade.

Of course, Zane must be an expert at wielding both. Which would explain how he'd survived with Mahmoud and his cronies for *months*. She had no business believing anything he'd said to her in the heat of their lovemaking, and she certainly couldn't believe any feelings he'd revealed to her.

Persephone rose from her desk, purse in hand, and nodded at Major Torsten. "If it'll help you protect Mark sooner, let's go right now."

It was decided that Tessa and Rebel would stay with Persephone at Piper's house—a neutral location not connected with Persephone Black's life in any way—

until FBI agents arrived to take her into custody. Torsten explained that the FBI would put her in a safe house or a hotel room at an undisclosed location and under guard around the clock until this crisis was over.

When they all arrived at her bungalow, Torsten agreed to let Piper take a quick shower and change into clean clothes while he made the arrangements with the FBI.

She shampooed her hair three times to get out the dirt and grime of that horrible basement and from running around in the woods for days. She scrubbed her body from head to toe with a loofah until her skin was red and tender—

Huh. Maybe she'd been more affected by her captivity than she'd admitted to herself. Go figure. She rinsed off and climbed out of the shower thoughtfully.

It was a little slice of heaven to put on clean clothes, blow-dry her hair and actually put on a bit of makeup. Finally. She felt like herself again.

She emerged from the bathroom and Zane rose to his feet. He'd been waiting for her apparently, sitting on the edge of her bed. Whether he stood out of general politeness or out of shock at seeing her cleaned up, she couldn't tell.

"Feeling better?" he asked quietly.

"Definitely."

He continued to study her intently, and she added, "It's a bit of a shock being here in my house with everything suddenly back to normal."

"I feel that way when I come off a tough undercover assignment," he offered.

"How do you settle back into your real life?" she asked curiously.

"I don't have a real life, so I'm not the guy to answer that."

She stepped closer, gazing up into his sober eyes. He wasn't being flippant. "How do you stay yourself when you spend so much time being somebody else?"

He flinched ever so slightly. She waited him out, though, and at length he answered, "Sometimes I don't know who I am anymore."

"Well, that sucks."

He snorted in what sounded like startled humor. Closing the distance between them, he wrapped his arms around her and buried his nose in her hair. "I feel like myself when I'm with you. I see the man you see when you look at me, and I remember who he is. For a minute or two, I'm back in my own skin."

"You're welcome, I think."

She felt his smile against her temple. Then he murmured, "I'm starting to think you saved me in the nick of time."

"You're the one who saved me," she protested.

"I might have saved you from Mahmoud and his boys, but you saved my soul, Piper."

Her arms tightened around his waist, and they stood like that for a long moment, silently sharing their relief at having made it out alive.

He commented reflectively, "You'd have figured out a way to escape on your own eventually. I just sped up the process."

"I'm not superhuman. They had me handcuffed to a steel pipe. That would have been hard to overcome."

"You'd have found a way," he stated confidently.

"We'll never know." She paused. "The good news is we're both alive and we're both safe."

"For now," he sighed. "I'll go back undercover to

identify the bad guys you and your team will chase down and take out. This momentary respite is just that—momentary."

Her stomach plummeted. He was right. If this was the real world, neither of them truly belonged in it. They both lived in the dangerous shadows beyond this shiny, safe place.

She had no business imagining them being together for the long term, imagining them finding some sort of permanent happiness, together or otherwise. This moment, this man, what they'd shared between them—it was nothing more than a sweet illusion.

Their realities bore no resemblance to this whatsoever. Her world was that basement, facing down bad guys. That forest, evading death. That farmhouse, shooting it out with terrorists.

Happiness with Zane had no place in that world.

Silently devastated, she stepped back, pulling away from him, slipping out of his embrace. Unable to look at him, she turned and headed away from him. Anywhere that wasn't the circle of his arms.

"Anyone hungry?" she asked everyone else.

Nobody wanted anything to eat, but she desperately needed to do something to keep busy. Her steps took her to her cheerful yellow kitchen.

It was a lie. All of it. The bright colors and homey touches. They were a big fat lie she told herself—that she could have a home. A picket fence and a dog and 2.1 kids. Maybe a husband. Family and friends. All lies.

When Zane followed her into her kitchen, she still refused to look at him. Instead, she stuck her head in her refrigerator and pulled out the makings for grilled cheese sandwiches.

"Hungry?" she asked Zane reluctantly.

"After the past few days of nothing to eat but bugs and weeds? That would be a yes."

She smiled in his general direction but didn't make eye contact. Her courage deserted her and she put her head down, buttering bread and stacking Swiss, cheddar and provolone cheese slices on the bread. *Damn. Nothing to do now but watch the sandwiches cook.*

Zane grabbed a quick shower while she got the stove heating up, and she was relieved to have the kitchen to herself to regain her composure. Everyone else had settled in the living room to wait for the FBI to arrive and take custody of Persephone.

By the time Zane came back, his hair damp and smelling like her shampoo, she'd managed to shove her feelings into a drawer in her mind and slam the damned thing tightly shut.

She said nothing, concentrating on slicing apples for the two of them.

"How are you doing?" Zane asked quietly.

"I'm glad to be home."

"Yeah, I got that. How are *you* doing?"

"What do you mean?"

"C'mon. It's me you're talking to. Your boss can blow off the past week by saying it was only what you were trained to deal with, but I know what you really went through. That kind of stuff leaves its mark on anyone."

She flipped the sandwiches and busied herself pulling out glasses and filling them with ice. "Something to drink?"

"Sure. Whatever you're having."

She poured sweet tea from the pitcher in her refrigerator. Napkins. They needed napkins

"Stop, Piper."

He snagged her hands and forced her to come to a

halt in front of him. Reluctantly, she lifted her gaze to his. She didn't want to do this!

"How are you doing?"

She huffed. She really, *really* didn't want to talk about it. But apparently Zane was prepared to burn the sandwiches black if she refused to answer him. "I've been better," she admitted.

He let her go when she tugged her hands away and turned to rescue the sandwiches from the stove. She cut them in half diagonally and plated them, along with apple slices and potato chips.

"Sit," he ordered. "And stop fussing."

Zane held her chair for her and she slid past him, so close that she could smell the earth-and-rain scent of him.

He moved his chair from across the table to beside hers and sat down. "I'm not letting you run away from what happened to you. If you don't face it and deal with it, it'll gnaw at you until it eats you up."

"Thanks to you, nothing really bad happened to me."

"I have to disagree."

She shrugged. "So I got slapped around a little. They could have branded me with hot pokers or shoved bamboo spikes under my fingernails. I'm healing, for the most part. And as for a sexual assault, it didn't happen, thanks to you."

He frowned as if he was searching for words. Then he leaned forward and spoke quietly. "Just because I didn't actually attack you doesn't mean that the mental—and emotional—damage wasn't done. You still have to deal with the very real possibility of it happening."

Was he right? She realized she was staring at him, and looked down at her plate hastily.

"Whatever you need from me to aid your recovery—

just let me know. If you need me to go to therapy with you, or you need me to go away and to never see me again—"

"No. Not that," she said quickly.

He fell silent, studying her intently. "You're sure?"

"I'm not sure about anything except that it feels supremely weird to think about being apart from you."

He gazed at her for a long time and then quietly said, "So be it."

Chapter 15

Zane always felt underdressed when he visited the Pentagon. A plain civilian suit just didn't impress when everyone else was running around in starched, spit-shined, beribboned-uniform glory.

He must have sighed aloud, for Piper murmured beside him, "What's wrong?" Either that or she was just that closely tuned to his emotional state. Which was entirely possible. Their morning of debriefing at the CIA had been a revelation.

She had an uncanny ability to know what he was going to say next, to finish sentences for him, supply the right word when it failed to come. And to correctly read every moment when he waxed uncomfortable, sometimes subtly touching his foot with hers under the table.

Not that they'd had a minute to themselves to talk in private, of course. The debrief had been thorough to the point of torture, and mentally exhausting. He'd walked through his months with Mahmoud's terror cell, and then through the kidnapping of Piper. She joined in at that point, and they gave their debriefs in parallel.

He described a portion of her captivity from his viewpoint, and then she told the same portion of it from hers.

Notably, she left out most of her fear and terror. But then, her boss and her teammates were also sitting in on the debrief. It wasn't like she was going to admit to being panicked and overwhelmed in front of them.

And it wasn't like he'd admitted to his own superiors how freaked out he'd been those last few days undercover, with his gut screaming at him to get the hell away from Mahmoud, but his head insisting he stick around to save Piper.

As for Mark Black, there had been no word from him. His supervisor on the international nuclear inspection team thought it was possible he'd gone on a short vacation over the weekend. In another eight hours or so, it would be Monday morning in Tehran, and they would find out if Black showed up for work or not.

In the meantime, they'd come over to the Pentagon to plan a rescue of the man in case he didn't turn up.

Zane had been included in the mission planning because he was an Iran specialist and fluent in Farsi. Also, he suspected Piper had spoken to her boss on the side and asked for him specifically.

Knowing her, she wasn't above playing the card of her recent trauma to get her way. Smiling a little, he opened the heavy glass-and-brass door for her and followed her into the Pentagon.

They were installed in a secure briefing room with a big-screen monitor on the wall flanked by two large whiteboards. The soundproof doors sealed shut, and Major Torsten turned to look at the three Medusas, his operations officer, who was a sharp guy named Beau Lambert, and Zane.

Torsten spoke briskly. "Okay, kids. The mission is

to infiltrate Iran, find and secure Mark Black, and ex-filtrate him…"

They brainstormed for a solid hour, and gradually a plan took shape. Personally, Zane thought it was freaking brilliant. He would never have thought of it himself. But then, he'd never had the tactical advantage of working with female Special Forces operators. They did, indeed, open up possibilities he'd never considered.

The whiteboards were carefully erased and washed, the browsing history of the computer attached to the big monitor deleted, and Major Torsten gathered up all his notes and locked them in his briefcase. He finished by saying, "I'll get the plan rolling. If the rest of you would like to stand down for now, I'll let you know when we're green-lighted."

"When will we know whether or not Black shows up for work?" Piper asked.

Torsten glanced at his watch. "Tehran is eight and a half hours ahead of Washington, DC. Black has a briefing at 9:00 a.m. Tehran local, so that'll be 12:30 tonight here."

Zane knew from long experience that a rescue mission could be green-lighted in a matter of minutes, or the decision could get mired in bureaucracy and take days or weeks to gain approval.

The first ride-share car to show up was small, so Zane suggested, "Why don't Tessa, Beau and Rebel take this vehicle? Piper and I will call another one."

To their credit, her teammates didn't rib him—or Piper—but merely sent her quick, questioning looks. She nodded slightly, and the others piled into a car and drove away.

"Thanks," she murmured. "I was getting claustrophobic sitting in that tiny, windowless, sealed room. I wasn't quite ready to get stuffed into a car yet."

Of course. It hadn't occurred to him that a side effect of her captivity might be fear of enclosed spaces, but it made sense.

A car showed up in just a minute or two, and he held the door for her. As he slid in beside her, he murmured, "Need a window open?"

"No, thanks. I have to get used to small spaces sometime."

"But you don't have to do it all at once, today."

She shrugged. "Actually, I do. If we get the go-ahead tonight, I may be trapped inside an airplane by tomorrow morning."

"Are you sure you want to go on this trip? You've had a rough week. Maybe you should stay home—"

"Don't coddle me. Aren't people supposed to get right back on the horse so they don't develop an irrational fear of riding?"

"They also say not to set yourself on fire to keep other people warm. The—" He broke off and glanced at the back of the head of the driver, then continued, "This party can happen without you."

She shrugged. "We work best together as a team. And I would hate to sit at home, staring at the walls, knowing I'd been left out of all the fun."

He huffed. But truthfully, he couldn't argue with that. Staying home when his teammates went out on a dangerous mission would drive him crazy, too.

They were silent for the remainder of the ride to a hotel in northern Virginia. They checked into rooms Torsten had arranged for them, and Zane stared around the bland, antiseptic space. It felt weird to be alone like this after months living in tight quarters with Mahmoud's men. His room phone rang, and he picked it up.

"Hi. It's Piper. Are you hungry?"

He laughed, "Yes. I'm still not caught up after our involuntary fast in the woods."

"Me, neither. But I don't feel like peopling tonight. Wanna come to my room and order in?"

Thank God. He replied, "I'll be there in two minutes."

They found an online food-delivery service and ordered Chinese from a local restaurant. They each ordered two entrées, and the grocery bag full of white cardboard cartons ended up holding enough to feed six people. They had a picnic, spreading the feast out on the floor by the big glass window in Piper's room and grazing until they were both stuffed.

He started packing up empty containers and Piper groaned, "Now I finally feel caught up on food. But I also think I can't move."

"A food coma is called for," he declared.

They stretched out on her bed, and she rolled over to put her head on his shoulder. He let her.

He should probably establish some sort of professional distance between them if they were going to be working on the rescue op together. But not today. Tomorrow would be soon enough.

For one more night, he was going to hold her in his arms and pretend that the two of them could have a future together. Pretend that he wouldn't head off to one end of the world on an undercover mission and disappear for months, and that she wasn't a commando about to be bombing off to the other end of the world, jumping into hot zones herself.

She snuggled a little closer, and her lush hair rubbed against his chin, soft as kitten fluff.

"Comfortable?" he murmured.

"Best spot in the world to be," she mumbled back. She sounded half-asleep. Did she even realize what she'd just said? Her breath settled into the light, shallow rhythm of sleep, and he followed after her, reveling in letting his eyes drift closed and his mind drift off into dreams of him and Piper doing other things besides napping together.

It was dark when Piper woke up. She felt safe, which registered as strange. She was very still so her captors wouldn't know she was awake—

Oh. Wait. She was free. She and Zane had successfully escaped. She sagged against her pillow. Then frowned. Her pillow was hot. Hard. Resilient.

She raised up on an elbow and it finally dawned on her she'd been sprawled on top of Zane the whole time.

"Hi, beautiful," he murmured in his deep, raspy voice that never failed to delight her.

"Hi. Sorry I woke you."

"I've been awake for a while."

"Why didn't you wake me up and shove me off of you?" she exclaimed.

"I was enjoying watching you sleep."

"That bad, huh? Do I snore like a freight train? Or drool? Or maybe talk in my sleep? Oh, God. What did I say?"

"You did none of the above. Although you did become restless while you were dreaming."

"I dreamed I was back in that van. And it hit a trip wire on the road and blew up."

"Jeez. That's dark. Was I in the van when it blew?"

"We both were. I was frantic to get the back door open so we could jump out before it—I don't know—hit the ground or something."

He rolled onto his side without removing his arm from under her ear and gathered her against him. "We're safe on the ground now. It's all good."

"Crud," she mumbled against his chest. "I'm a wreck, aren't I?"

"Not at all. Everything you're experiencing is normal after a traumatic event."

"You say that like this isn't your first rodeo with trauma," she commented.

"It's not."

"Tell me about it?"

"I've been undercover for most of my career. First with a couple religious cults, and then with several supremacist groups. Then Mahmoud and company."

"Who was the scariest?"

He thought about that for several seconds. "Depends on the kind of scary you mean. The cults were scary because of how subtle they were. They played on people's minds like nobody's business. Lost, naive people got sucked in like dust bunnies into a vacuum cleaner. The supremacist groups were scary for how violent they were and how truly ugly their beliefs were. Mahmoud's crew was terrifying because of how incredibly disciplined they were. I had no idea who they were or what they were here to do, and I lived with them for *months*. What kind of a fanatic does a person have to be to maintain that level of focus for so long?"

"Are you talking about yourself having to focus not to blow your cover or about them maintaining operational security like that?" she asked.

He stared down at her. "You think I'm a fanatic? I'm

doing the same thing you are—serving my country by doing a hard job very few other people could handle."

She frowned thoughtfully. "I don't think of myself as a fanatic, but I guess an outsider might see the Medusas that way. We have to go to some pretty extreme lengths to prepare for the work we do. Particularly since we're women."

"I was startled by the brainstorming session with your team today. Having an entire group of women operatives opens up all kinds of unique possibilities for missions."

"You have no idea. In today's meeting we only scratched the surface of the sort of stuff we can do."

"Tell me more."

She stared down at him from the lofty perch of her elbow. "Well, we're trained exotic dancers, and we wear fancy gowns with guns strapped to our thighs, drink champagne and play baccarat and seduce heads of state. It's all very glamorous."

"Stop," he chuckled.

"Isn't that what people think you do when they find out you're an undercover operative?" she retorted.

"People don't find that out about me. Ever."

"Really? You told me without having any idea who I was."

He used one finger to gently tuck a strand of her hair behind her ear. "I had a good idea of who you were. I spotted that class ring of yours—"

She glanced down at her West Point class ring, which Tessa had returned to her this morning.

"—and the quality of your character was evident in how well you handled yourself in a crisis. Most women, or men for that matter, would have been completely panicked. You kept your cool and worked with me instead of against me."

"Well, yeah. You were helping me," she replied.

"You let me help you, and that made all the difference. It's why we both made it out alive," he responded soberly.

"Was it that close a call?" she asked reflectively.

"I was told nothing, as in *nothing*, about the attack on the school. They set up the getaway van without my knowing, and when it came time to sexually assault you, I was chosen to do it because they didn't want to leave behind any DNA evidence to incriminate themselves. You tell me what that sounds like."

"They didn't trust you, did they?"

"Nope. Had it not been for you, I would have bugged out and called in the authorities to grab them as soon as I realized we were going to attack the school. Had Mahmoud and Yousef not barged into the office when they did, I was going to ask you to call the FBI while I delayed their getaway."

"Why didn't you?"

"They were focused on finding Persephone Black at all costs. They would have shot everyone in that office, including you, if that was what it took to get her to show herself to them. I hoped they would take longer searching the school room by room before they came back to the office, but they were too fast."

"It's not that big a school. And I imagine the teachers were quick to volunteer the information that she would be in the principal's office and not in any of the classrooms. Their focus would have been on getting those gunmen out of their classes as soon as possible."

"I can't blame them," Zane muttered.

"How close was Mahmoud to killing me when you and I escaped?" she asked curiously.

"My guess was that, as soon as he handed over that fake rape tape, his bosses had everything they needed from you to secure your 'husband's' cooperation. You had become expendable."

"And they had a violent end planned for me?" She knew the answer, but she wanted to hear him say it. She needed to hear Zane say it. After all, she'd killed a man in those woods.

He shrugged. "You were trapped in that farmer's house with me and then hunted through the woods. I think they made their intentions toward both of us crystal clear."

Indeed, they had. Hassan's death had been necessary. It had been a kill-or-be-killed situation. She took no pleasure in killing, but she could live with the necessity of it.

"How did you find Hassan, anyway?" Obviously, Zane's thoughts were paralleling hers as he processed yesterday's events.

She shrugged. "Once we were out in the woods, I flipped the script and hunted the hunters. The Medusas are taught to believe their training is superior to the other guy's, and that we'll be underestimated because of our gender. Often, we're actually the aggressors when people are chasing after us in the mistaken belief that we're the prey."

"Handy, that."

She smiled at him. "Yes, it is."

His hand slipped under her silky hair, cupping the back of her head and very gently urging her down to him. It was more of an invitation than a demand, and she appreciated his continued gentleness and restraint.

She leaned forward, propping herself on his chest and kissing him leisurely.

His mouth was warm and gentle, his kisses as lazy as a wide river on a hot summer day. She sank into him, into the lure of his mouth, loving how the attraction between them simmered today, easy and sure.

It was a relief to discover that the attraction between them wasn't solely about fear and survival. And it was doubly a relief to discover that they still wanted each other now that they had returned to the real world.

Missions were fraught with danger and tension, and it was inevitable that the stress would find outlets. She'd been worried their hot sex in the woods had been nothing more than that to him, and nothing more than trauma recovery for her.

But the desire building in her now, filling her belly like magma flowing into an underground chamber, was reassuringly insistent. And frustrating in the best possible way.

This time, Zane took the lead, slowly undressing her, taking time to taste every new bit of skin he uncovered as he peeled off her T-shirt and stripped off her jeans. She returned the favor, savoring the soapy, male scent of his skin and the faint savory-sweet taste of soy sauce lingering on his tongue.

Tonight, they got to know each other's bodies more thoroughly. She learned the textures and tastes of him, and he learned where all her most sensitive spots were and what felt the best to her.

He murmured words of praise and encouragement, and she murmured words of trust and assurance back to him. Eventually, she laughed.

"What?" Zane asked quickly, looking up from her belly button.

"We're both being so careful we're starting to sound like a pair of nervous old ladies."

"Speak for yourself. I am merely sensitive to the trauma you've experienced."

"You can help me get past the trauma by treating me like a flesh-and-blood woman and not a crystal statue."

"Done," he murmured.

He drew her into his arms once more. But he still kissed her lazily as if he didn't have a care in the world, no expectations of anything more from her. Thankfully, his erection was thick and heavy against her hip, or else she might have wondered if he found her attractive at all. The man had the patience of a saint.

Not so herself, however.

"You taste like sweet-and-sour," he murmured.

"You're rocking *moo goo gai pan*," she replied, smiling against his lips. "But can we move this along?"

He laughed quietly, "But I like driving women crazy with desire. Trust me. I have a plan."

"*Crazy* being the operative word," she grumbled.

He eased her onto her back, smiling down at her and murmuring, "Let me have my moment with you. Imagining this kept me going for a lot of our trek from hell."

"How's that?"

"I spent hours thinking about what I was going to do with you once I got you naked. And after that night in the rain, I vowed that someday I would get you into a real bed and do every one of the things I'd imagined."

"What happened by the campfire was premeditated, was it? And this? Do you have every bit of this planned out?" She looped her arms around his neck and pulled him down to her for a long, deep kiss that left her gasping for air and extremely impatient for more.

"I'm open to a little spontaneity," he murmured against her lips.

"I'm relieved to hear you're not *entirely* unable to change your plans," she teased.

"In my line of work? That's all I do." He drew his fingertips down her body slowly, starting at her throat, caressing her neck, stroking down the valley between her breasts, then down her belly, culminating in a delicious stroke between the soft folds of her feminine flesh that had her arching up off the mattress and struggling to remember the thread of their conversation.

With some effort, she managed to say a bit breathlessly, "It would make sense in your private life if you wanted complete control and predictability."

Toying with the hard little pearl of her desire, and stealing at least forty points off her IQ in the process, he commented, "I like control and predictability, but not like how you mean them. It's rare that I get to turn off my internal alarms and be fully at ease. That's what I crave. Safety, so I can relax."

"What do you like to do when you're fully at ease, Mr. Cosworth?"

"I'd rather show you," he whispered as his lips closed on a rosy peak of her breast and laved it into a tight little bud.

"Feel free," she gasped.

"Mmm. I'd like to spend weeks wooing you." A gentle suck and a flick of his tongue made her cry out. He continued, "I would take you out to nice dinners. Some movie nights. Maybe a concert or two."

"You wouldn't want to stay in? Be unseen?"

He didn't answer right away. Instead, he lavished the same attention on her other breast until she was nearly sobbing in need. Then he murmured, "I know this great jazz club in DC that I'd love to show you—"

She interrupted him, tugging his head up to her mouth so she could kiss him, showing him just how desperate she was for him to get on with business. "I appreciate your willingness to put in some time on me—"

He interrupted in turn. "You're not a project to be managed and completed. But I want you to be comfortable with me. To feel safe."

"Me? I feel plenty safe. I could incapacitate or kill you in any number of ways, thank you."

He rolled onto his back beside her and laughed under his breath. "God. I never thought I'd hear a woman in my bed say *that*."

It was her turn to wince. "I'm sorry. I suck at romance."

"Lucky for you, I don't," he replied, humor vibrating in his voice.

"I sincerely appreciate you planning out how you would romance me, but all I really want is you."

"Are you telling me you don't have any interest at all in romance?" he responded, sounding surprised.

"Oh, I love being romanced as much as the next girl. But I have a weird sense of what constitutes romance."

"Like what?"

"I thought you letting me use the restroom after I tried to escape from you that first morning was shockingly chivalrous. And you always fed me and made sure I had plenty of water. You helped me out of the van and checked to make sure my handcuffs didn't chafe my wrists. You covered me with a blanket when I passed out in the basement."

"You caught all that, huh?"

She answered softly, "Yeah. I did. And thank you."

Frustration crept into his voice. "I felt so damned helpless to protect you. I wanted to tell you who I was so you wouldn't feel alone and you would know you were going to make it out of there, but I worried that you would slip up if they put you under enough duress and that you might reveal who I was."

She smiled up at him. "We Medusas are tougher than we look."

"Oh, yeah? And here I was thinking you're so much softer than I expected."

"Hey! I stay in good shape!"

He grinned down at her, stroking his palm across her stomach and up to cup her breast gently. "I dunno. You feel like all woman to me." His mouth hovered barely a millimeter from hers. "And I love the idea of a woman who's strong and fit and capable, too."

"You're just saying that because you want in my panties," she teased.

"Darlin', we're already way past your panties."

"I dunno. You're spending a whole lot of time talking and not getting busy."

He laughed down at her. "You did *not* just challenge my manhood."

"I might have…"

Their laughter mingled as they kissed, gradually transforming into something more serious. More passionate.

But still he moved slowly, treating her with care. She appreciated him taking it slow with her. It gave her plenty of time to check in with herself and make sure nothing along the way freaked her out.

She loved the way his hard body pressed her down into the mattress. His muscular thighs tangling with hers were sexy as hell. And when his hard, hot length filled her ever so slowly, the only thing that went through her mind was a wish that he would go faster and deeper and harder.

She moved against him experimentally, and it was good. Very good. Bordering on outstanding, in fact.

They found a rhythm easily this time, their bodies accustomed to each other and finding synchronicity immediately. She had time to register liking being tall enough that their bodies fitted so nicely and to register liking that he was fully as strong and fit as she was, which made her feel at ease showing her eagerness for more from him. She wrapped her legs around his hips and welcomed him into her strong embrace, and he met her on equal ground.

Gradually, he let go of the caution he was exercising with her and unleashed his full passion into their lovemaking. And that was when it blew right past outstanding into the realm of epic.

They were unabashedly athletic with each other, surging into each other until their bodies were slick with perspiration and they were both gasping for air. Riding a wave they built between them, they rushed all the way to completion, a lovely race with only winners and no losers.

The pleasure built and built until it finally toppled over, crashing down around them in delicious destruction that left her breathless, her limbs languid, and her mind and soul sated.

It was fully as magical as she remembered, maybe even better this time around because they were more comfortable with each other, not to mention they were dry and warm and in a proper bed. Not that she minded sleeping on the ground or sprawled across his chest as the case might be. But this was better.

And falling asleep cuddled up next to Zane, replete with pleasure and relaxed with knowing he would look out for her while she rested, was even better yet.

Chapter 16

Zane woke up gradually, reveling lazily in the happiness that washed over him. That was not a feeling he really ever ascribed to himself. But he was definitely feeling great tonight. It was a weird contrast with his normal wake up, where his mind would turn immediately to the day's work, to the threats at hand, to remembering the identity he was supposed to be living in from the moment he opened his eyes and started his day.

Happiness had no place in his work, and his work had been his life for a decade or more.

But there were no immediate threats at hand, and the only identity he had to assume was the rather unfamiliar one of Zane Cosworth. Even better, the only work at hand was to enjoy the amazing woman sharing his bed.

What had he been missing, denying himself this feeling for so long? Piper brought up a good point. Was doing his duty to the exclusion of all else really worth it? Was there a way to make time for happiness—for her—in his life, too? Could he have his job and a personal life?

It would take exactly the right woman to be sure. One

who understood the importance of his work and how much it meant to him. One willing to sacrifice time with him, willing to put up with long silences when he was undercover, willing to worry and wait and have faith that he would survive and make it home once more.

A woman like Piper.

If only she would give him some indication that she was willing to consider a longer-term relationship than just this time together. But she'd never said a single word about what came after this mission.

He got that people like the two of them needed to live in the moment. They both needed to be able to focus completely on the task at hand, on the dangers directly in front of them. It was how they both stayed alive in their respective lines of work.

Her house had been cozy. Clearly a personal and private sanctuary, not set up for anyone else to share. He knew: he'd searched the place for pictures of other men. For hints about her family, about her past, about her life before the kidnapping. The place had been completely bare of any such mementos.

Yup, she was an operator through and through. Her life revolved one hundred percent around her work.

Exactly like his life revolved around his work.

Or more accurately, like it had until he'd met her.

Huh. He'd never expected to fall for a woman who hadn't fallen for him first. He was always the one to break things off, to move on to the next mission, to the next identity, to the next false life.

But Piper made him think about settling down. About resuming life as Zane Cosworth. About home. Family. Love. All the things he'd given up and hadn't realized he missed until this very moment.

"You're thinking pretty hard over there, sailor," Piper interrupted from her pillow beside his.

"Sorry. I didn't mean to wake you up."

"You didn't. I set a silent alarm on my watch to wake me up, and it's due to vibrate in a few minutes. My mental alarm clock usually beats my watch by five minutes or so."

He glanced over at her quickly. "Why did you set an alarm for half past midnight?"

"Mark Black is supposed to show up for his Monday morning briefing in a few minutes."

Right. The mission.

Obviously, for Piper the mission came first, and Zane came in a distant second.

The realization tasted bitter in his mouth. Not that he could blame her. It was just strange wearing the shoe on the other foot. He was always the one who made the glib excuse, slipped out of the woman's bed and disappeared, never to look back. But tonight, it was her citing the mission to slip out of bed, collect her clothes and efficiently get dressed.

Zane rolled out of bed and pulled on clothes, as well. No way was Mark Black showing up for that meeting. And when the guy was officially declared missing, a manhunt would be initiated. Quietly. Which meant the CIA would probably green-light the op Torsten had proposed to find the guy.

Piper's phone rang, and they both stared at it.

Then she jolted into motion and picked it up, listening for a few seconds. "Roger. On my way," she replied. She disconnected the call.

"Black didn't show up, did he?" Zane asked.

"Nope."

"I'd better get back to my room. My phone's going to blow up in a minute or two."

She nodded, her face set in serious lines, her mind obviously already at work on what came next.

He kissed her quickly and left, striding down the hall and slipping into his room.

Must not look back.

Let her go.

No regrets.

Maybe in another time, another place, they could've been good together for a long time. Maybe a lifetime. But duty called them both.

He'd been in his room perhaps thirty seconds when someone knocked quietly on his door. He opened it cautiously, leaving the chain on and barely cracking it open.

Shit. Gunnar Torsten.

He threw the door open.

"Five minutes. Out front," Gunnar murmured.

"I'll be there."

As Zane closed his door, he heard Gunnar knocking quietly on another door down the hall.

Zane used three of his five minutes to leap into the shower and try to wash Piper off his skin, out of his heart, out of his life.

It didn't work.

He swiped a razor across his cheeks, tossed the razor in his prepacked bag and was out the door with a minute to spare. He jogged down the hall and took the stairs, arriving in the lobby exactly five minutes after Gunnar's knock.

A dark blue government van was just pulling up, and the three Medusas and Torsten nodded to him.

"Where's Beau?" he asked.

Piper murmured, "He's gone home to plan the party from his end."

They piled into the vehicle, and he was surprised when the van didn't head down I-395 toward the Pentagon. Rather, it wound north, ending up on Rock Creek Parkway.

"Are we going to Langley?" he blurted in surprise.

Gunnar nodded. "Your guys are going to be running this show. They want you and Piper involved, since you have personal knowledge of possible operators involved."

He and Piper? They got to work together on this op? *Yes.* His gut leaped with joy. A little longer to savor what could have been before it was ripped away from them for good. Hell, he was so desperate to be with her that he would take whatever morsels of time he could snatch with her.

It took several minutes to pass all their government IDs through the window to the gate guard and for them to be waved through to the parking area at CIA headquarters. He had only his fake IDs generated for the Amir legend, but those were on file, and he was approved to enter without delay.

He led the way through long corridors to the briefing room the guy at the front desk told them to report to.

It was a bland conference room with bland paneling and bland furniture that belied none of the massive technology and intelligence resources pulsing around them in this, the living brain of the US intelligence apparatus.

A bland-looking man in a suit walked into the room, and Zane recognized one of the senior Iran analysts, a guy several pay grades above him, Dominic Farris.

Dominic nodded at Zane and said in a bland tone,

"Welcome back. Good work on your recent mission rescuing Captain Ford."

Zane snorted. "It's entirely possible that she ultimately rescued me."

Piper's gaze snapped to his, and he belatedly realized that his comment could be taken both literally and figuratively. He shrugged, silently owning both interpretations.

Torsten leaned forward, asking Dominic, "What can you tell us about Mark Black?"

The analyst picked up a remote control, and a section of the paneling slid back to reveal a backlit screen. An awkward official portrait of a man in perhaps his midthirties, wearing horn-rimmed glasses and an ill-fitting suit, popped up on the screen. It could've been straight out of a high school yearbook were it not for the guy's age.

"Mark Black. Nuclear physicist and propulsion engineer by education. Senior field inspector for the Global Atomic Inspection Team, or GAIT. He has been in Iran for three months, monitoring and inspecting various facilities there for GAIT. His boss is this man, René Descarnes. French. Long-time Interpol asset. Sharp guy."

Zane leaned forward as a picture of Black walking on the street he recognized to be in Tehran flashed up on screen. "And Black? Is he an asset to anyone?"

"Not officially. Obviously, his GAIT reports come across our desks, compliments of Descarnes. But Black's just a nuclear inspector."

Piper interjected, "Then why was his wife targeted for kidnapping?"

"Black is scheduled to be the first inspector inside a new Iranian scientific facility in a few days. Place is called the Iranian Center for Materials Research. We believe her—your—kidnapping—" he nodded in Piper's direction "—was an attempt to pressure him into not reporting something the Iranians expect him to see at that facility."

"Like what?" Zane asked quickly.

Dominic shrugged. "We can speculate all day long, but until Black gets inside those labs, we'll have no way of knowing."

"Where is Black now?"

"We believe he's a guest of the Iranian government."

"Meaning what?" Torsten snapped.

"Meaning they will hold him in their custody until he has inspected the facility and issued the report they want him to make."

Torsten asked briskly, like the military man he was, "What's our mission?"

"Go to Tehran. Find Mark Black. Let him go to the Center for Materials Research and, after he's out, retrieve him and bring him home. We need to know what he sees in there. While you're at it, make sure he knows his wife is safe. He may not cooperate with you otherwise. Once you've got Black's debrief, at all costs, he must not fall back into the hands of the Iranian government. We do not want a high-value hostage situation to develop."

Zane leaned back hard in his chair. Damn. The powers that be wanted Black dead rather than in Iranian hands? Just what did the CIA think was inside that lab, anyway?

"Any other mission parameters?" Torsten asked briskly.

"Don't get caught."

Torsten threw Dominic a "duh" look. "That's why we're here. The Medusas specialize in being invisible.

Speaking of which, do you have your own plan in place to get this team into Iran, or are we on our own to arrange it?"

"Did you have something in mind?" Dominic asked with interest.

Torsten grinned, and Zane was struck by how wolf-like an expression it was. The major continued, "Yes, actually we do. An air show is scheduled to start in Tehran the day after tomorrow. Business jets are being flown in by all the big global airplane manufacturers to Mehrabad International Airport downtown and shown off to various government officials. The Iranian government plans to buy a new fleet of small jets and is accepting bids from companies all over the world."

"And?" Dominic asked.

"We'd like to fly in on one of those jets. We'll pose as crew members and corporate representatives, which will give us a reason to be in Tehran and to be doing nothing for most of our time in country while we wait to fly the jet out. We'll use real pilots to fly the plane, of course. They can fly any demonstrations Iranian officials want."

"And you'll bring Mark Black out on that plane with you?" Dominic asked.

Torsten nodded. "Correct. Mehrabad is very close to the city center. It'll be a lot easier to get there than Imam Khomeini International Airport, which is well outside of Tehran."

Zane murmured, "It's about thirty kilometers southwest of Tehran. Good roads. Traffic's not too bad out that way. But plenty of time for security forces to catch up with a person. Security's tight at Mehrabad, though. We'll need a subterfuge to get Black onto the airfield."

Zane's boss nodded thoughtfully. "I'll need a list of

equipment and support you'll need to mount the operation, and a time frame for execution."

Torsten replied, "The equipment list is already built. I'll email it to you as soon as we're done here. We can be ready to go as soon as you pull the trigger."

Zane added, "All we need now is the go-ahead to get Mark Black."

"Stay here. I'll be back," Dominic ordered.

Piper looked over at Zane. "Where'd he run off to?"

"Hopefully, he's getting us approval to roll."

The team opened the printed dossiers on Mark Black and went through them in detail, studying every picture of his face, memorizing each angle and look carefully. Zane hoped the knowledge would be put to use identifying the guy and not having to shoot him to keep him out of Iranian clutches. Persephone Black seemed like a nice lady who would appreciate getting her husband back in one piece.

Dominic was back within about ten minutes to announce that they had, indeed, been green-lighted to proceed with the rescue mission. He nodded at Zane. "You'll be the CIA liaison officer for this joint operation. Use your usual contacts."

Dominic passed him a Tyvek envelope taped shut, and Zane signed for it. He recognized a legend package when he saw one. Inside would be fake IDs, a passport, perhaps some jewelry or a distinctive possession, emergency phone numbers and email addresses to memorize, along with challenge-and-response codes to use with those emergency contacts. And most important, there would be a printed packet of information on his new identity. An entire team of cyberspecialists sat around day in and day out building identities just like this one and maintaining them for when operatives needed a quick cover story.

He would memorize everything inside the envelope over the next few days and accustom himself to answering to the new name inside. Goodbye, Zane. Goodbye, Amir, the wannabe terrorist. Hello, Rashid Farouk.

"The folks down in the photography shop would like to see you before you leave the building so they can get to work creating identification documents for all of you," Dominic commented.

Zane would undoubtedly get his hair dyed, wear colored contact lenses, maybe start growing a beard, and then he would be photographed for his—Rashid's—new passport, driver's license, library card and whatever other IDs were in the package.

Piper and her teammates were taken away to be fitted for their uniforms for the mission—costumes, actually. They would also be photographed for their fake IDs.

The hair dying, fittings and interminable photographs, fingerprints and even dental X-rays took the rest of the night. They reconvened back at the hotel in Torsten's room for breakfast and to quiz each other on their legends. Zane stared when Piper walked in. He'd assumed she would also go dark haired, but in fact, just the opposite had happened. Her hair, already antique gold in color, was now platinum blond.

"Well, hello, Barbie," he drawled.

She stuck her tongue out at him, while Rebel and Tessa laughed. Tessa, naturally olive complexioned and dark haired, had not had her appearance appreciably altered. Rebel, naturally a fair-skinned brunette, had been taken red haired. It was actually a good look on her.

He understood the thinking of the beauticians in the basement at Langley. Blondes and redheads were exotic creatures in a country like Iran, where most of the population was Persian in descent. Piper and Rebel would be treated like celebrities anywhere they went, but all that anyone would remember after seeing them would be their hair colors and not their faces.

The women all carried zippered vinyl clothing bags, which they hung in Torsten's closet. Their uniforms were already tailored and ready to go? That was fast. This mission must have a higher priority at Langley than Dominic had let on to them.

Now, why wouldn't Dominic be honest about something like that? Zane hated it when the higher-ups withheld information from field schmucks like him. The more he knew, the safer he was and the better he could do his job. But without fail, the brass kept secrets and played coy with the truth.

He sat beside Torsten, who was digging into his pancakes with gusto. Zane waited until the guy had slowed down to murmur, "Have folks in your intel channels given you any additional information about this op?"

Torsten looked up at him sharply. "Most of what the military has comes from your people. Why would we have more?"

Zane shrugged. "I know Dominic. He wasn't telling us everything. I got the distinct feeling that folks up the chain of command from us are holding back something important."

"Like what?"

"Maybe something about Black, or maybe about the facility he's supposed to inspect."

Torsten nodded. "I noticed how coy Dominic was about guessing what the Iranians don't want Black to see." He paused and then added quietly, "Only bit of hot intel I've seen recently on Iran has a major arms dealer coming back from the dead and supposedly doing a deal with the Iranian government."

"What dealer?" Zane asked quickly.

"Abu Haddad."

"Haddad? Well, hell. I was hoping that bastard was well and truly six feet under."

Torsten lifted his chin in Tessa's direction. "Tessa and Beau are the ones who took him out. We all thought for sure we got him, but apparently, he managed to slip away. Either that or one of his flunkies has resurrected his business and is invoking his name to get clients."

Zane picked up his cell phone, put it on secure mode and placed a quick phone call. "Hi, Antonia. It's Zane." He chatted with the Turkey-Cyprus-Greece specialist for a few minutes and then casually shifted topics. "Hey, Toni. I heard a rumor that Haddad may be back in business. Has anything crossed your desk about him recently?"

The analyst expressed surprise that Haddad was alive but had nothing else.

"Do me a favor," Zane added. "Don't mention his name in connection with mine. No need to go out of your way poking around to find out more."

"You don't want me to raise any red flags?" the woman asked shrewdly.

"You know me too well," he replied ruefully.

"If I happen to run across any information, I'll pass it your way."

"Thanks, love."

Piper's eyebrows raised fractionally across the room.

Zane disconnected the call and said to the group at large, "Antonia has been around practically since the CIA was founded. I'm convinced she personally knows every single person living in Greece today. And she is related to at least half of them by blood. Last time I heard, she has about thirty grandchildren."

Piper's expression abruptly shifted to one of total disinterest, and Zane glanced over at Torsten, who was, indeed, looking back and forth between him and Piper.

"Did she have anything to say?" the major asked.

"No. Which is telling. She knows *everything* about Turkey. Whatever's being withheld from us is happening at a very high level."

Torsten swore quietly. "There's possibly nothing on earth I hate worse than going into a mission half-blind."

Zane laughed without humor. "I dunno. Direct congressional oversight on a mission sucks pretty hard."

Torsten groaned. "God save us all from meddling politicians."

Around midmorning, a call came in to Zane that the airplane and two pilots requisitioned by the agency would arrive at Dulles International Airport in a few hours. They would cross the Atlantic and stop in Europe for twelve hours of crew rest for the pilots and then continue on to Tehran.

Zane asked the group, "Any preference as to where we stop over in Europe?"

Torsten pulled up a map on his laptop, and a good-natured argument ensued. It was eventually settled that they would stop over at a US Naval facility in Sicily. It was far enough off the beaten path that casual informants shouldn't spot them, and the food was apparently first-class. Mount Etna, the volcano that rose up to tower over Sicily, had been quiet recently, as well.

The entire group went to the Pentagon to work out in its gym before their ride arrived, and Zane took pleasure in being less shocked than the other gym rats as Piper, Tessa and Rebel commenced tossing around weights like candy and generally embarrassing the men in the big facility.

A group of silent men working out together in one corner recognized Torsten and invited him and the women to come over and play with the big boys. Zane was just as happy to stay on his treadmill, stretching out his legs for a quick hard run today.

As they rode in the van back to the hotel, the women talked excitedly about getting to work out with and measure themselves against a SEAL team. He was gratified when Piper slid her hand surreptitiously between them to squeeze his in reassurance.

No need for her to worry. He was confident in his own masculinity.

They each went their own way for supper, which meant he was able to collect Piper and take her to that jazz club downtown. They sat on the same side of a banquette table, and he lounged back, listening to an improv band while she half lay on his chest, relaxing.

He couldn't remember ever being this at peace in his own skin.

He couldn't ever remember being this scared.

Which was exceedingly strange to him. He didn't do scared. He'd stared down fanatics and terrorists; he'd been chased by spies and run for his life without ever feeling half this terrified.

But then, he also didn't spend much time living in his own skin, either. He'd spent a good chunk of his adult life pretending to be someone else.

"You're messing with my head, Piper," he murmured as the level in the bottle of wine in front of them dropped.

"You're messing with mine, too," she replied.

"How?" they both asked simultaneously.

"You first." He beat her to saying it.

"I wasn't looking for a relationship," she confessed. "I'm still not looking for one. But here you are, and I have no idea what to do about you."

He set down his wineglass and twined their fingers together. "I would never come between you and your work. I have a decent idea of how hard it was for you to land an assignment with the Medusas. It's a once-in-a-lifetime opportunity."

"You're not wrong. I've devoted my entire adult life to this goal," she replied. "But then, I imagine you had to do the same to become what you are, too."

He shrugged. "It's possible that it was easier for me to hide behind all those other personas rather than face my own life and deal with it."

"Is there some trauma in your past? Something that made you want or need to run away from it rather than face it?"

He replied quickly, "Nothing like that. My family is affluent. Successful. Relatively normal if you accept the premise that no family is actually 'normal' and that all families have their problems."

"What problems does your family have?"

He shrugged again. "Nothing radical. My father is a control freak and ordered around my mom, my brother and me. My older brother went along with the program and did what he was told. I…didn't."

She nodded. "Rebelled as a kid. Check." A pause. "Did you get in trouble with the law?"

"No. My old man was the district attorney and was always able to have a word with the police chief and get any charges dropped."

"What kind of stuff did you do?"

"I drove too fast and drank too much. Partied too hard and made too much noise mostly."

"Why the choice of your current employer?" she asked curiously.

"They were looking for risk takers. People who could function in danger and were willing to put their necks on the line. It seemed like a good fit at the time."

"And now?"

He looked up, making eye contact with her. "For the first time, I'm questioning my life choices."

She jolted. "Why? Because I'm a bad choice?"

"Not at all. Because I may actually have found something—someone—worth living for. Someone more important to me than my job."

"Oh." Her gaze slid away from his, and in the dim lighting he wasn't sure she blushed. But he thought she did.

After a long pause, she looked back at him. "You said before that I'm messing with your head. Is that what you meant?"

"Partially."

When he didn't explain, she asked hesitantly, "What's the rest of it?"

He sighed, "This is going to sound stupid, but I have no idea who I am."

She frowned. "How's that?"

"I went straight from college to the agency. All that growing up and self-discovery you're supposed to do in your twenties didn't happen for me. The next thing I knew, I was pretending to be all these other people."

He tossed back the rest of his wine and refilled their glasses.

"The thing with deep cover is you have to become your legend. You don't get a break to go home and put your feet up on a coffee table, read your mail and catch up on your life. You don't report in to your boss or touch base with your colleagues. Anything that might link you to your real life is strictly off-limits. You're cast adrift without any anchor whatsoever to your reality."

"That sounds scary," she murmured.

"After a while, it becomes normal. You stop thinking about your real life, your real family and friends, your real identity. You become the cover story."

"Would you say you actually became a white supremacist or a religious fanatic?"

He took another slug of the excellent wine, swirling it around in his mouth and savoring its dry bite.

"While I was that other person, I was both of those things. I had to be. There's no room in an undercover operation for hesitation or equivocation. You have to commit to the role, both in action and in thought. You have to believe you're that other persona."

"I don't think I could do that," she replied.

"It's like being a method actor and completely immersing yourself in the role."

She smiled sadly. "I still couldn't do it."

"I'm starting to wish I hadn't done it," he replied in a low voice.

"Why not? You've done your country a great service. You should be proud of your work."

"But at what cost? I don't even remember who I am anymore. I don't know what I think, what I like or dislike, what I believe in. I'm...empty."

"How do you feel right this minute?" she asked urgently.

He considered for a moment. "Relaxed. Happy. Relieved that I get to spend more time with you before our careers rip us apart. Worried about the mission."

"Why are you worried?" she asked quickly.

"I'm a known Iran expert. I have to assume that Mahmoud sent photos of me back to his superiors. After I escaped with you, he also surely told them I was at best a traitor to their cause and at worst a plant of some kind. The odds of me being recognized when I enter Iran are fairly high. And the consequences of that…" He shrugged.

"You'd be lucky if they only killed you," she finished for him.

"Exactly."

"How good is the disguise the agency worked up for you?"

"It'll have to be good enough, won't it?"

"Can I help you be less recognizable?" she asked.

"I don't know."

"What if we pose as a married couple? That would throw them off, wouldn't it?"

"Our IDs would have to be redone—"

"Not necessarily," she interrupted. "You know us aggressive, out-of-control American women. We don't take our husbands' names anymore. It's scandalous. All that would have to happen is one of the cyberidentity folks would have to enter a marriage license for us in some database." Warming to her topic, she added, "We could have eloped to Las Vegas recently."

"It might help. And it would have the added benefit of forcing you to stay near me during the mission."

She reached in her purse for her cell phone and placed a call. "Beau, it's Piper. I need you to marry me."

Even Zane heard the squawk at the other end of the phone.

"Not like that," she laughed. "I need you to plant a marriage for me in whatever system it needs to be planted in. Yes. Part of a cover legend. Zane. His name will be Rashid Farouk."

She glanced up at him. "How's that spelled?"

He relayed what was on his new passport, and she relayed it to Beau.

She put her phone away and picked up her wineglass. "A toast. To our long and happy fake marriage, Mr. Farouk."

"To us, Mrs. Farouk."

Except it didn't feel the least bit fake as they clinked glasses and drank, smiling deeply into each other's eyes.

Chapter 17

Piper tugged at the annoyingly tight red suit the CIA had seen fit to provide for her. "When I signed up to be a Medusa, I didn't think I would end up saving the world in pantyhose and high heels."

Zane and Torsten laughed, and she threw them a dirty look. "Next mission, you two get to wear the pencil skirts and stilettos."

Zane threw up his hands. "No, thank you. I don't know how women stand upright in those monstrosities, let alone walk in them."

She glared at him. "Clearly, it's because we are the superior gender and have exceptional balance."

He grinned. "You'll get no argument out of me."

Tessa rolled her eyes. "It's this stupid hat that's going to be the death of me."

All three women had been given dopey little red pillbox hats that had to be pinned to their hair to even stay perched on their heads.

Torsten grinned. "Think of them as your big red buttons. Someone hits one of those, I give you full permission to take out the transgressor."

"Done," Piper muttered.

"You may regret telling them that," Zane commented. The two men traded wry smiles.

"How much longer till we land?" Piper asked no one in particular.

Torsten got up and walked forward past a half-dozen plush armchair-style seats to ask the pilots. He wore an identical uniform to those of the two men in the cockpit, and his hair was cut to match theirs. She had to admit he wore a suit well. But then, all military men tended to. They had the right physiques for it.

"About an hour left," Torsten announced, returning through the snazzy, tricked-out passenger space. "Any last-minute questions before we land?"

Piper shook her head. They'd been over the mission parameters so many times she could probably recite them in her sleep. Zane sat across from her, wearing an exceptionally well-cut suit. He was posing as a sales representative of the TrevAir Jet Manufacturing Company. Poor guy had had to memorize more information about airplanes in the past two days than she could even begin to imagine.

Luckily, her job was to act like a bubblehead and flirt with the Iranian officials. The challenge would be to flirt enough to disarm them without flirting so much as to offend them. Zane had spoken with all three women at length about it, explaining that, as infidels, they would not be perceived as fully human. They were something…less. Particularly with the ultra-conservatives who tended to populate the government.

He avoided using words like *whores* or *sluts*, but Piper got the idea. And it left a sour taste in her mouth.

The descent and landing at Mehrabad, in downtown Tehran, went uneventfully. Out her window, Piper spotted a row of tan C-130s, American military cargo planes sold to Iran in another age, when the shah was still in power and a friend to the United States. On the other side of the runway from the military ramp was a blocky, ugly 1970s-style terminal. And in the distance, dry, dark mountains rose above the skyline of Tehran. High-rise apartments and offices rose in clusters growing out of the lower, older sprawl of the ancient city. The contrast was stark.

The airport's tarmac was crowded with business jets from all over the world, every major aircraft manufacturer angling for this lucrative contract with the Iranian government. The Medusas had timed their arrival for after most of the other airplanes arrived, giving them a big, chaotic crowd of jets and crew members to blend into.

The air tasted like bitter dust and thick diesel exhaust. A wall of city noise struck Piper as she paused on the top of the steps to the jet—vehicles and people living in overcrowded proximity. Over eight million of Iran's not quite seventy-five million citizens lived in Tehran.

They passed through customs control without issue. The immigration officers had spent the past two days checking in crews for the air show and were overworked and sloppy.

Thank God. Piper noted that the customs agent didn't look twice at Zane with his black hair, dark beard stubble and thick, horn-rimmed glasses, nor at his papers declaring him to be the crew's translator.

The first hurdle was crossed. She and Zane had made it into Iran without incident. Now to make it out the same way.

Piper rolled around the unfamiliar gold wedding band on her left ring finger and glanced sidelong at him. She murmured, "Should I drop back three steps behind you as befits a proper wife?"

"Don't you dare."

He had a quick conversation in Farsi with two cab drivers at the front of the taxi queue outside the main terminal, and then he loaded Torsten, Tessa, Rebel and one of the pilots in one cab, and Piper, the second pilot and himself in the second. She was careful not to touch him because he'd stressed that public displays of affection between men and women were deeply frowned upon.

The taxis delivered them to a nearby hotel, and Zane efficiently checked them in and passed out room keys. Piper followed him to their shared room.

The decor was hopelessly outdated, but the unit was clean. She commented, "Well, it's better than that last place we stayed in."

He shot her a rueful smile. He'd also told everyone to expect their hotel rooms to be bugged and to guard their speech accordingly. "Are you tired, darling, or would you like to go out and see a bit of the city?"

They had a short window of three days to find Mark Black and arrange to sneak him out of the country. Which was to say they didn't have a minute to spare. "Ooh, I'd love to go sightseeing," she gushed. "Just let me get out of this uniform and into something a little more appropriate."

Appropriate being loose long pants, a high-collared blouse, a loose long sweater and a scarf tied around her head. Thankfully, it was a cool day in the city and she wasn't going to swelter under all the clothing.

Zane gave her a quick once-over and nodded in approval at the modest attire. He drew her into his arms for a quick kiss that ended up being a long, slow affair that left her rethinking having turned down a nap with him. She was pleased to see him breathing a little hard when he finally broke it off.

"I can't ever get enough of you," he whispered against her temple before he stepped back from her and opened the door.

"Ditto," she murmured as she moved past him into the hall.

Tehran was crowded and dusty, but the streets were bustling and energetic.

"I've never seen traffic this bad," she commented as she watched a group of pedestrians nearly be run down by several motorcycles diving between gridlocked lines of cars.

"The city was designed for about three hundred thousand cars but has more than five million vehicles on the road. You do the math."

"Aren't you just a font of information?" she teased.

"We'll have to take traffic into account when we... need to get anywhere."

He was referring to their plan to kidnap Mark Black back from the Iranians. Torsten had wanted to rent a large, covered truck to move the whole team covertly, but now Piper understood why Zane had insisted that motorcycles would be more practical.

They walked to the bazaar, an old but charming covered market in the old city. A huge white dome decorated with blue and gold mosaic tiles rose over the ancient wooden structure, shading the heart of the open-air marketplace.

"You look like you need a cup of coffee," Zane announced as they wandered through the shops, full of textiles, brass and cheap electronics, while the scents of cinnamon, saffron and sewage swirled around them.

"Um, sure," she replied.

He steered her into a grimy little coffee shop with plaster walls painted peach, faded turquoise ceilings and cobalt blue tables. This country was a full-on assault to her senses, noisy, brightly colored and smelly. Zane tucked her at a table in a dark corner and then went to fetch tiny cups of what turned out to be tactical nuclear espresso.

Thick and strong and bitter, it nonetheless left a pleasant aftertaste, and she definitely felt the zing of its caffeine punch within a few minutes.

Zane lingered over his cup of coffee and then wandered away again, bringing back sweet pastries this time, and warning her to take her time eating hers.

"What's up?" she muttered from behind unmoving lips.

"Contact's late."

Whoa. This was a meeting, then? She smiled and nodded, leaning back in her chair and feigning exhaustion and relief to be seated and resting. Zane picked up a newspaper abandoned on the table beside them and began browsing through it.

"Can you read that?" she asked, eyeing the Arabic script.

"Of course I can. Just because my family lived in the United States for a while doesn't mean I didn't learn my family's native tongue."

"I'm sorry. That was stupid of me. Of course you would have learned your family's language and culture."

He shrugged. "It came in handy in college in my Middle Eastern studies."

He said that like she was supposed to know what he'd majored in at university. Oh, right. They were married. Did he think they were being eavesdropped on, even here? She had to give him credit; he was flawless at maintaining a cover.

"And here I thought I knew everything about you," she replied.

Approval shone in his eyes, but he said smoothly, "I have to keep a few secrets from you, darling. How else will I keep you on your toes?"

They traded affectionate smiles that felt entirely genuine, and he went back to reading his newspaper.

Thankfully, she still had a few bites of the dry, stale cinnamon bun left on her plate when a young man approached their table. Zane stood up, exclaiming in pleasure, and hugged the man, warmly inviting him to share a cup of coffee with them.

She'd already noted that the locals generally seemed animated and demonstrative. They tended to talk loudly, laugh a lot and argue good-naturedly. Although the greeting was wildly out of character for reserved Zane, it was wholly in keeping with how everyone else was behaving. Yet again, she was impressed to death by how well he blended into his surroundings. The man was *really* good at his job.

Zane bought a round of espresso for all three of them, and Piper braced herself to have the jitters for hours to come.

The new man was introduced as Samir—an old friend of the family—although what family was never specified. And she didn't ask.

Samir and Zane chatted in casual, quick Farsi for perhaps ten minutes. Just long enough to finish their coffees and trade pleasantries. Then Samir excused himself, citing not wanting to be late for a class, and rushed off. As far as she could tell, not one bit of useful information had been exchanged. There had been no message passed, no dead drop, nothing that would help them find Mark Black.

Zane was in no hurry to leave, but when they finished their drinks, he led her outside once more. "Wanna see something amusing?" he asked her.

"Sure."

They walked a few blocks until they came to a blocky office building made of pink brick with iron bars on the windows. "What is it?" she asked.

"It's called the US Den of Espionage Museum."

Her gaze snapped back to the facade. "Is this the old US Embassy? Where the hostages were taken?"

"The very same."

"Well, that's…gruesome."

"You should see the inside. There's a huge painting covering a wall, of the Statue of Liberty with a skull face." He muttered under his breath, "It's creepy as hell."

"No, thanks."

"That's okay. I want to show you the Negarestan Garden, anyway. It's only a few blocks from here."

The garden turned out to be more of a park, but it was green and shady, with fountains sending the sound of tinkling water into the air. It was a pleasant break from the cars, jostling crowds and thick traffic fumes.

"What are we doing here?" she asked from behind unmoving lips.

"Dead drop to fetch," Zane answered in the same fashion.

The CIA must have arranged this before they left Washington. Efficient bunch, those spooks.

They stopped in front of a turquoise blue pool of water shaped roughly like an embellished square, with elaborately swirled and curved edges in the ancient

Persian style. "Let me take your picture in front of the fountain," Zane announced.

"Uh, sure." She took her place, obediently smiling. She suspected he had spotted someone following them and was snapping a picture of the unlucky tail.

They strolled a bit more, and then he suggested they take a rest on a bench under a row of young trees beside a long, narrow lawn. "I gather grass is a bit of a luxury in this part of the world?" she commented.

"Water's in terribly short supply. Hence grass is, too."

Zane leaned back, stretching his arm across the back of the bench behind her but not touching her shoulders. Still, the move was possessive, and sent warm fuzzies through her tummy. "It's good to be home," he sighed.

"Do you miss it?" she asked, playing along. Rashid Farouk had been born here, according to his legend, which she, as his "wife," had memorized along with her own.

"I miss the big family gatherings. And the food. There were always cousins around to play with. Although there were also always aunts and grannies around to grab your ear and tell you to behave, too."

She smiled wistfully. "That sounds nice."

"It was a good way to grow up." He paused, then added, "You'll see for yourself in a few days, when you meet my family."

They'd agreed that it would look strange for a native Iranian not to visit his family if he was in the country. The CIA had undoubtedly arranged for some family in the suburbs of Tehran to pose as his relatives and go through the motions of preparing for a big family get-together. She'd already figured out the agency was nothing if not thorough in building cover legends.

"Would you ever consider moving us back here?" she asked Zane speculatively.

"Would you come with me if I wanted to live here?"

"Of course. You're my husband. I'll follow you to the end of the world and back."

His gaze snapped to hers, and the look they traded was loaded with intensity. And questions. Did she mean that for real? What would their life together be like if they were really married?

A slow smile unfolded across his face, growing to encompass all his features. "I think it's time for us to go back to the hotel, Mrs. Farouk."

"Indeed, Mr. Farouk."

They left the gardens, and he surprised her by hailing a cab. In a hurry to get her into bed, was he? More warm fuzzies coursed through her. Good. She was in a hurry to get naked with him, too.

Not that a cab ended up being much faster than walking. The traffic really was incredible. Their driver yelled out his window and honked, and she was pretty sure he went the wrong way on a one-way street before they finally made it back to the hotel.

When they got back to the room, Zane announced that he wanted a shower and disappeared into the bathroom. After a few minutes, he called, "Can you come scrub my back, wife?"

That was a strange request. Nonetheless, she played along and slipped into the fog-filled bathroom. The shower ran loudly, but he sat on the toilet, fully clothed and holding a wrinkled strip of paper. He passed it to her, and she realized it was thin onionskin that could fold into a tiny space.

Holding it open, she read aloud. "'MB, guest of

honor. Appears at Club Musika Retro tomorrow. Don't miss it—one-time show!'"

She looked up at Zane, frowning. He stood, took her in his arms and whispered in her ear, "MB is Mark Black. *Guest of honor* means he's under arrest, as in he's a guest of state security. Club Musika Retro—CMR—Center for Materials Research. Tomorrow is when he's due to inspect that facility. And the one-time show comment undoubtedly means that he's expected to see the facility only once and then disappear after his report on the CMR is delivered to the Iranian government."

"How did you know to pick this up?"

"Samir showing up at the café meant the message had been successfully dropped. All we had to do was go collect it."

"Was the pickup point prearranged?"

"No. Samir and I talked about playing as children in the park and he remembered that fountain and liking to sit and listen to the sound of water."

She smiled at Zane. "Well, aren't you clever."

He smiled back at her, and then he stood up, drawing her into his arms. Their smiles mingled, turning into a kiss fully as steamy as the shower.

Breathless and distracted, she pulled her mind back to business with great reluctance. "What time will Black be at the lab tomorrow? How much security will be around him?"

"No idea. If the CIA's informants knew it, that information would also have been in the note. This is the part where we get to improvise."

"Weapons?" she asked in a low voice.

"Gunnar's going over to the airport later today to get the equipment out of the plane."

That had been the hardest part of getting ready for

this trip—asking the manufacturer of the airplane to quickly build in a hidden compartment large enough to carry all the operational gear for an entire special operations team. Apparently, a team of cabinetmakers had worked around the clock to finish the construction and installation.

She asked, "Do we have wheels yet?"

"No. We have to go take care of that tonight. We have supper with the Iranian contract officials this evening, and after that, we'll need to go over to Club Musika Retro in case the message was discovered. We'll sneak out of there, get transportation and then meet up with the others."

She nodded in understanding.

He said gently, "Time for you to leave the bathroom if we don't want to arouse suspicion. If you want to take a nap, I'll join you when I'm done in here." His hands fell away from her and he stepped back, but reluctantly. Her heart warmed. She knew the feeling.

When she glanced back over her shoulder at him as she slipped out of the bathroom, though, his eyes were alight with the promise of delights to come.

Yes.

She stripped out of her tourist clothes and washed off with a damp cloth. Refreshed, she lay down on a mattress only marginally softer than concrete. But having slept on concrete recently, she was able to perceive and appreciate the slight difference.

She was half-asleep when Zane slipped under the sheet beside her, gathering her into his warm, slightly damp embrace and murmuring, "I never get tired of how you feel in my arms."

She noticed he made no effort to keep his voice

down. *Right. Act married for the people on the other end of the bugs in the walls.*

"I never get tired of being in your arms, my love."

His gaze snapped to hers, and a slow, possessive smile took over his features. He liked the *L*-word, did he? She'd never been in love, but she was starting to wonder if it didn't feel pretty close to how she was feeling now.

"You're so good for me. You ground me in the present," he said, staring at her significantly. Clearly, he meant more than that. But, leery of any bugs, he wasn't going to say anything more aloud. She got the message, though. In the midst of running from cover story to cover story, she reminded him of who he really was. She grounded him in his real identity.

"I hope you'll always do the same for me," she replied carefully. She wasn't likely to spend the majority of her career in undercover roles, but she was likely to spend a lot of time away from home in dangerous places doing dangerous missions. She, too, could use the reminder that moments like this were real and waiting for her when she got home.

"Always," he agreed solemnly.

Had they just agreed to try a long-term relationship with each other? If only she could ask him outright!

Instead, she kissed him passionately, pouring all the feelings she dared not speak aloud into their kiss. She desperately hoped he felt her genuine desire for him, her wish to be with him, her willingness to commit to a full-blown relationship.

She traced her hands across his muscular shoulders and relished the smoothness of his skin sliding under her palms. He was so warm and vital, and he made her feel vibrantly alive.

He smiled at her, a whole host of emotions flitting through his expressive eyes, and she smiled back.

"Don't let me lose myself," he breathed.

"Never. I'll be your anchor as long as you need me to be."

They made love slowly, tenderly even. When it had shifted from great sex to deeply emotional lovemaking, she wasn't sure. But this was entirely different than what they'd shared the other times they'd been together—and it had been pretty special then, too.

In the midst of a dangerous foreign land, they created between them an island of safety and belonging. If only she could tell if it was a real promise. Had some sort of deal been sealed between them or not?

Or was she interpreting great sex by a considerate lover to mean more than it really did? Assailed by doubts and bedeviled by her silent hopes and dreams, she made love to him with all the intensity of feeling that she could express. No surprise, she felt tears on her cheeks when they finally fell back on the mattress, side by side, to catch their breaths.

Regardless of what it meant for the long term, it surely had satisfied the curiosity of whoever was listening on the other end of the bugs. If that didn't sound like a married couple genuinely enjoying each other's company, she gave up.

They had time for a short nap together before Zane's alarm clock blared, announcing it was time to dress for dinner.

The supper meeting with government officials responsible for choosing which airplanes to buy was a complete bore to Piper. She was expected to smile politely, look nice and say nothing. At least she got to dust off her rusty Farsi as she listened to the conversation flowing around her. Zane was kept busy through the meal discussing airplane performance parameters and dancing around possible discounts that the aircraft company—ostensibly a Swiss firm and politically neutral—might be willing to slip to the Iranians on the down low.

After the interminable meal with course after course of heavy sauce-laden fare, each spicier than the last, Zane finally escorted her out of the restaurant to the hotel lobby, where Tessa and Rebel were waiting.

"Shall we go, ladies?" Zane asked.

He led them outside, hailed a cab and gave the name of the nightclub, Club Musika Retro. The odds of the dead-dropped message being intercepted were low, but just in case, they needed to follow through with visiting what turned out to be a discotheque, complete with mirror balls, flashing lights and dreadful Persian remakes of Western music from thirty years ago. Piper was totally going to have a headache before they got out of here.

Under the cover of the pounding noise, she leaned over to ask Tessa, "Did Gunnar get the toys okay?"

"No problem. Did you get a nap this afternoon?"

Piper felt her cheeks heating up and hoped her teammate would put her flush down to the mass of hot bodies around them. "Um, yes. A nap. Uh-huh."

Tessa grinned knowingly. "Makes life easier when you finally work out all that romantic confusion, doesn't it?"

"I'm not sure it's all worked out. And it's not as if we can have heart-to-hearts about it here and now."

"He's crazy about you. Never takes his eyes off you. Always looks half enthralled and half ready to leap to your defense at the slightest provocation."

Piper stared at her teammate. "Really?"

Rebel jumped into the conversation, rolling her eyes. "The poor guy's completely head over heels for you."

Piper knew the feeling.

Zane came back from the bar to their booth, juggling four sodas without ice. "We're in luck," he announced. "There's a men-only hookah lounge in the back. I'll slip through there and head out to pick up the keys to our motorcycles. You three party hard while I'm gone, and don't forget to flirt with our tails."

"We were followed?" Piper exclaimed.

"They picked us up leaving the hotel," Zane retorted.

"You'll have to teach us how to spot them better," Tessa interjected. "I didn't see anyone, and I was looking."

"Me, neither," Rebel admitted glumly.

Zane murmured, "Once we get home, it would be my pleasure to up your field ops games. In the meantime, it's the two guys on the bar stools right where the bar turns toward that wall."

"One guy has his back to us and the other is facing us?" Piper responded. "Big, beefy dudes in suits, with the funny bulges under their left arms?"

"Those are the ones," Zane laughed over his tepid drink.

Piper sipped without relish at the flat, oversweet soda. Zane stood up and dropped a chaste kiss on her forehead. "Don't have too much fun without me."

"Ha!" she replied in fake indignation. "Do you know who you're talking to?"

He looked around at all three women. "Yes. I do. Hence the caution."

Piper rolled her eyes at him and grabbed Tessa's and

Rebel's hands. "C'mon, girls. I feel some *Saturday Night Fever* moves coming on."

All three women actually danced carefully, not wanting to draw too much attention to themselves. They followed the lead of the local women in how to dance. It wasn't just that Iranian women moved only a tiny bit. They also looked strange doing it in clothes that would not have been out of place at a Catholic school dance presided over by nuns. Piper and her teammates wore thick leggings underneath calf-length skirts, long-sleeved turtlenecks and sweaters over those.

When traditional, Iranian-flavored music came on, everyone on the dance floor, male and female, shifted to more traditional Middle Eastern dances. The young men twirled cloth handkerchiefs over their heads, while the women mostly clapped and laughed.

Piper and the other Medusas joined in for close to a half hour with no sign of Zane. Then Rebel leaned close to Piper to shout in her ear, "Problem—our tails are looking at their watches and at the entrance to the hookah lounge."

Crud. A distraction was called for.

"C'mon!" she shouted at her teammates. They made their way across the floor until they were directly in front of the tails. And this time, when an American dance tune blared, they broke into American-style dance moves, still being careful not to do anything that might be perceived as overly provocative. Zane had warned them that nightclubs were a recent experiment by the government and tightly monitored for obscenity.

Piper hoped that, by ignoring their tails and dancing in a tight triangle facing one another, they wouldn't get arrested by whatever religious police might be lurking in the corners.

"There's Rashid," Rebel called to Piper, just as the song ended.

Thank God. Piper was nearly out of dance moves that wouldn't get her arrested. The women strolled back to the booth to rejoin Zane, who brought them another round of drinks. This time he set down bottles of water. They all sipped, using the bottles to shield their mouths from any lip readers or cameras.

"Success?" Piper asked him.

"Indeed. Having fun?"

"I'm ready to get out of here. Our tails are enjoying watching our, um, tails, a little too much."

Tessa added, "We're supposed to meet the boss in an hour. We'll need that time to make sure we're not followed."

"We'll split up to leave," Zane commented lightly from behind his water bottle. "Our minders will be forced to split up, too, and it's a lot easier to lose a solo tail than a team who can pass you off from one person to the next."

Piper asked her friends, "Do you girls know how to get to the rendezvous point?"

Rebel grinned. "I speak Arabic. Even if we get lost, I'll be able to make myself understood enough to get directions. That, and I memorized a map of the city. We'll be fine."

Piper lifted her bottle one last time. "All right, then. We'll see you in an hour or so." She drained her water and nodded at Zane. Time for the new Medusas to go into action for the first time as a real team on a real mission.

Chapter 18

Zane watched Tessa and Rebel slip out behind a couple that actually looked quite a bit like himself and Piper. He was impressed at how quickly the two women managed to exit the bar without looking like they were in the slightest hurry. It was a departure worthy of an experienced CIA operative.

Even better, one of the two men seated at the bar left moments after they did. The lone tail left behind in the club looked disconcerted. Excellent.

"Time to go," Zane muttered to Piper. "Before our friend has time to call in reinforcements."

She gathered her sweater and he ushered her outside, making no secret that they were leaving the club. The moment they stepped out into the cool evening, he and Piper turned left, hurrying away from the noisy disco.

He lengthened his stride to a near run, relieved that Piper could keep up with him. They swerved into the first alley they came to and took off running. She ran lightly on the balls of her feet, making very little noise. Thank God for her excellent training. Or more accurately, thank Torsten.

However, when they dodged out of the far end of the alley, she tugged his sleeve for him to stop. He glanced at her and was shocked to see a pair of black, rubber-soled loafers emerge from somewhere under her coat. She changed shoes quickly, threw a dark scarf over her blond hair and nodded her readiness to proceed.

If he'd thought she was quiet and fast before, she was twice as silent and quick wearing flats instead of high heels. Which was fortunate, because he ran her all over the old city, winding through warrens of narrow streets, narrower alleys and connected courtyards.

He defied anyone to successfully follow the two of them without revealing himself or herself as they darted across the city on foot. The tricky bit was actually going to be circling back to where their motorcycles were waiting for them.

He and Piper slowed down, moving stealthily as they backtracked into the old city. At this time of night the walls and tall iron gates, so abundant in Tehran, were mostly closed. It turned the streets into long tunnels with a single entrance and one exit. Their only option was to sprint down each street, slowing only to slip around corners into a new tunnel and then sprinting down it.

Eventually, he found what he was looking for. A gate stood open into a courtyard bordered by several old apartment buildings only four or five stories high. Tehran sat on two major fault lines, and these old buildings were squat and built of heavy stone to survive earthquakes.

As they darted across the deserted courtyard, Piper snatched a woman's chador off a clothesline. The traditional garment was made of a large semicircle of black cloth. Piper wrapped it loosely about her head and upper body, letting it fall nearly to her knees.

Following her lead, Zane stripped off his blazer and exchanged it for a sweater drying on the same line. It was still damp and smelled like lye, but it changed his physical appearance and made him look even closer to native.

They darted to a gate on the opposite side of the courtyard, at the end of a dark tunnel through one of the buildings. He paused to peer out before stepping into the street with Piper.

They continued to peer around corners and randomly pause in dark doorways to check behind them for the next several minutes. Even he didn't spot anyone following them. They were in the clear.

He approached a row of motorcycles, chained together and parked in front of a small storefront with its metal grate pulled down and locked. Using the key he'd collected earlier, he unlocked the motorcycle on the end and relocked the chain looped through rest of them.

He threw his leg across the seat, and Piper climbed on behind him, clasping her arms around his waist. He picked up the ratty baseball cap hanging from the handlebar and tugged it down low on his head. The street was rather quieter than he would like, but there was no help for it. He started the engine, and it roared to life, sounding shockingly loud in his ears.

He pulled away from the curb and turned the corner. "Hide your face," he ordered Piper tersely.

She instantly buried her nose against his back, letting the flapping chador do the rest. Her entire torso pressed against his back, and she felt warm and feminine and sexy. Memories of their afternoon in bed flooded through his mind's eye, and he nearly drove over the curb in his distraction.

Dammit. Focus on driving.

"Good thing you're my wife," he muttered as he drove past a man in a dark suit standing on a street corner and looking around suspiciously. Maybe the guy was a state security agent, maybe not. But either way, Zane wasn't taking any chances with Piper's safety. "Otherwise you'd go to jail for holding me like this."

"I'd happily go to jail to keep holding you like this," she muttered back. He wasn't sure if she'd meant for him to hear her or not, but her comment caused a burst of warmth in his gut nonetheless.

The strangeness of having a partner, and of worrying about that person's safety more than his own, struck him. It wasn't that he minded working with her; it was just weird not being a lone wolf.

Truth be told, he could get used to this business of working in a pack of wolves.

"Okay. You can sit up," he announced, when the guy on the corner disappeared from view behind them.

"I don't know," she murmured. "I kinda like it right here."

"Don't distract me," he half laughed.

She lifted her face, but her hands slipped lower, sliding below his belt buckle and coming perilously close to parts of him that were all too ready to perk up with interest.

Thankfully, they came into a more lit area soon, and she moved her hands back up to a more decorous position. He turned onto the Besat Expressway, then headed southeast out of Tehran on Highway 44. The idea was for the other team members to meet up and make their way out of the city center, where police and security forces would be thickest. The rendezvous point was in a small city called Mamazand, about forty-five minutes outside Tehran.

The Center for Materials Research, where Mark Black should be making an appearance in the morning, was just beyond Mamazand.

The trip out of Tehran and into the barren desert was uneventful. He guided the motorcycle to the house where their rendezvous had been arranged, and the tall iron-paneled gate, painted light blue, opened for him as he approached it. He drove into the courtyard and cut the engine.

Torsten locked the gate behind them as Piper climbed off the motorcycle, and Zane followed suit.

"Everyone's here now," the major said quietly. "We'll head out as soon as you gear up."

Piper had already moved over to the weapons and body armor laid out on the ground, stripped off her chador and was arming herself efficiently, stowing flashbang grenades, spare ammo magazines, det cord and other gadgets and tidbits in the utility belt she'd strapped to her waist.

Zane joined her, familiarizing himself with the equipment before stowing it on his person. "You look pretty comfortable with all this stuff."

"Tools of the trade," she commented with a shrug.

"This is the first time I've seen you in full commando mode," he commented back.

"Welcome to the Medusas in combat mode."

"You ladies really are full-blown warriors, aren't you?"

Piper stopped what she was doing to stare at him. "After everything you've seen me do, it's just now dawning on you that I'm a real soldier?"

He frowned. "It's one thing to know you can do all this stuff. It's another thing to actually see you do it."

"You saw me engage in a firefight with Mahmoud's guys. I killed Hassan, for crying out loud."

"I know. I know. But this…" He spread his hand over the tarp filled with weapons. "This is an imposing array of killing power."

"And that's why the Medusas are successful in general. People, particularly in places like this, can't compute that women can use all this gear effectively. Heck, you're American and have seen me in action, and you're still having trouble buying it. Imagine some Iranian dude who's never seen a woman say boo to a mouse."

He nodded, impressed in spite of himself. Only now was he fully grasping the scope of her training. No wonder she'd been such an emotionally strong and mentally disciplined prisoner.

"I'm just glad you women are on my side in this mission," he said fervently.

Piper smiled. "Let's go find ourselves an American engineer and bring him home."

"Amen," Zane said under his breath.

Piper shifted slightly beside Zane. Their surveillance hide was low to the ground and dusty as they peered over a slight rise toward the research facility Black would be inspecting any minute now.

The lab was a freaking fortress. Shortly after they'd arrived here in the wee hours, the team had determined that no way could they infiltrate the facility, snatch Black from his captors and make it out alive. The place bristled with electronic signals, there were cameras everywhere and alert Iranian Special Forces types were crawling all over the place.

The revised plan was to spot Black from here and follow him to wherever his captors took him next. They would have to keep him alive long enough to film him or have him type out an email. It would be during that transfer when the rescue team nabbed Black.

Problem was, they had no idea where the Iranians planned to take him after this. Which meant they were going to have to improvise on the fly. It was nobody's idea of a good mission, but it was the only option they had to save the guy.

Tessa's muttered voice sounded in Piper's earbud. "I've got dust on the horizon. Caravan of three SUVs inbound at high speed."

Torsten whispered, "That's probably Black. Get me license plates and a head count of people inside the vehicles when able."

"Working on it," Rebel replied absently. She was flying the team's tiny overwatch drone, while Tessa watched the live feed from the drone's high-powered surveillance camera.

In a few minutes, Tessa called out license plate numbers and started counting heads inside the SUVs. Four men in the first one. Three in the second…and a possible facial ID on Mark Black in the back seat with one other man. Three men in the third vehicle.

Black plus nine hostiles. Not bad. They'd been expecting more like a dozen guards.

Tessa, Rebel, Torsten, Zane and herself made five. Five on nine with their training and their equipment was a piece of cake. Assuming they could isolate the group transporting Black. And assuming the Medusas could engage in a firefight without excessively endangering

Black. It was entirely possible that his captors would try to hide behind him. It was what she would do.

"I can hear you thinking, you're doing it so loudly," Zane murmured.

"I was just thinking about how I'd use Black as a human shield if I were the tango."

"How much training do you ladies have in close-quarters marksmanship?"

"I'm good down to about a four-inch-wide target. Tessa can shoot consistently into one-inch windows." Meaning if Tessa had a one-inch-wide target behind a hostage, she could still hit the bad guy without nicking the hostage.

"Nice," Zane commented. "I'll leave that shot to you and Tessa, then."

"Let's hope it doesn't come to that," she replied.

Silence fell between them as, in the distance, a puff of dust became visible. She gauged that it was still several minutes out.

"Tell me something," Zane said in a low voice. "Do you enjoy doing stuff like this?"

"Love it. You?"

"This is a lot easier than being undercover. It's straightforward. Kill or be killed."

She smiled briefly. "We like to think in terms of kill…or kill."

He grinned. "Fair enough." A pause. "I like being here with you like this. I'm enjoying being part of a team."

"It's nice…weird but nice…having you here." She focused on the length of his muscular body pressed against her side and took comfort in his steady breathing and contained power. It wasn't that she needed a big, strong man to protect her. Far from it. But it was nice having a big, strong man work with her as an equal, respecting her capabilities and ready to cover her back.

"Vehicles are slowing," Tessa reported, at the same time as at least a dozen guards swarmed out of the lab to await the arrival of the caravan.

Zane muttered, "Black's sure getting the VIP treatment."

"The prisoner VIP treatment," Piper corrected.

They watched through their field binoculars as the SUVs halted in front of the lab and a Caucasian man was ushered out of the middle vehicle. Black was escorted toward the building.

Torsten said tersely, "He's ambulatory. Appears healthy. Anticipate an able-bodied hostage."

That was good news. Having to carry out a badly injured hostage slowed a team down. A lot.

Black disappeared into the building and Torsten started a stopwatch. The longer Black was inside, the more the CIA hoped he would be able to see and report on.

When Torsten's stopwatch hit the thirty-minute mark, Zane let out a sigh of relief. "Black's getting the full tour of the place. Which means he knows what the Iranians are so hot and bothered to protect that they kidnapped his wife."

"Why wouldn't they not let him into the lab at all and just coerce him into writing up a fake report?" Piper asked Zane.

"The report has to pass for real. He has to include enough technical details that the Global Atomic Inspection Team bigwigs believe he actually did the inspection. And for all the Iranians know, the West is watching on satellite feeds as Black arrives and goes inside the facility."

"Or a surveillance drone," Piper remarked dryly.

"Exactly."

They traded warm smiles. Zane seemed as happy to be here with her as she was to have him here. Something had shifted between them since they arrived in Tehran. They'd both settled into the idea of being in a relationship with each other, and they both liked how it felt.

Who'd have guessed she would find a man of her own who was okay with what she did and who she was? She didn't know where this would go or what the future would hold, but for once, she was hopeful. Maybe her dreams of someday settling down with a man who could accept her life choices, dreams of maybe even having a family, might come true, after all.

"Here they come," Tessa announced.

The lab's front doors opened and a large group of guards streamed out with Black tucked in their midst. Piper saw several of the guards glance up at the sky, and she grinned. The overwatch drone was barely a foot long, its underside was painted pale blue and it was loitering several thousand feet up, completely invisible to the naked eye.

Tessa reported that Black had again been loaded into the second SUV, this time with three escorts instead of two. Piper and Zane slid backward from their hide and raced down the sandy hill to their motorcycle. They jumped on and took off down the road.

Their job was to get in front of the convoy in case it headed back toward Tehran. If it went the other way, heading away from Tehran, they would turn around and ride in the trailing position. It was also their job to hunt for a good spot to ambush the SUVs and to call for the actual attack.

"We're away," Piper reported into her microphone.

"First SUVs pulling out now," Tessa stated.

"In position to fall in behind them," Torsten reported. He, Rebel and Tessa each had their own motorcycle. That way, they could all carry weapons, ammo and gear in bags behind them.

As it was, Piper felt like a porcupine underneath her billowing chador. This morning, she'd added a maqnaeh to her clothing. It was a hooded scarf that had a tiny protruding bill, like a baseball cap. It would keep the chador from sliding down over her eyes and obscuring her sight. She also wore loose black trousers, black socks and her black tennis shoes. There would be no bare flesh to draw the attention of the religious police, no, sir.

Even though it was only midmorning, the day promised to be a hot one, and the sun baked her beneath the layers of dark clothing. No help for it, though. She needed the chador to cover all her weapons. Tessa and Rebel were similarly dressed.

Torsten had laughingly declared them all BBMOs last night: Badass Black Moving Objects.

Zane sped up as Torsten reported that the SUVs were driving back toward Tehran at nearly a hundred miles per hour. The wind tore past Piper, cooling her a little, at least. No way could they ambush vehicles moving that fast.

Which was, of course, the point of driving that rapidly. They would have to wait until the convoy slowed to jump it. When that SUV caravan hit the horrendous city traffic, it was going to have to drop to a crawl. That would be the best time to rescue Black.

She leaned forward and yelled into Zane's ear, "Slow down when we approach Tehran and let them catch up with us."

"My thoughts exactly!" he shouted back, without taking his eyes off the road.

Into her microphone, she called, "Have we notified the pilots to crank up the jet and be ready to go?"

"Affirmative," Torsten replied.

The roar of the engine beneath her lessened as Zane throttled back, slowing the cycle to a more sedate speed as they hit the suburbs. She kept watch over her shoulder for the SUVs.

"Convoy in sight," she reported over her radio.

"Let's let them get as far into the city center as we can before they make a turn away from the vicinity of the airport," Torsten ordered.

"Contact on the traffic jam," Zane reported. All of a sudden, their motorcycle slowed to a few miles per hour as they hit the wall of cars, taxis, mopeds and people that clogged the Tehran streets.

Piper took one last glance over her shoulder and spied the three black SUVs a dozen cars back. She dared not look back again lest the front driver see her watching him and grow suspicious.

"We're weaving through traffic to close the gap," Tessa reported.

Piper and Zane inched forward through an intersection. The SUVs cleared the traffic light.

"Caught by the light," Torsten grumbled. "Don't move until we've caught up to you again."

Zane reported tightly, "First SUV turned behind us. I'm going to turn now to try to meet up with the convoy at the end of the next block."

"Convoy in sight. We're turning, as well," Torsten responded.

A cacophony of car horns erupted behind them, and Piper looked back as Zane cut across traffic to turn the corner. She saw three motorcycles running the red light and cutting in turn—not that they made the congestion any worse.

"They're through the light and in pursuit of the convoy," she reported.

"Targets acquired," Zane stated as they shot out into the next street in front of the SUVs, but perhaps only a hundred feet ahead of them now.

"We need to take them as soon as the others are in place behind the tangos," she called in his ear, off mike.

"Agreed," he called back.

She clutched her chador close so it wouldn't flap and reveal the rifle strapped across her back. Zane wove expertly between lanes of traffic, ignoring the occasional shouted epithet. She was glad he was doing the driving. Even she wouldn't have been as bold as him.

They passed the SUVs going the opposite direction, and Zane made a quick U-turn. "Don't look at them," he bit out over his shoulder.

He actually drove directly past the SUVs, close enough for her to reach out and touch them. She turned her face away and counted the seconds until Zane muttered, "We're clear."

Into her mike, she said, "Call when in position."

"We're there," Torsten replied. "Anytime now."

"Next intersection," Zane said. "Hang on tight, Piper. When I tell you to, jump off the bike and make your move for the tangos. I'll cause a distraction."

"Roger," she replied in a clipped voice. Here it went.

"Now!" Zane called out.

She slid off the back end of the motorcycle, jumping clear of the rear fender just as Zane punched the throttle and slammed into a produce truck in the middle of the intersection. Somehow, as the bike slid under the truck's wheels, Zane came off it, and one of the wooden slats of the truck bed miraculously gave way, spilling melons all over the intersection.

The chaos was instant and spectacular. People shouted. Horns honked. Drivers got out of their cars to shout some more and wave their arms. Where Zane was in that mess, she had no idea.

Piper turned, ducking low between cars, and ran back toward the SUVs. She approached the second one from the passenger's side and pounded on the front door. The window started to roll down.

"Help! Help!" she screamed in her best Farsi. "My husband is dying! He needs a hospital. You have to drive him!"

"Go away," the man inside shouted back at her.

Through the open window, she spied Tessa pounding on the driver's window, and Rebel doing the same on the left rear-passenger door.

The doors of the front SUV opened. Tessa, hardly looking to the left, paused her tirade for just a second. Piper was at exactly the right angle to see Tessa fire a silenced handgun under her left armpit at one of the security guards emerging from the front SUV, shooting a dart coated with a high-powered chemical that caused instant shock and paralysis. The other two front guards went down, as well. Torsten and Zane had hit their targets successfully, too.

Time to cause total chaos. Piper pulled out two flash-bang grenades and threw them as hard as she could in opposite directions. Other Medusas did the same, and a half-dozen explosions rocked the entire intersection.

As smoke filled the air, people screamed, abandoning their cars and running for cover. Whipping out her sound-suppressed handgun, Piper shot the front passenger in the temple—with a bullet—while Tessa took out the driver.

Piper had to expose herself to lean in the front window, and the shot was at an awkward angle, but she targeted the third guard, in the rear. She hit him in the face, and blood and gore exploded everywhere. Mark Black shouted from the back seat.

"Open your door, Mr. Black!" Piper yelled over the din. "We're Americans here to rescue you!"

The rear door opened and she moved swiftly to intercept Black before he could emerge from the vehicle. The four security guards from the rear vehicle had yet to be neutralized, and he needed to keep off the street until Torsten reported that the other tangos were down.

"Stay inside," she snapped at Black, who'd already started to climb out.

"Who are you?" he demanded, sounding close to losing his cool.

"I told you. Americans. Put this on." She handed him a maqnaeh. He merely stared at it, and she took it from him and yanked it down over his head. Leaning into the SUV, she sloppily wrapped a chador around his torso.

"What are you doing?" he asked.

"Rescuing you. Do what I say and don't ask any questions until I tell you we're in the clear."

"Rear guards are down," Torsten reported.

She didn't know how he'd done it and didn't stop to ask. "Come with me," she ordered Black. "Quickly."

He stumbled out of the vehicle, getting twisted up in the chador. She yanked it free and pulled it down around his thighs, then grabbed his hand and took off running along with the other panicked civilians.

Torsten fell in on Black's other side, and a woman in a chador closed in directly behind them, keeping up with the killer sprint Piper was forcing Black into. One of the other Medusas.

They turned the corner into a smaller street filled with fleeing people and made their way to one side, letting the flow of civilians pass by.

"Any sign of Zane?" Piper panted into her microphone.

Rebel answered, "I'm about to…" a pause, then the sound of a pop came over her mike. "…take out the cop trying to detain him." Another pause. "Zane's running."

"Turn left, Zane," Rebel said tersely. "Then take your second right."

"Get out of there, Rebel," Torsten ordered.

"On my way."

"Strip down," Torsten ordered. Piper took off her chador and maqnaeh, switching them out for a bulky, knee-length coat. It was wool and hot as blazes, but it allowed her to wear her utility belt and hide a short-barreled urban assault weapon across her back. She probably looked deformed, but whatever. She wasn't giving up that weapon until Black was on the jet.

They waited for a long, tense minute until Piper spied Zane's familiar face coming around the corner. In a few seconds, Rebel came around the corner in turn, stripping off her chador to reveal a red coat and a colorful head scarf.

"Move out," Torsten ordered.

Together, they moved back into the street, turning away from the accident, the smoke and the renewed round of chaotic screaming as civilians began to realize a bunch of men lay in the street and in their vehicles.

Quickly, they fetched Torsten, Rebel and Tessa's motorcycles, and the six of them climbed onto the bikes and drove away from the scene.

They headed directly for the airport and didn't stop until the tall hurricane fencing surrounding it was in sight. They swerved into a small grocery shop and headed for the restrooms in the back, the women piling into one room and the men in the other. Quickly, all three women changed into their flight attendant uniforms. When they emerged, Zane wore the suit he'd arrived in, and Torsten and Black wore identical pilot's uniforms.

Quickly, the women dumped all their weapons into the canvas bags their uniforms had been stowed in and passed the bags to Torsten and Zane.

"I can't go with you," Black announced.

"Why not?" Torsten blurted. "You'll die if you stay here."

"The Iranians have kidnapped a woman. They thought she was my wife, and they're torturing her. I won't let that woman die."

Oh, for crying out loud. Piper stepped right up to Black. "That woman was me. Look at me carefully, Mr. Black. I escaped my captors, and now I'm here to rescue you."

Black stared hard at her. Recognition dawned in his eyes. "How did you escape…and get all the way over here… Who *are* you?"

"Later," she bit out. "Right now, we've got to get you out of Iran. Your wife is in a safe house with the FBI guarding her, and she'd very much like to see you."

"Right, then," Black mumbled. "What are we waiting for?"

Everybody laughed and turned for the exit.

The young man at the cash register stared at them suspiciously until Torsten tossed a fat wad of bills across the counter on the way past. Avidly, the young man turned his attention to counting it.

It was awkward as hell climbing onto a motorcycle in a tight pencil skirt, and Piper had to hitch the stupid thing practically up to her hips. They'd better get to the airport soon because someone was sure to arrest them *fast* for this lewd display of legs.

They raced up to the guard shack where crews for the air show could access the flight ramp directly, bypassing the terminal on the far side of the airfield. The three women leaped off the motorcycles and yanked their skirts down hastily. Then, as a group, they approached the guard shack on foot with their credentials in hand.

The guard checked them off on a clipboard. Black had been given Torsten's credentials and stepped through to the other side of the shack with Zane and Piper, while the guard hunted through the clipboard in search of Torsten's new fake name.

"I'm sorry. You're not on the list," the guard announced.

Torsten frowned. "I've been back and forth through this checkpoint a half-dozen times. Hell, son, I remember you. Don't you remember me? I'm the guy who brought in the coffee and box of pastries yesterday morning."

"Oh, yes! That was you!" the guard exclaimed.

"Just write my name down, and when the next list of air crew members is printed up, add me to it. It was obviously a clerical oversight."

Piper was impressed to death by how casual and calm Torsten was. Not even the slightest hint of tension was visible in his stance or demeanor.

The guard waved Torsten through, and Zane breathed beside her, "Damn, he's good."

The group started the long walk across the ramp toward their ride out of here.

Another plane was just pulling in and parking, and Piper idly watched it as the steps lowered and a pair of men, acting a lot like security guards, jogged out and took positions on either side of the steps. A third man stepped into the doorway, and Piper gasped. Her footsteps slowed, and the others pulled ahead of her.

Zane, who'd kept pace beside her, glanced at her quickly. "What's up?" he asked out of the side of his mouth.

"Is that Abu Haddad?" she muttered back without moving her lips.

Zane glanced toward the new arrival and swore under his breath. "The mission is to get Black out of here."

"The jets flown in for the air show were granted diplomatic status. As soon as Black's on our jet, he's in Swiss territory and can't be touched," she retorted. "We can't get this close to Haddad and let him get away."

"Torsten will kill you."

"He'll forgive me if I take out Abu Haddad. He seriously hates that guy."

Ahead of them, Black jogged up the steps of their Swiss jet and Torsten waved for them to catch up.

"Do you still have the bag of gear?" she asked quickly.

"Yes."

"Come with me," Piper muttered, making a rapid decision.

"This is crazy," Zane warned.

"*Crazy* is my middle name."

"So I heard."

"We'll never get another chance like this. And isn't

this what we've both trained for? To capitalize on opportunities that come our way?"

"That interpretation of our missions is open to debate—"

"I went along with your kidnapping. You need to go along with this for me."

"That's a low blow," he muttered.

"I'm right and you know it."

Zane huffed and then nodded tersely. She veered to the left, with him on her heels. They paused to peer under the nose of a low-slung business jet.

Three pairs of male legs were striding away from them, heading in the general direction of a big white hangar at the edge of the tarmac.

"C'mon," she called over her shoulder to Zane, taking off running herself, swinging wide of Haddad and his men.

She spied a maintenance pickup truck parked beside another plane and headed for it. She ran up to the driver's window and looked in. *Yes.* The keys were in the ignition. She and Zane hopped in, and she drove as fast as she dared across the open space between the planes and the hangars. She veered between two hangars and raced around to the back of the one Haddad and his men were approaching.

While she drove, Zane emptied the bag, slamming magazines into both assault weapons and laying out Piper's utility belt. She stopped the truck, snatched the keys out of the ignition, grabbed the gun and belt, and took off running after Zane, who was already racing for the man-sized entrance door.

He eased the door open as she swung into position behind him. Moving low and fast, he spun right, leaving her to spin left. They were in an office with a big window looking out into the hangar.

Two limousines with dark windows were parked off to the left side, and a sleek jet took up the right side of the hangar. Along the left wall was a second-story metal loft housing shelves full of tools and aircraft parts.

As Haddad and his guards stepped into the cavernous shadows, a half-dozen men emerged from the limos, and four more exited the jet.

Zane swore under his breath. He must recognize them. Piper didn't know any, but this had to be some insanely high-powered meeting.

Haddad walked up to the group of men, shaking hands with several. The others, obviously guards, fanned out around them in a loose circle.

Zane ducked down below the windowsill and Piper knelt beside him. "We're badly outgunned here," he muttered. "What's the plan?"

"Take out Haddad and run like hell?" she suggested.

"The other men he's meeting with are a who's who of terrorists, arms dealers and criminals. We need to take out the whole bunch or we won't have made any difference at all."

She thought fast. "We'll have to split up. You tell me which targets are mine and I'll make my way to that platform on the left. It looks like there's a staircase up to it from an office. You stay here. Take your shots and then head back to the truck and get out of here." She passed the keys to him.

"I can't leave you behind!" he exclaimed under his breath.

"Either I get off my kill shots and make it off that platform to join you, or I die," she said matter-of-factly.

"I'll take the five men nearest the jet. You take the others."

"I don't like this. Let's just leave. We can have the agency's eyes in the sky track Haddad after he leaves this place."

"This is a once-in-a-lifetime opportunity, and you know it," she whispered back. "Would your bosses deem the loss of two American agents' lives worth the trade-off of killing all the men in there?" she challenged.

Zane huffed. "Yes." He paused and then said grimly, "But I'm taking the platform. You stay here with the easy egress."

"But—"

"I'm not arguing with you. That's my final take-it-or-leave-it offer."

It was her turn to huff. "Fine. Go."

"Give me three minutes to get into position and then fire at will. And, Piper?"

"Yes?"

He kissed her hard and fast, and then raced over to the doorway, stopping only long enough to say, "Good hunting. I love you."

She stared at the door in shock as Zane left the office the way they'd come in.

He *loved* her? What in the hell? Why on earth would he drop that bomb on her here and now? The only possible explanation was that he expected to die in the next few minutes.

No way did he get to make a declaration like that and then *die*! The big jerk hadn't even given her a chance to tell him she loved him back! Irritation rushed through her, along with furious determination to see to it that both of them got out of this alive so she could return the favor.

Swearing in a continuous stream under her breath at Zane, she moved stealthily into position by the window. She would take two quick shots from this corner of the window, and then would move to the other side for the next shots. The window was a good eight feet across and she calculated distances and angles from both spots as she waited for Zane to get into position. Using a glass cutter, she carefully and quietly scribed two small circles in the glass. Her first shots at each position should blow out the pieces of cut glass without shattering the whole window. In theory.

Zane should be past the long hallway behind several more offices and on his way upstairs soon. She watched the metal staircase like a hawk and caught the barest hint of movement at the top of the steps. Dang, he was smooth. She lost sight of Zane as he worked his way into the stacks of spare parts. Her watch said he had one more minute to get into position.

She checked over her weapon quickly and then settled into her first shooting position, emptying her mind of everything but her targets and her weapons.

He loved her?

Well, she loved him, too—

Stop. Focus.

And then she inhaled, counted to four and exhaled slowly.

Showtime.

Chapter 19

Tessa jumped as Torsten barked without warning, practically in her ear, "Where in the hell are Zane and Piper running off to?"

Torsten leaned across her, staring out the windows of the jet, apparently trying to spot his operative and the CIA liaison, who'd just gone AWOL without warning.

"She must have seen something," Tessa answered.

"But what?" Torsten demanded. "We have to get Black out of here before the Iranians decide to cause an international incident and storm a Swiss-flagged aircraft."

"It must be important or she wouldn't have run off," Rebel offered. "And the Iranians have no idea where Black is right now. We made a clean getaway. It'll take them hours to sort out where we went, even assuming they do have full closed-circuit television coverage of downtown Tehran. Which I highly doubt."

Torsten straightened to his full height and glared at both women. "It is unacceptable to go off script in the middle of a freaking operation."

Tessa replied gently, "Which means it must be a matter of life and death, or she and Zane wouldn't have taken off like that."

Her boss moved over to another window to stare out, grumbling, "You Medusas are going to be the death of me yet."

He sounded ticked off enough that Tessa refrained from a snappy comeback.

"Son of a bitch," Torsten grunted. "There they are. Driving across the damned ramp in a truck like bats out of hell." He whipped around and pointed a finger at Black. "You. Don't move a muscle. You're a dead man if you set foot off this jet. Understood?"

"Um, yes," the engineer said nervously.

Torsten snapped at Tessa and Rebel. "Gear up, you two." He strode forward and poked his head into the cockpit. "If you gentlemen see anyone except me and my teammates approaching this jet, taxi out and take off. Immediately."

"We can't just take off. We have to get clearance first—" the copilot started.

Torsten cut him off. "You'll die if you don't get the hell out of here. Use this jet like a weapon, get to the runway and get airborne at all costs. Do you understand?"

The captain replied crisply, "I'm ex-navy. I hear you loud and clear."

Torsten grabbed one of the canvas bags of weaponry and ran down the plane's steps. Tessa and Rebel were close on his heels with bags of their own. He said tersely, "Last I saw, Piper and Zane were driving toward that big white hangar."

Tessa peered where he pointed. "You mean the one with all the security guards coming out of it right now to surround it?"

Torsten swore again.

"The guards don't look alarmed, at any rate," she reported.

Rebel spoke up. "There's a luggage carrier off to our right. What if you drive that, boss, while Tessa and I hide in the back behind the curtains?"

"Done," Torsten replied. Quickly, he stripped off his pilot's uniform coat, leaving him wearing a white shirt and black slacks.

While he hot-wired the tug vehicle, Tessa and Rebel hid themselves in the covered luggage cart, carefully pulling the curtains closed and then quickly unpacking guns and the last of their concussion grenades. The luggage carrier lurched into movement.

"Here we go," Tessa muttered. "Charging into battle at a solid five miles per hour, wearing skirts and heels."

"And sassy hats," Rebel added.

"Torsten did say we could kill anyone who messed with the hats," Tessa retorted.

"Game on."

They traded grins, and then they both picked up weapons and put on their game faces.

Piper didn't even have to think about which target to choose first. Haddad. The bastard had slipped through the Medusas' grasp once. No way was he doing it again. She aimed at his head, going for the kill shot. All the weapons provided for the Medusas would have been precisely tuned to fire true, so she would aim right at the middle of Haddad's face.

Her watch said Zane had ten more seconds to get into position and commence firing. She placed her eye on the rubber cup of the sight, counted down the remaining time in her head and exhaled. Three. Two. One.

Bang-bang.

Her shot rang out at almost the exact same moment Zane's did. Haddad dropped to the ground, a fine red mist hanging in the air where his face had just been. She'd hit him. Whether he was dead or playing possum, though, she had no way of knowing.

Men jumped all over the place, shouting and diving for cover, which she'd expected and anticipated. One of her targets dived behind a limo, taking cover from Zane, but still a clear shot for her. She exhaled and fired again.

Two down.

But then the security guards started shooting back. The window in front of her shattered, and she spun away, taking cover behind an old-fashioned metal desk. Rounds pinged off of it.

She slipped around the end of the desk and moved to the other firing position. She spied a target clambering into the plane, and then going limp on the steps. Zane must've shot him. She took aim at the man trying to climb over the body and shot again.

A pair of security guards took off running toward her.

Well, damn.

She took aim at one and shot him. He doubled over like he'd taken a bullet but then continued running.

She shot twice at the second guard, who staggered but also kept coming. New plan. She had to retreat from the office.

Grabbing her spare magazines of ammo, she flung the bag over her shoulder and ran out of the office, closing the door behind her. Darting down the hall, she tried a door. Locked.

Sprinting on, she tried the next door. And the next. Finally, an unlocked door. She spun inside, caught her breath for a second and then cracked it open just far enough to point her muzzle down the hall and see to aim.

The guards burst out into the hallway. She fired quickly, sending nearly a dozen rounds at them in a burst.

One man slid down the wall to sit motionless on the floor, while the other cried out and retreated into the office. But she'd seen enough blood from the second guy to know he wasn't going to be chasing after her anytime soon.

This office had no window into the hangar. Checking the hallway quickly, she darted out and continued running down it. From inside the hangar, she heard car engines starting.

Veering into the next unlocked office, she was relieved to spy a window, and rushed over to it. She was just in time to see a concussion grenade explode directly in front of the first limo. Zane must have thrown that.

She also spied guards shooting up at the second-floor platform where Zane was trapped.

Oh, no, you don't kill the man I love.

Using the butt of her weapon, she knocked out the window glass and dropped into a firing crouch, spraying the backs of the shooting guards with a burst of lead. She was going through ammo fast, but this would all be over in the next minute. There was no use conserving ammo.

A power unit of some kind started to make noise from the jet, and she took aim at the tires, shooting out both nose tires and one set of main tires before returning her aim to the men, most of whom who were running around the hangar like panicked chickens.

What they were trying to accomplish, she couldn't

tell. They certainly didn't have the discipline of trained Special Forces types. She picked off three or four of them before someone got wise to her new position and rounds started coming her way.

The red pillbox hat flew off her head. Good riddance. But she was more careful about showing herself as she shot at the melee in the hangar.

The jet's engines screamed to life, and the steps lifted as the passenger door closed. The plane started to taxi, leaving behind strips of rubber that had once been tires. They had to stop that jet!

She fired at the one engine she could see, but to no apparent avail. The jet rolled forward and was almost clear of the hangar when, without warning, a vehicle pulling a big metal luggage cart rolled directly in front of the aircraft.

The luggage vehicle slammed into the nose gear of the business jet with a screech of metal on metal. It startled everyone inside the hangar into looking that way.

Piper took aim and dropped two more men before the firefight resumed. She slammed her last mag into place.

Three men had been organized by a fourth, and raced toward the metal steps leading up to Zane's position. They moved out of her line of fire and she swore. Leaping to her feet, she jumped over the windowsill and ran toward them, firing in bursts at the men, heedless of her safety.

Nobody was killing her man! Not on her watch!

The trigger clicked and nothing happened. Out of ammo.

She continued running forward, reaching into her belt for a concussion grenade. Designed mostly to create noise and smoke, it would nonetheless have enough punch to knock a grown man off his feet at close range.

Arm raised and screaming like a banshee, she charged toward the last cluster of resisting guards.

Zane swore as he saw Piper charge out of an office near the far end of the hangar. He saw the moment when muzzle flashes stopped spurting from her weapon and she tossed it aside.

"Turn around! Turn around!" he shouted at her. But she either didn't hear him or didn't listen, because she was running straight at Haddad's personal bodyguards. They were the best-trained of the security types now littering the hangar floor in pools of blood. They'd stayed together, crouched over Haddad's body, and had dragged Haddad over to the limo in between shooting at him and Piper. They almost had their boss stuffed into the last limo.

It happened in slow motion below him. One of the men saw or heard Piper coming and pulled a sidearm, turning around to shoot her. Zane aimed and fired all in one frantic, blindingly fast motion, and the guy pitched forward. But not before his weapon discharged.

Piper spun to the side, hit.

No-o-o!

Off to Zane's right, a tremendous explosion rocked the whole platform beneath him. Bastards must have found the trip wire he'd left at the base of the stairs.

He grimly regained visual on Piper, and saw her right herself and alter course to charge the limousine. Zane pointed his weapon at the cluster of men beside the limo and mashed the trigger, emptying every round he had left at the guards.

They had the good sense to duck, which removed them from his line of fire behind the limo. He swore and stood up, coming out of hiding and racing for the stairs, yanking out his own sidearm as he went. Fourteen rounds. That was all his pistol held. And they had better be enough to get him to Piper's side and save her life. He leaped over the gap and the dead bodies left over from his trip wire trap and sprinted toward the woman who was his whole reason for living.

Piper felt the round hit the meaty part of her upper left arm, but didn't register pain. Only a vague burning sensation. A few more steps.

In range now.

She lobbed a grenade at a cluster of men, who were now crouching beside the limousine, unsuccessfully trying to manhandle another man's limp body into the vehicle.

She had one more grenade. She threw it with all her strength, drawing on everything she'd ever learned in fast-pitch softball in high school, and flinging the grenade through the open door into the black cavern of the limousine's interior.

The vehicle's windows lit up as the grenade exploded. The doors opened and the men inside poured out, coughing and doubled over.

She heard the pops of a nearby pistol, but couldn't see where they were coming from in the thick smoke.

She stumbled over something big and soft. A body. She dropped to her knees and searched the corpse by feel. Bingo. She felt the cold, hard barrel of a weapon. Scooping it up, she spun away from the cloud of smoke now enveloping the hangar.

Out of the fog and shouting and gunfire, a familiar voice merged from the din. "Get out, Piper!"

"You get out, Zane!"

And then she ran, zigzagging back and forth as she

headed for the open hangar doors. As she got close to the light outside, she realized that her zigzagging had turned into staggering, first to one side and then the other.

She made out red shapes spilling out of a luggage cart and squinted, confused, as they rushed toward her.

"Get down, Piper!" one of the shapes shouted.

She dropped to the ground, but whether it was voluntary or her legs just gave out from underneath her, she wasn't sure.

In front of her, the red shapes erupted into flashes of light. She identified it fuzzily. Muzzle fire.

And then everything happened very fast. Someone came up behind her and scooped her off the ground. She bounced like she was on a trampoline. There was a luggage cart for a minute or two, and then the back of a pickup truck. And then they were racing across the airfield toward…the runway?

She didn't understand.

A male voice nearby murmured a continuous stream of soothing words. Something about hanging on and staying with him.

"Zane?" she mumbled as her eyesight gave out and gray crept across her field of vision. "You'll never get rid of me. I love you, too…"

Chapter 20

Piper woke up slowly. The room around her was white, and the whole wall beside the bed was made of glass blocks that let in a lot of light but didn't allow her to see out. She tried to move, but her whole body ached, and she sighed in pain, subsiding.

"There's my girl. Welcome back."

She blinked several times, and Zane's face came into focus, bending down over her.

"Hey." Her voice was strangely raspy. Her throat felt desert dry.

Zane reached out of her field of view and came back with a glass of water and a bendy straw that he put to her lips. She took a sip and then another. She collapsed back against the pillows.

"Am I in huge trouble for going after Haddad?"

"Torsten was pretty mad, but he had the whole flight back to Switzerland to cool off. By the time we landed here in Geneva, the CIA confirmed that not only did Haddad die in the fight, but a half-dozen other major arms dealers and terrorists, as well. It was a hell of a haul. Since we all made it out alive and mostly in one piece, and he's being hailed as a genius, I suspect he'll get over any lingering irritation."

"Are you okay?" she asked in concern.

"I'm fine. But, darling, what were you thinking, charging out into the middle of a firefight like that?"

She frowned, thinking back. It took a few seconds to retrieve the memory. "I saw those men racing toward the stairs. They were going to kill you." She shrugged, but it turned into a wince instead. "I wasn't going to let you die."

"I was fine. You should have stayed undercover, or better yet, headed for the truck like you said you would, and bugged out of there."

She snorted, but it came out a weak sound of disgust. "As if I would ever leave you behind in a firefight."

He stared down at her, the frustration fading slowly from his gaze. "Yeah. I get that," he finally allowed. "I charged down the stairs into the middle of the battle when I saw you get hit. I guess I can't expect any less of you than I would of myself."

She smiled up at him. "Now you're getting the idea. The Medusas operate just like you would."

He gently pushed a stray lock of hair back off her forehead. "Well, not just like me. I think your heroic streak may be even more pronounced than mine." He bent down and brushed his lips very gently across hers. As he started to pull away she tried to reach for his shirt to tug him back down, but frowned when her left arm didn't budge.

She glanced down at it and was startled to see it encased in a cast. "How bad is it?"

"Not bad. It was a through-and-through shot. Bone got nicked. Your humerus has a hairline fracture. They only casted it to keep you from going crazy with it. Your

arm will heal fully. If," he added significantly, "you behave yourself for a few weeks."

"Oh, yeah? Who's gonna make me behave?" she
teased lightly.

"That would be me." The smile slipped off his face,
leaving him staring down at her seriously. "Would it
help if I said I have a project for you that should keep
you busy for a few weeks?"

"What's that, Mr. Cosworth?"

"How would you feel about planning our wedding?"

She stared up at him as the words refused to compute. She heard them, all right. *But them? Her? Him?*

"A wedding?" she echoed in a small voice.

"I'm fine with going to a justice of the peace's office if you don't want the whole wedding thing." He
picked up her left hand and clasped it between his warm
ones. "But either way, I'm putting a ring on this hand
if you'll have me."

"Oh, I'll have you," she breathed.

A huge smile broke out across Zane's handsome features. They kissed, and it was so sweet that tears came
to Piper's eyes. When Zane realized she was crying,
he sat up and wiped the tears off her cheeks with his
fingertips.

He said reflectively, "Who'd have guessed when I
told Mahmoud you were the one in that school office
that I was actually right? You really were the one. The
one for me."

Who'd have guessed, indeed? On the very day she'd
decided that no man would ever be able to live with her
career, a man who not only could live with her career
but who shared her work, had blasted into her life and
swept her off her feet.

"Zane?"

"Hmm?"

"In case you didn't hear it when I shouted it to you in the hangar, I love you. To the moon and back."

Staring deep into her eyes, he leaned down toward her. Their breath mingled as his lips hovered over hers. "I love you, too, Piper. To the stars and beyond."

And then he kissed her…and took her to the stars with him.

* * * * *

*Be sure to check out the next
Mission Medusa romance,*
Special Forces: The Operator,
available next month.

Other books by Cindy Dees:

Navy SEAL Cop
Undercover with a SEAL
Her Secret Spy
Her Mission with a SEAL

Available now from Harlequin Romantic Suspense!

Rebel asked more seriously, "How should a woman be treated, then?"

Avi smiled broadly. Now they were getting somewhere. "It would be my pleasure to show you."

She leaned back, staring openly at him. He was tempted to dare her to take him up on it. After all, no Special Forces operator he'd ever known could turn down a dare. But he was probably better served by backing off and letting her make the next move. Not to mention she deserved the decency on his part.

Waiting out her response was harder than he'd expected it to be. He wanted her to take him up on the offer more than he'd realized.

"What would showing me entail?" she finally asked.

He shrugged. "It would entail whatever you're comfortable with. Decent men don't force women to do anything they don't want to do or are uncomfortable with."

"Hmm."

Suppressing a smile at her hedging, he said quietly, "They do, however, insist on yes or no answers to questions of whether they should proceed. Consent must always be clearly given."

He waited her out while the SUV carrying Piper and Zane pulled up at the gate to the Olympic Village.

Gunnar delivered them to the back door of the building, and Avi watched the pair ride an elevator to their floor, walk down the hall and enter their room.

"Here comes Major Torsten now. He's going to spell me watching the cameras tonight."

"Excellent," Avi purred.

Alarm blossomed in Rebel's oh-so-expressive eyes. He liked making her a little nervous. If he didn't miss his guess, boredom would kill her interest in a man faster than just about anything else.

Avi moved his chair back to its position under the window. The hall door opened and he turned quickly. "Hey, Gun."

"Avi." A nod. "How's it going, Rebel?"

"All quiet on the western front."

"Great. You go get some sleep."

"Yes, sir," she said crisply.

"I'll walk you out," Avi said casually.

He followed Rebel into the hallway and closed the door behind her. They walked to the elevator in silence. Rebel was obviously as vividly aware as he was of the cameras Gunnar would be using to watch them.

"Walk with me?" he breathed without moving his lips as they reached the lobby. Gunnar no doubt read lips.

"Sure," Rebel uttered back, playing ventriloquist herself, and without so much as glancing in his direction.

It was a crisp Australian winter night under bright stars. The temperature was cool and bracing, perfect for a brisk walk. He matched his stride to Rebel's, relieved he didn't have to hold it back too much.

"So what's your answer, Rebel? Shall I show you how real men treat women? Yes or no?"

Don't miss
Special Forces: The Operator *by Cindy Dees,*
available July 2019 wherever
Harlequin® Romantic Suspense books
and ebooks are sold.

www.Harlequin.com

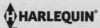

Need an adrenaline rush from nail-biting tales
(and irresistible males)?

Check out **Harlequin Intrigue®**,
Harlequin® Romantic Suspense and
Love Inspired® Suspense books!

New books available every month!

CONNECT WITH US AT:

Facebook.com/groups/HarlequinConnection

 Facebook.com/HarlequinBooks

 Twitter.com/HarlequinBooks

 Instagram.com/HarlequinBooks

 Pinterest.com/HarlequinBooks

ReaderService.com

**ROMANCE WHEN
YOU NEED IT**

SGENRE2018R

Happily-ever-after.
It's our promise,
whatever kind of love story you're seeking—
passionate, dramatic, suspenseful,
historical, inspirational…

With different lines to choose from
and new books in each one every month,
Harlequin has stories to satisfy even the most
voracious romance readers.

Find them in-store, online or subscribe to
the Reader Service!

HARLEQUIN®

ROMANCE WHEN
YOU NEED IT

A SECRET AGENT KIDNAPS
AN UNDERCOVER OPERATIVE!
THE MISSION MEDUSA SERIES CONTINUES...

To maintain his cover, spy Zane Cosworth kidnaps Medusa
member Piper Ford. She might be trained to endure a
hostage situation, but when one of her kidnappers continues
to protect her from harm, she finds herself losing her heart.
They flee for their lives, and the lines between enemy and
lover begin to blur. But will they survive long enough to
explore this new passion?

$5.75 U.S./$6.50 CAN.

ISBN-13: 978-1-335-66202-6

50575

9 781335 662026

EAN

S

CATEGORY
SUSPENSE

HARLEQUIN®
ROMANTIC
SUSPENSE

harlequin.com